Two Feet Press

UNCOVERED

An UNLIKELY SERIES Novel

Book 2

JB SCHROEDER

Enjoy, Lily

Two Feet Press
PO Box 351
Chatham, NJ 07928-9991

Cover photographs ©teamtime/depositphotos,
©lanych/depositphotos and ©Digital Vision/Thinkstock

Digital Edition 1.0

ISBN-10: 1-943561-05-2
ISBN-13: 978-1-943561-05-6

To Bethany
With love and gratitude

~

No one understands you like your sister does.
And no one can make you laugh as hard, either.

PROLOGUE

NO ONE DARED speak the word *suicide* aloud. Not here, graveside, but Eddie sensed the weight of it in the chill air—pressing at the neck and shoulders of his dress uniform. Accusation seemed to hover behind the sympathy in every set of eyes, gathering together in his mind like a tangible mass.

Under the tight band of his cap, Eddie wore his combat face. Jaw straining forward, lips tight but parted, breath soughing through the gap, and nostrils flared. Skin tight with tension, eyes dead, yet hyperaware. Because this felt like a war zone. An emotional one. Guilt, horror, incomprehension...

He was disoriented physically, too. His eyes felt like sandpaper, as if he remained in the arid desert. His ears still strained for the crunch of rock under the enemy's tread; his hands constantly sought the solid rigidity of his weapon; his chest ached for the comforting press of body armor laden with ammunition and gear.

There hadn't been time to acclimate. He'd been called to the commander's tent, told his wife was dead, sent to pack his gear, spent a sleepless night awaiting transport...

Fucking *wrong* on so many levels, he'd struggled to process the news.

Kathleen dead. By suicide.

Her family had pushed for a fast service near their hometown on Long Island—a plot already reserved. Hours blurred, and now, suddenly, here he stood surrounded by mourners and headstones.

He was unable to focus on the minister's murmured words of condolence, attuned as he was to both his body and the press of people from a cavalcade of cars arriving behind the family at the cemetery.

Kathleen's employers were in the lead—the mayor of New York City, somber and dressed in a black suit, and his wife, a tiny thing in a tailored black skirt and jacket, wearing a hat with one of those nets you only saw in movies. Next came a classy auburn-haired woman, gripping the hand of a young man, both faces pale. Then a few more staffers, he assumed, all ages, eyes downcast.

There were some old pals from the early New York days. People he hadn't seen in years, ones Kathleen hadn't even bothered to send him news of after a while. Surely, too, some of Kathleen's current friends. He wouldn't know.

A white plastic chain held back numerous people wearing ribbons pinned in loops to their chests. They picked apart white bouquets, passing the flowers along their ranks until everyone held one. Lesser staff from the city offices? Or friends from some cancer support group? It hardly mattered.

Slinking around the far reaches were the newspaper photographers. Kathleen had worked directly for the mayor's wife, as her personal assistant. She'd also been part of some marketing campaign for the mayor, in which she'd been dubbed the Face of New York. Eddie could only assume that anything that happened in the mayor's office made news. The suicide of a well-known staffer would make it front page news. Although the reporters were attempting to be discreet, Eddie still found it distasteful and intrusive. Throwing them out would only make more crap news, however, so Eddie focused on pressing his soles into the soft ground. Feeling the earth. American soil.

He tried not to see Kathleen's family: her mother especially, looking stricken, her father, so deathly pale that Eddie was afraid he'd keel over. Both faces bloated from crying and hollow-eyed from lack of sleep. Grief and shock. Cousins, aunts, uncles, too—weeping, frowning, stoic.

Yet Eddie felt no solace from the presence of Kathleen's clan.

One foot in the door for this morning's viewing, and Eddie had barely hugged Kathleen's parents before blurting out, "Why didn't you tell me Kath had cancer?"

"Don't you dare walk in here and blame us," her father had said, shocked. "We had no idea you didn't know."

"I would have *been here* if I'd known." Eddie had wanted to tear his hair out. It was so obvious—he would have put in for a discharge immediately and come home.

"Why didn't *she* tell you?" Kathleen's mother had asked, accusation causing her voice to shake. "What went on between you two?"

Dammed if he knew. He'd thought that despite the distance, he and Kathleen were all right. Or at least that they would be, later, when they had time to reconnect.

So no, Eddie felt no comfort from Kathleen's family. Anger? Hell yes—mostly toward Kathleen. Along with disbelief, confusion, and guilt—although he hardly knew what for.

The words of the service washed past him, pushed aside by his efforts to control the riotous emotion threatening to overwhelm him. He was strung tight, on the breaking point, like a hair trigger.

Luckily, his best friend, Aiden, stood shoulder to shoulder with him, a brother in spirit, as always. Aiden's mere presence held him up, kept him steady—much like his combat team. Support intrinsic, words unnecessary, strength in spades.

Eddie stood ramrod stiff in his uniform and made a concerted effort to think of the lives he'd saved. From the idiotic young soldier, too frozen with fear to return fire or even duck, to some future gaggle of Middle Eastern shoppers who frequented a terrorist-targeted marketplace.

Not the one in the ground. The life he hadn't saved.

Not because he hadn't been able to, but because he hadn't known he'd needed to. He should have, though. She was his *wife*.

Aiden's hand settled on his shoulder, the weight an alert. Eddie blinked and came to. Stepped forward and reached for the short shovel held out to him. On autopilot, he bent, sticking it in the mound of earth. Dust to dust. He tipped it, dirt thudding and sliding off the shiny curve of the coffin.

Loud, messy sobs erupted and grew—machinegun fire to his soul. He clenched his teeth so hard they hurt, and had to stare at his fingers to make them uncurl from around the shaft of the shovel. He passed it on without making eye contact and marched back to his place, but not before catching sight of the mayor taking his wife's arm. The wails were hers, Annette Thompson's, Kathleen's boss. They must have spent a hell of a lot of time together, Eddie thought, and flinched before he could stop it.

From the corner of his eye, he saw the mayor leading his wife away, toward the limos, looking both grim and embarrassed. She keened and convulsed with sobs, and he supported her slight frame. As they passed the roped-off section, where so many people wiped their eyes with handkerchiefs, one of them patted Mrs. Thompson on the arm. She howled, grief palpable in the wail.

The same reverberation came from his own wounded heart.

CHAPTER 1

A year and a half later

EDDIE SLAMMED the heavy-duty plastic mailbox shut and considered kicking it into oblivion. He'd had all the mail from the New York apartment forwarded here to the Poconos. Logical, right? You forwarded mail so you didn't miss a bill, a final paycheck, a notice from the IRS. Except he fervently wished he hadn't.

Twice a week he forced himself to stop the car at the bottom of the drive and take the shit inside. He loved this property—all green, nestled in a riot of trees and bushes and overgrowth—and this house—not large, but modern, slung into the middle of nowhere like it'd been airdropped from a helo. A contemporary feel, clean lines, natural wood grain, muted colors, an open floor plan…

But he hated bringing in the mail. It felt like carrying handfuls of mini IEDs. Paper couldn't kill him, but there might be one or two sheets in there that'd blow him off his feet, ring his bell and send him reeling for hours.

He'd been managing all right. The karate school he and his friend Aiden had opened kept him busy, social, and fit. Aiden, his oldest friend, made things bearable. Residing in New York, where he and Kathleen had met and married, simply hadn't been an option. Too many memories, too stifling, too loud, too tight. He was, of course, accustomed to missing Kathleen; they'd lived on different continents for much of their marriage. But he struggled nonetheless—the return to civilian life, coupled with the idea that she was no longer here *somewhere*…

Because although they'd grown apart, he hadn't given up on the marriage. He'd believed they had time, believed that after he retired, they'd get back on track. And now he couldn't seem to reconcile that she'd been dishonest with him. That she was gone. That he wasn't married. That there was no fixing it, no second chance.

He banged into the house and dumped it all on the kitchen table for a cursory look before hiding most of it in the spare room.

Kathleen's passing generated loads of mail, still. Various financial institutes requesting a certificate of death. Slews of condolence cards from people he'd never heard of—all from New York, and so many that he'd stopped reading them. And yet he couldn't make himself throw them out.

Today, yet another of Kathleen's insurance statements had arrived. No matter that it'd been a year and a half—every time medically-related mail came, a fresh wave of guilt climbed up his throat. It was the same feeling he had when he'd been told how she'd died—like thick tree roots slithered up his torso to wrap around his windpipe.

Because—according to the medical examiner, at least— she'd committed suicide.

Bull-fucking-shit.

Yeah, Kathleen had had a hard time for a while. Christ, 9/11 and its aftermath was brutal on everyone. They'd already had their issues. She'd been on shift work as a paramedic, and he'd been on early hours at a trading desk. Half the time they were at home, one or the other of them was sleeping. Then, after the tragedy, she pulled doubles at Ground Zero, and he—mourning coworkers—either paced the apartment like a caged animal or walked the city like a zombie. When they crossed paths, it seemed they had nothing to talk about. Then, when he'd told her he wanted to join the service they'd fought. Big time. She understood his need to *do* something, but couldn't help feeling abandoned. She was proud of him, but terrified for him. Round and round they went.

Frankly, by the time he'd actually left, he thought it'd been a relief to both of them. And not long after he'd begun training, she made a seismic shift in her own life as well. She quit her job, and quickly found something entirely different, something that alleviated facing life and death every day—the job for the mayor's wife.

They talked via Skype when he could, and she sent letters. She'd made peace with him being away, sounded content with her life, and loved her new work. She'd proven her strength and resiliency time and again.

As for their marriage, they'd hit a rocky patch, but found their way through. And there'd been a plan, at least in his mind. Having served his country and done his duty, he was supposed to come back to her. Smooth out the jagged edges of their relationship; make their marriage even stronger.

Barring that, he was the one who'd left—he was the one who was supposed to die. He'd been in a goddamn war zone, for fuck's sake.

Yet here he stood, in one piece and breathing. Still grappling with the fact that *she* was the one who was gone. And how.

It was seriously messed up. But what could he do about it? His conviction that Kathleen was emotionally healthy, that she'd had a deep well of strength inside, that cancer or no cancer there was no way he could see her committing suicide—none of that was going to make a medical examiner change the death certificate.

Eddie sat on the back deck for at least an hour, watching the woods. A couple of empty beer bottles sat at his elbow, and Stripes, his Shepherd-mix puppy, lay at his feet. His thoughts churned, until he finally faced the truth. Aiden was right. Despite opening the studio and getting a dog, he'd been sitting still, eyes shut, trying not to breathe, as the past swirled around him like a Middle East sandstorm.

It was time to move forward, find a way through. Ignoring the details of Kathleen's last days hadn't gotten him anywhere. Maybe addressing them would.

Eddie headed for the kitchen, slapped together a sandwich as a late lunch, and ate it over the sink. Then he headed for the second bedroom, empty save for boxes of Kathleen's stuff.

He eyeballed the liquor box full of personal notes addressed to him or the "Family of Kathleen Mackey." He grimaced and looked away, gaze landing on the DVD in a sleeve on the floor next to it. A video from his wife, filmed by a Miranda Hill at a company called the Goodbye Angel. Sucky name, if you asked him, and a damn depressing business. At first, he'd watched Kathleen's goodbye to him over and over. Eventually, he'd relegated it to this room, tossing it through the door to lie where it landed.

Jaw tight, Eddie scrubbed his hands over his buzzcut. He'd ease in, take this tactically. The box of insurance statements first, as they seemed less…emotional. He dropped to the floor, and, using the wall as a backrest, began to sort by sender and postal date. Next, he retrieved his utility tool from the kitchen counter where he always unloaded his junk—keys, wallet, shades, utility knife—in order to slice open the envelopes. The house was too quiet, so he grabbed his phone and chose a streaming station—classic rock for this task—and immediately sound filled the space. Another reason to like a modern house; the place was wired for sound in nearly every room.

Soon enough, he had three working piles. Trash, keep, address. Most of it was junk—duplicates and privacy notices, crap like that. Some he figured he should file, which would involve a trip to the store for a file cabinet, folders, etcetera. The third stack he'd have to deal with.

Eddie stretched, then gathered what he needed and went to the kitchen table, where he usually left his laptop, checkbook, phone, and login information, picking up another beer on the way to make this bearable.

He called the health insurance company and was speaking with a real babbler, when she said something that yanked him out of his stupor.

"Congratulations on your wife's recovery."

He winced. These bills were old, and it'd been easy to ignore the details thus far, as Kathleen had her own insurance through the mayor's office. This woman obviously didn't know—though what he'd said to make her think Kathleen was still alive, he had no idea.

"...reminds me of why I wanted to go into healthcare in the first place, to help people," she chirped. "Of course, I ended up on the phones, but I'm still happy when I see proof like this. Cancer-free. I mean, that's so great, right, that—"

"What?" Eddie choked. This was the first he'd heard that word in conjunction with Kathleen. "Where do you see that?"

"Right there on page two. Cancer markers near thirty."

Eddie flipped the sheet and dragged a finger down the page. "That's good?"

She snorted. "Absolutely. Even people who've never had cancer can test up to thirty."

Holy shit.

He had never really believed Kathleen had committed suicide, because he knew that she was a fighter, with a solid core of inner strength and resolve few people possessed. Even the video she'd made for him seemed to him more a measure of insurance, against the cancer, than a firm goodbye. But there'd been only his conviction. Even her parents had seemed to accept it. No one else would even utter otherwise. Not when the cause of death had been suggested by the NYPD and subsequently confirmed by the ME. Not when everyone believed she was dying of cancer anyway.

Here, in black and white, was just as near as he was going to get to proof that Kathleen *wouldn't* have taken her own life.

CANCER-FREE.

———

Once the gravity of his discovery began pressing in around the initial relief, Eddie called Aiden. A good workout would take the edge off. They'd been sparring for a while when he finally scored a hit, nicking Aiden in the gut with his heel. Eddie popped out his mouth guard and joked, "You're losing your touch. That pretty wife of yours keeping you up late again?"

Aiden and Tori were only recently married. Aiden said, "Don't even picture my marital bed, man, or we're going another round so you can eat your teeth."

"Easy, Miller, easy." Eddie smiled. Having trained together since they were kids, and being equally matched, it was rare one or the other managed a point. Eddie would enjoy it while he could.

He tossed Aiden a water bottle. By unspoken agreement, they headed out the back door of the studio to the wooden bleachers that overlooked a cleared field and a prime piece of Pocono woodland. A perfect place to watch the sun rise or set. That and the early hours they both often kept had led to the name: Sunrise Martial Arts.

Aiden had been Eddie's one and only phone call since he'd learned that Kathleen had been cancer-free when she died, so he wasn't surprised when Aiden asked, "So what's the plan?"

Neither one of them were the type to let grass grow under their feet. The fact that Eddie had been sitting on his duff, doing exactly that, reminded him just how off kilter he'd gotten.

Eddie twisted his lips and cocked his head. "Can't exactly call it a plan, more like an unexpected fishing expedition."

Aiden raised an eyebrow.

"I spoke with the doctor at Sloan Kettering in New York. When she'd had little result with standard treatment, Kathleen was approved for some new drug. It worked—like a fucking charm. She responded better than they ever dreamed." Eddie shook his head, still astounded.

"For starters, I want to go talk to the coroner. Maybe with new information, they can take another look at her file. Reopen it or something." Eddie ticked items off on his fingers as he spoke. "I also want to see that woman Miranda Hill who filmed the goodbye video, and Kathleen's boss."

"The mayor's wife?"

Eddie nodded. Kathleen had been Annette Thompson's personal assistant, so she worked in the Office of the Mayor of New York City, otherwise known as city hall. Eddie recalled Kathleen telling him that it was odd for the mayor's wife to have an office there. Apparently, space was at a premium, yet the mayor had booted someone else to a satellite office, preferring to have his wife nearby given all the hours he worked. It seemed the man was whipped.

Eddie said, "She and Kathleen would have spent a hell of a lot of time together." That alone made Annette worth talking to. "Figure I'll start calling some of her better friends, too, but"—he shrugged—"at the funeral, I realized she hadn't seen much of the ones I would have expected her to lean on."

"During tough times," Aiden said, "you tend to find out who your real friends are."

"Well said, old man."

Aiden snapped Eddie with his towel. Eddie could have moved but didn't—it was an old ritual between them.

"Why the video woman?" Aiden asked.

Eddie rubbed his hand over his morning scruff. "Filming that would have been pretty emotional, so who knows? Maybe there's more footage. Maybe Kathleen confided something else off tape." He could only hope. "Beyond any of that, I don't know where this will lead."

Eddie felt tension building to something palpable, like wearing the weight of full combat gear, but inside his skin.

"Doc say whether she could have been out of it enough to mix up doses? Accidentally overdo it?"

Eddie was shaking his head before Aiden was done asking. "No way."

Trained as a paramedic, Kathleen wasn't likely to *accidentally* take a mega-dose of painkillers, even while reeling from cancer. He'd had trouble conceiving of it in the first place, but now, knowing her health outlook had improved dramatically? No friggin' way. "The doctor said she wouldn't have been in pain at that point."

Aiden grimaced. "Addicted, maybe?"

Eddie didn't take offense—he knew Aiden was only ruling out possibilities, same as he himself had done. "I checked. No extra prescriptions, no multiple doctors, urgent care visits, or anything. All the same primary team on all the medical papers. I even checked her bank withdrawals. No big ones, and not an unusually large amount of small ones. Besides, I just can't see it. Can you?"

"Nah, not with Kathleen."

Eddie concurred, but he'd ask her friends as well just to be thorough. Hell, she barely even drank. One was her limit because, as a paramedic, she always wanted to be clearheaded enough to help a person in need even when she was off-duty. He doubted she'd throw that personal rule out the window just because she'd switched careers.

So, what the hell did that leave? His gut—which had served him well during three tours of active duty in the Middle East—cried foul play. But who would want to hurt her? And why? Kathleen had been...well, overall a good person. Not perfect, of course, but no bad habits, no dicey connections, no checkered past.

But if it wasn't suicide, and it wasn't an accident...

"Taking this all the way, then?" Aiden asked, expression grim.

Eddie nodded. "Have to."

Because he hadn't really been there for her at the end. Shit—long before the end. And because if he didn't make it right, who would? So yeah, he'd see this through.

CHAPTER 2

MIRANDA SHOVED her client out the door and leaned against it in relief. Then she straightened and shook herself like her childhood dog Cocoa used to do after he'd been in the pond. If only she could dislodge the feeling of filth and betrayal like a dog shed water.

Most of the people who came to her to craft goodbyes just wanted to leave something of themselves behind. Full of love, forgiveness, and yes, often regrets, they came for the right reasons. To make amends, share words of comfort, pass on family stories, or express their love.

Occasionally, though, she got someone toxic. Someone who ranted or blamed. And sometimes she'd had to hear terrible secrets from the past. Thankfully, though, never anything that needed to be shared with the police.

Miranda stomped across the room and snatched up a can of aerosol disinfectant. Silly, she knew, but the ritual—needed rarely—made her feel better, as if she could symbolically eradicate the lingering creepy-crawly feeling in her space.

"Begone, filth," she said as she raised the can. Yep, far simpler than having a priest come bless the place or perform an exorcism.

Mr. Kornow, though—she scowled as she sprayed—had seemed like the sweetest thing. Older, but appearing to still have a long life ahead of him, she'd assumed maybe the video was an anniversary or milestone birthday present. He'd gushed about the love of his life for a full thirty minutes until he finally blew the lid off. The video was for his mistress, whom he'd finally "found" after years of "other side pieces." He'd gotten way too graphic cataloguing them all, despite Miranda's attempts to redirect him. But when he began bashing his wife, that'd been it. Miranda declared time was up. This was exactly why she relied on her digital watch, instead of a visible clock in the filming area.

That poor wife, Miranda thought. She probably despised the man, between having to worry about catching diseases from her own husband and knowing he valued nothing beyond his version of worthwhile sex—eewww.

Miranda cringed and sprayed another round.

Most of the time she loved this work—found it satisfying, emotionally uplifting, and often it even restored her faith in humankind.

But sometimes the job was damn hard. She did not appreciate being used to pass on dirty secrets. That just plain sucked.

"Room, you are restored to goodness and harmony," she declared, and bent to stow the Lysol behind the counter.

Then she turned to the video camera to eject the memory card. She wasn't even going to duplicate this one for safekeeping, though she would have to work with the video long enough to sync up the sound. Then the jerk-off could have it. She was tempted to refuse to finish the film, but reminded herself that his money would spot someone who couldn't afford it.

Standing behind the camcorder, she realized Mr. Kornow had left his glasses on the side table right next to the lav mic that'd she'd clipped to his collar.

"Dammit." Cheap readers or expensive prescription?

The intercom buzzed and her tension level flared back up. She snatched up the spectacles and prepared herself to deal with the man one last time. Wrenching open the door, she held out the glasses and held her breath as well—as if she didn't breathe in the air surrounding him, she'd stay clean.

But the torso in front of her outstretched hand was not paunchy Dennis Kornow's... But a very solid, trim waist in worn army-green cargo pants.

Her gaze slid up inch by inch. Black, fitted T-shirt—lean and, whoa, muscular chest. Tanned and ripped biceps. All the way to a strong, clean-shaven jaw, wide lips just curving in a smile, and deep blue eyes under a buzzcut of blond hair.

Miranda's breath whooshed out all at once, and she blushed. My God, she'd looked this man over like he was— well, a page out of *Military GQ* that happened to come to life on her very own doorstep.

His nose twitched, and she realized she'd brought a cloud of disinfectant with her to the door.

"Miranda Hill?" he asked.

His eyes sparkled like he knew she liked what she saw. No surprise there. Hot as could be, he probably left a wake of drool behind him daily.

Or maybe all that sizzle had melted the locks, because it'd just occurred to her that she'd never answered the intercom or pushed the button to release the door.

She narrowed her eyes. "How did you get in here?"

He gestured toward the entryway. "Some guy held the door open for me."

Another strike against that creep Kornow. The snake could easily have let in a mass murderer, or a rabid-eyed fan— though thankfully that kind of attention had waned.

"You're Miranda? The Goodbye Angel?" He waved a DVD in one of her preprinted sleeves.

She nodded. "Yes, but I work by appointment only." Though for this hunk, she might bend some of her rules.

"I'm Eddie Mackey." He stuck out a hand.

On autopilot, she transferred Kornow's specs to her left hand to shake his. Warmth and strength enveloped her, shooting right up her arm, derailing her attempt to place his name. Realizing they'd held hands too long, she pulled away hastily.

"My wife—"

She didn't hear any more, because her own voice was suddenly shouting in her head. Mackey. This was Kathleen's husband. What had the woman been thinking? And shit—what was he doing here?

"I don't need an appointment," he said, his tone a mix of smooth and do-me-a-solid-please, while his eyes held a heavy sorrow and a faint gleam of...what? determination? "Just a few minutes to ask you some questions."

She couldn't—just simply could not—handle this right now. Not after Kornow.

"Still need an appointment. Number's on the case."

And she slammed the door—right in his face—before her brain even caught up to what her body had just done.

Only then did she realize that he wouldn't have known.

No one would. No one but her—because she was the only one who'd ever seen Kathleen Mackey's last taping.

———

"Goodbye to you too, angel," Eddie muttered as he shoved through Miranda Hill's vestibule. He was sorely tempted to dial her for an appointment the minute he hit the street. Just to be a dick.

He gritted his teeth. For now, he still needed to play nice, needed her amenable—if the woman could even attain such a reasonable state.

Then again, before he'd spoken, she'd looked more than friendly, even *interested*. Those fern-green eyes had been full of heat after they'd tattooed a wake of tingles from his fly right on up. Bursts of pink on her cheeks and parted lips meant she was definitely picturing him naked.

Ooh-rah.

He could easily picture her telling face showing every reaction to his touch on her long-legged body. Damn her. He blew out a breath laced with a twinge of guilt. Now was not the time.

Eddie headed west on Eighty-fourth, his boots eating up the seams of the sidewalk, passing stoop after stoop of prewar apartment buildings. Much like Miranda's, they were essentially the same size and shape, though the facades, railings, and window styles differed. The Upper East Side was a nice neighborhood. Fairly quiet all the way over here near York Avenue, and about as bland as you got in New York City. Perfect for families and new-to-New-Yorkers.

Small businesses, like markets, delis, pubs, and restaurants fronted every avenue, and Eddie ducked into a bagel shop on Second. Nothing like a New York bagel—something about the water here that made them better than anywhere else.

Inhaling the familiar fresh-baked scent, he surveyed the case of puffed, golden brown circles piled in metal baskets behind the glass, and went with an old favorite.

Everything bagel. Piled high with turkey and Swiss. Mayo, yellow mustard, pickles, and lettuce.

Friggin' delicious. Made killing time here almost bearable.

And yeah, he probably could have waited until Sunday night to arrive in the city. But he was a marine and he had a new mission. There was no sitting around with his thumb up his ass. Simple as that.

He hadn't expected Miranda Hill to be much help, but the fact that she'd turned to ice when she found out who he was? Shot him down and shut the door—literally slammed it—in his face? Seriously, if he hadn't jerked back that fraction of an inch, she'd have smashed his nose in.

Yep. She'd just moved herself up to the top of his list of people to question. Although the next time, he'd have a boot strategically placed in her doorframe.

Eddie crumpled up the paper wrapper from his sandwich, and watched the street activity as he thought over his schedule.

Tomorrow he had an appointment with the coroner, and he'd take some time to call on Kathleen's family on Long Island. He had managed to secure an appointment to see Annette Thompson Monday morning.

A slot in Sloan Kettering's full schedule had been impossible, but the doc, Baladeva Malik, had twice squeezed out five minutes over the phone to answer his questions. Malik had insisted Kathleen was healthy, nearly clear.

"I can't give you certainty." The Indian accent was light and lilting, gentling the serious subject matter. "There are never guarantees when it comes to trial drugs, or a person's health, for that matter."

He'd gone on to give Eddie a brief lesson in the numbers—red blood cells and white, and an illustration of just how miraculous Kathleen's drug seemed. Then he'd admitted, "A person's mental health, their desire and will, do factor in. Of course, a big no-no to admit in a scientific field, but I'm saying to you your wife was glowing the last time I saw her. All good news. Celebration, you see?"

Eddie left the shop feeling more solid, the dense mass of carbs and protein in his gut rallying him, and headed for the subway. He'd parked his truck—which sucked for tight street parking—down near the hotel because they had a long-term deal with a connected garage. Check-in for his room wasn't until 1500, but there was no reason to hang around the Upper East Side.

He figured the best use of his time this afternoon was to try and connect with some of Kathleen's friends. As he walked, he scrolled through his phone, looking for Charise's contact information.

Kathleen's best friend from her paramedic days answered with a question mark in her voice.

"Charise, it's Eddie Mackey."

"No way! How are you?"

Eddie said, "Doing all right. You?"

"I'm good..." Charise said. "God, I still miss her, you know?"

A heavy thump hit his chest, and he sucked air. Charise never was one to beat around the bush. "I do."

"So, what can I do you for?"

"I need to pick your brain." With luck, straight-shooting Charise would have something he could use.

Several hours later and an easy walk from his hotel on Fifty-first and Eighth, which he'd now officially checked into, Eddie headed for the Hell's Kitchen neighborhood to meet Charise. Four Brothers, an aging but comfortable pub with decent, hearty food, drew a heavy crew of police, EMS, and firefighters, along with the neighborhood locals, especially at happy hour.

When Eddie walked in, he swore the only thing that had changed under the neon signs and red plastic tablecloths was the placement of the crumbs. Even the waitress was the same. She called everybody "hon" in a heavy smoker's rasp, and he recalled that she wouldn't bring condiments, ever.

He'd attracted notice from the regulars, when a short woman with dark hair dyed deep red turned and threw out her arms. Charise.

"Hey, old friend." She wrapped her arms around him and hung on tight. "How you doin'?" She pulled back to stare at him with her sharp gaze.

"Doin' okay." Eddie smiled. He'd always liked Kathleen's favorite EMS partner. "But the question is how are you doing, and who is this?" Eddie smiled and put his hands to her very pregnant middle.

She laughed. "Abigale or Anaia, depending on which one of us gets our way."

"Charles isn't very smart, is he?"

Charise's eyes went wide. "Oh boy, it has been a long time. That jackass Charles has been outta the picture for years. This here baby is my Frank's."

Had it been that long since Eddie had seen Charise? Had Kathleen told him at some point that her friend had a new guy and he'd forgotten? Introductions followed, and Eddie was glad to find that Frank, a city firefighter, seemed like a good guy.

Eddie recognized several other old friends of Kathleen's and bought a couple of rounds of beers before he got down to business, subtly working around to the questions he wanted to ask.

Most seemed happy to catch up and expressed their sympathy, but none seemed to have spent much time with Kathleen in the last couple of years before she'd died.

Eventually, he claimed a barstool next to Charise. They faced out, watching the action, but their conversation was their own.

"No, no way was she using," Charise insisted, shaking her head. "I know addicts—you see an awful lot of 'em in our line of work—and Kath wasn't one."

Eddie agreed wholeheartedly. Charise continued, "Once she stopped all the disaster relief stuff and knew you were settled in where you needed to be, she seemed lighter, more content. Loved that new office job. Didn't see her much, though, as time went on. Seemed to want to stay home and lie low, mostly, and eventually, she stopped hanging with us." She waved a hand at her crew. "Enjoyed her new work people. I missed her, but it seemed natural to me, you know?"

"Anyone particular in the new crowd that I should talk to? Anyone she mentioned spending a lot of time with?" His shoulders were tense with frustration, and he willed her to remember something helpful, something concrete.

"Oh, I don't know. She talked highly of her boss, but beyond that..." She shrugged.

"Mrs. Thompson? Or the mayor?"

"The Mrs. She didn't say much about the mayor."

"And the cancer? Did she tell you?"

"Not right away, but yes," Charise said. "I came to see her now and then. Offered to bring meals, but she said her coworkers had been doing that, and that her boss had helped her get an aide who could be there daily." Charise must have seen something in his face, because she patted his arm and said, "It sounded like the radiation and drug therapy combo they had her on wasn't as wicked as chemo would have been."

Still, Eddie tried not to let guilt swamp him. He should have been there to make sure Kathleen ate well, didn't have to cook or clean up, and felt cared for, every day. Whether she felt smothered or not. But he hadn't been given that choice.

"Kathleen struggled some, sure," Charise said. "Jeez—what person isn't terrified of cancer, huh?" More shaking of the stiff, bright hairdo. "But she seemed strong. Inside, you know?"

Charise didn't wait for an answer. "I wasn't worried. That girl was tough." Her eyes sought Eddie's, held them. "I couldn't have been more shocked when I heard the word *suicide*."

And there he had it. Proof that he wasn't the only one that thought Kathleen wouldn't have taken her own life.

CHAPTER 3

MAKEUP ON, her curls as tame as they'd get, Miranda was dressed for a night out. Skin-hugging jeans showed off her long legs and her rear. A printed, sleeveless blouse, loose and very current. Big silver hoop earrings. She'd bring a black wrap for the fall chill—she could easily shove it into her cross-body purse, since oversized bags also happened to be in style.

It should have been a typical Friday night in the Big Apple with Maxine, her best friend since college, who'd be here any minute. Normally, they'd hit their favorite bar. Always fun, whether they met friends, met men, or ended up talking solo.

Tonight, however, she didn't wear her bright red flats, but her sneakers. She needed solid footing and rubber soles. She needed to be steady on her feet.

Miranda bit her lip and frowned at her reflection. All except for the shoes, the outfit screamed modern woman. Single, but not necessarily available, and sexy, while still projecting secure, confident, and capable.

She was no longer that woman. The one who could walk into a bar and search out the faces of her friends and an open seat—without first cataloguing exit signs and escape routes. A video journalist—a shooter—who was ready at a moment's notice to run all over this city for a story, jumping into whatever transportation was fastest. At all hours, in all neighborhoods, any venue. Dilapidated buildings, scary weather, billowing smoke, dark tunnels, high-rise rooftops.

Heck, she'd felt practically invincible some days. Savvy, intuitive, decisive, and fearless.

Miranda stuck her tongue out at the mirror—it was either that or cry. She looked the same, but she wasn't. These days confident and capable was a mirage.

She wasn't feeling it. And she knew exactly why. She was an intruder. A scared one.

Miranda sucked in a bracing breath and stared herself down. She had to remedy all that. Rebalance the scales. And it had to be tonight.

The buzzer sounded, and Miranda exhaled that big breath with a whoosh, wrenched her gaze away, and headed for the door.

Max had her key in the lock before Miranda got to the living room. The buzz had been courtesy only, as they'd once been roommates and were now family in all but blood. In fact, Miranda only used the 1B door for herself and her closest family and friends. Everyone else entered through the client side, 1A.

"Oooh, I like the new top," Max said after they'd exchanged a hug. She was the real fashionista. Miranda didn't care much as long as she could claim the right decade in an always-hip, ever-current New York.

"Thanks." She waved a hand over herself like a magician prepping for a trick. "I'm not loving it."

"Shut up, it's perfect."

"It's not the outfit," Miranda said. She sucked in a great big gulp of air and blurted, "I don't think I can do this. It's been two whole years since I set foot underground. One night is not going to suddenly—"

"Shhh—you can do this, I know you can," Max said, and reached for Miranda's hands. "You are going to make it down those subway steps, and then we are going to celebrate like nobody's business."

Miranda shut her eyes. She couldn't even imagine it.

Max said, "Listen, let's just *try*. It's not your fault that that posttraumatic stress counselor dude was a schmendrick—"

That got a shaky laugh out of Miranda. The jerkiest of all jerks, Miranda knew she meant, as she'd learned all Max's quirky Jewish phrases—and her Italian ones, too—years ago. "He wasn't that bad. Maybe just a schlump," Miranda said. Although she had wasted precious time with him for no real gain.

"You won't be alone. I'll be right there with you." Max squeezed her hands, then let go.

Miranda bit her lip.

Max changed tactics. "Listen, I ditched Giorgio for you, so you have to at least *try*."

"Who's Giorgio again? So many men, so little memory space," Miranda quipped.

"Ha ha." Max tossed her satchel—purple leather with tassels—on the kitchen counter.

When Miranda had renovated last winter, she'd eliminated the wall between the living room and kitchen. She didn't use a table, just stools at the peninsula, and this was where she and Max nearly always began.

"New to the city. Divine Italian accent?" Max prodded.

Miranda smiled. "That's right. You bonded over soppressata at the Italian market."

"That's the one."

"I thought you were passing on that."

Max leaned a hip on the counter, cocked one shoulder, and made a small pout, and Miranda couldn't help but smile.

The move was so totally Max. Inherently sexy, all confident woman. She couldn't turn it off if she tried.

And then there was Miranda…not nearly as confident anymore as she should be, though sex appeal was the last thing on her mind. Even when she wasn't working, she used to enjoy the city, and the myriad of people and cultures and events in it, so much. She'd never minded going out of her way to document something interesting. The Mermaid Parade in Coney Island, the Hispanic Day Parade or the Harlem EatUp! Festival. A hot new artists' studio that had cropped up in DUMBO or an ancient Polish butcher downtown someone had mentioned. Now? Well, she was always weighing transportation, crowds, escape routes…

"Stop stalling," Max said.

Miranda frowned. "Maybe you should call Giorgio and see if he's still free. I'm good."

Max scowled. "I'm not leaving you home on the second anniversary of the E-Train Disaster to edit teary videos or whatever the hell it is you do in here when you are holed up."

Miranda placed a hand over her heart. "It's Friday. I promise I won't work." Except she knew her voice wasn't as light as it should be.

Miranda expected Max to hoist her over her shoulder any minute, but instead she cocked her head, black waves—very fifties starlet—dipping well past her shoulder. "It's up to you. Your choice whether we go or not."

Miranda's shoulders sagged and she sank onto one of the stools.

Max narrowed her eyes, then spun on black, high-heeled half-boots and headed for the wine rack.

"Vino and takeout it is." She dug in the drawer for the bottle opener.

"You don't mind?" Miranda asked.

Max waved manicured fingertips—the shade a near match to her vivid purse. "Of course not. There's more where Giorgio came from."

Miranda couldn't argue that point. Max was like a magnet. It wasn't so much that she was gorgeous—although she was. Instead, boldness set her apart. Sure in her sexuality, bold in style, and full of attitude. She *never* lacked for male attention.

Max handed her a glass of red wine, raised in a silent toast, then suggested, "How about Antonio's?"

Miranda grinned. "Still in the mood for Italian, huh?"

"One way or another."

"Good by me." Antonio's never disappointed.

Max said, "Let's schlep over and pick it up instead of using delivery." She slid Miranda a glance out of the corner of her eye.

Miranda huffed. The Eighty-sixth and Lexington Avenue subway entrance was on the way. She should have known Max wouldn't give up that easily, but she'd been too wrapped up in her anxiety to catch on quickly. "You think I'm going to change my mind."

Max just leaned a hip against the counter and waited, watching her steadily, that perfectly groomed, dark eyebrow raised.

Miranda realized she was gnawing on the side of her thumb, and stuck her hand under her butt.

Her eyes full of sympathy, Max said, "You are going to regret it if you don't even try, honey."

Miranda held up a hand, and then took a fortifying swig of wine. She'd heard from Aggie, Max's grandmother, today, and Aggie's sister, Cora, who was, for all intents and purposes, a grandmother to the both of them. They knew about Miranda and Max's plan to try going underground together, and they were ready to put on their brightest lipstick and join them for a huge celebration afterward—even if she only managed half a flight of stairs.

What would tomorrow bring if she didn't even attempt this tonight?

She didn't want more sympathy or another pep talk or any more well-meaning suggestions.

She simply wanted to stop counting.

She'd been walking the date, counting down daily, pounding the numbers into her body through her soles for weeks—the triple digits climbing, taunting her—but she still hadn't managed to pre-empt the official "second anniversary." True, she'd given herself a pass the first year, so she hadn't really started counting until she'd started counseling. But if she was facing facts, today was seven hundred and thirty days. Two whole years since the incident that had painted her a hero. Ha—she'd been petrified, and still was.

Fingers on her wine glass, she spun the stem, watching the liquid undulate. Finally, Miranda whispered, "Okay."

"Okay, then." Max slid her own glass forward to touch Miranda's. "To conquering demons, and reclaiming what you've lost."

Miranda's eyes welled as she locked eyes with her dearest friend. She couldn't speak, only nodded. But Max knew. She always did.

Thirty minutes later, Miranda shook her head. The glass of wine hadn't helped at all.

Yes, she was standing on Lexington Avenue at the top of the stairs to the Eighty-sixth Street metro station. Her toes even pointed in the right direction, only an inch from the diagonally patterned tread at the first step.

But every muscle in her body was on lockdown, her breathing was shallow, and sweat had broken out on her forehead and under her breasts and arms.

"Miranda."

Her ears were roaring, making Max's voice seem far away.

"Look at me, honey. Hold my eyes."

It took effort, but Miranda tore her stare away from her own toes. Max had moved up a couple of steps, from the fourth to the second, close enough to reach out and touch. Except Miranda couldn't. She had both hands on the square, solid metal endcap of the railing, and she wasn't letting go.

"Okay, good girl. Now breathe." Max modeled a long inhale and longer exhale. "With me."

Miranda tried, she did, but her breath felt jerky and she didn't get much air in.

"Again."

Eyes locked, they breathed, and it helped—a little—to concentrate on that small action.

"Now just take my hand. I'm right here, see?"

It didn't matter that Max's fingers were right in front of her. Miranda's insides shook, and her hands clenched every bit as tight as the vise on the workbench in her dad's barn. But her palms were getting slick, making her fear she'd lose her grip if she reached for Max. Ridiculous, she knew, but nothing about this was rational.

"Breathe. One hand only."

She didn't have to do this. She could live with no subway, no basements, no underground shopping malls, no down escalators.

But she'd never be whole, would she?

Miranda's eyes welled and she clenched her jaw. She tore her eyes from Max's and looked at her fingers on the chipped green rail. Forced the pinky finger of the top hand up, then the ring and middle fingers. Sweat poured down her temples now, and she thought she'd puke.

"You can do it. I know you can."

Last was the pointer and thumb. She made sure she knew where Max's hand was—only a foot. Probably less, but it seemed like every inch was a mile.

Miranda bit her cheek hard and did it—like forcing rusted metal—grasping fast for Max.

But that action—her arm straight ahead instead of crossed over her body—left her chest exposed. Unprotected. Vulnerable.

Panic seized her—her lungs gulped and adrenaline spiked. Miranda yanked her slick hand from Max's, scrabbled for the endcap, and launched herself around the side to grip the upright posts hard with both hands. She stared at the little metal spikes at the top and felt the comfort of the ledge pressing hard into her kneecaps. All of it together, a wall of solid security between her and a terrifying pitch into the dark.

Her legs buckled, and she sobbed. "I can't, Max. I just can't."

———

The phone rang, waking Miranda from a doze, the aborted attempt at conquering her phobia having completely drained her. Max, who'd refused to leave Miranda alone and was watching a movie at the other end of the couch, said, "Stay asleep. Let it go."

"It's all right." Miranda tossed off the throw blanket, rubbed her face, and scrambled up. She'd been too upset to go on to Antonio's—even to just order to go—and had barely touched the pizza they'd called in for delivery. But between another glass of wine and the shut-eye, she was feeling stronger now.

Max muttered, "Ten o'clock on Friday night? These people know no boundaries."

Miranda waved a hand as she reached for the phone. "Yeah, but honestly, it's easier to pick up than to call everybody back." She pushed her hair off her face. "Hello?"

"I'm calling for an appointment." Deep voice, gruff and curt. "Officially."

A wave of hot shame suffused Miranda's face, and she tucked her chin. "Mr. Mackey?" Though she hardly needed to ask. He'd left numerous messages earlier that she'd ignored, and his voice was unmistakable—a cross between sandpaper and rich honey, if such a thing existed.

"Eddie."

She cleared her throat. "I apologize about earlier today. That was, um, uncalled for. You caught me at a bad time, and I... Well, I'm sorry."

"Maybe make it up to me?" His voice held a slight teasing note now, and even though she'd only laid eyes on him once, she could picture that sexy curve to his mouth. "I do need an appointment, but..."

Her breath lodged in her throat. Holy crap, was he coming on to her? About to ask her out? Her eyes darted to Max, who would know exactly what to say here.

"I need it soon," Eddie said, voice full of apology and heavy on charm. "I'm only in town for a few days."

"Oh. Uh, okay. Give me a sec to pull up the calendar." She scooted out of the room and took the phone with her to the office. She didn't speak—and tried not to think about what questions Eddie Mackey might have about his wife as she checked Saturday's appointments. "I'm sorry. I'm full up on Saturday, and out all Sunday, and at my other job on Monday."

She imagined she could hear him grinding his teeth. "I have a spot Tuesday evening at seven."

"I'd hoped to be gone by then."

Definitely a bite in his voice. "Maybe a phone conference instead?" Miranda asked, hoping to hell he wouldn't want to do that *now*.

"No. Put me down for Tuesday, but call me if you have a cancelation, even last minute." He paused. "Please."

"Will do."

Miranda put down the phone, entered the appointment, and stared at his name, frowning.

She jumped when Max's voice came from behind her. "What was that about?"

Miranda stood. "Just an appointment."

"What about the something uncalled for?"

She gave her friend a wry smile. "I slammed the door in the guy's face earlier today."

Max's eyes went wide. "You? He must really have been asking for it."

Miranda shook her head. "Nope."

Both eyebrows shot up over her friend's eyes.

Except Miranda was way too fried to adequately navigate around *why* she didn't want to talk with Eddie Mackey. And Max was way too perceptive. "It's a story for another time."

Miranda wouldn't tell her clients' secrets, though. Not even when they were already dead.

Not even to Max. And certainly not to the deceased client's husband.

CHAPTER 4

EDDIE HAD BEEN asked to wait in a small interior office in the NYU Langone Medical Center Campus on First and Thirtieth—one of the family services branches of the Officer of the Chief Medical Examiner. Apparently, Winston Chang, the coroner who'd handled Kathleen's...case—Eddie tried hard not to think of her as a body—was in the middle of something. Eddie twitched his shoulders to dislodge the thought of what exactly. He'd just be thankful he was killing time in a regular old office, not anywhere near a wall of person-sized sliding drawers. Eddie had seen more death than the average Joe, and he didn't care to add to his visual catalogue if he didn't have to.

A good twenty-five minutes had passed by the time Chang walked in.

"Sorry to keep you waiting. Never a slow day here," Chang said by way of greeting, chomping on a piece of gum. He was nearly the same height as Eddie but half as broad, probably mid-thirties, and was bald on top with the rest of his hair shaved close.

"No problem," Eddie said.

The smell of...embalming fluid, Eddie guessed...clung to the guy, and the realization made Eddie hesitate a second when shaking his hand. Then—surprise—Chang's hand was warm, when somehow Eddie had expected meat-locker cold.

The shake was almost too brief, bordering on rude...or hurried? Uncomfortable, perhaps? Did Chang recognize the name Kathleen Mackey as an employee of the mayor, or was he just awkward around the living?

Chang sat behind the metal desk and placed the manila file folder he held on it. A series of numbers were on the sticker, with the words *Mackey, Kathleen*. Eddie sat in the same chair he'd been occupying before—one of two guest chairs.

"I'm not sure what you're looking for here," Chang said, glancing up but keeping his eyes largely on the folder. He had terrible posture, almost curling over the folder, which made him seem small. "This suicide was fairly straightforward. Large amounts of benzodiazepines and alcohol. Too large to be accidental."

Eddie hadn't said much when he'd made the appointment—he hadn't wanted to be barred from visiting. And, of course, he'd requested the autopsy report long ago. He knew what was inside. He'd have to walk a fine line now, too. "I'm having a hard time reconciling that. Suicide," Eddie said.

Chang looked up then quickly glanced away. He didn't say anything, his jaw working away on the gum. Orange-flavored, Eddie thought.

"Suicide is extremely difficult on those left behind," Chang said quietly.

"It's more than that," Eddie said. "Kathleen was strong. Stronger than anybody I know. You know that she'd undergone cancer treatment."

Chang nodded, despite the fact that it hadn't been a question.

"Her oncologist says she was winning that battle. She'd pretty much been given a new lease on life. Right before she died." Eddie tried hard to keep his voice level.

Chang smoothed his fingers over the folder and shook his head slowly. "Everything in here points to suicide."

It would, Eddie thought, gritting his teeth, if you were doing simple addition. Way too many Valium, plus way too much vodka to increase the effect, and even a big dose of grapefruit juice to speed up absorption? Yeah, that equaled suicide. And just in case, draw a nice full bath to sink into when you get sleepy...

Eddie pried open his jaw far enough to speak. "Listen, I don't mean to say you don't know your job, but is there any way you could have missed something?"

Chang continued to shake his head.

"Maybe she was forced to take the pills? Or held under the water? Maybe there was bruising or—"

"No." Chang didn't look up.

"Maybe she was coerced—threatened verbally—and so he didn't lay hands on her. Maybe—"

"I'm very sorry. I did a thorough exam," Chang said. "I went over her case very carefully because..." He paused, seemed to shift his gum around. "Well...she was somewhat high profile. The Face of New York thing."

Eddie ignored that thorn in his side. "I'd like you to take another look at the file. See if—"

"No. I can't."

"Please," Eddie said, fisting his hands to keep from shaking a yes out of this skinny yet imperturbable guy. "*Please*," Eddie said once more with all the pent-up emotion he felt.

Chang shook his head, picked up his file, and stepped around the desk toward the door. "So sorry," he said quietly.

"That's not enough," Eddie said as he stood.

Change hesitated, moved toward the door, then hesitated

again. He didn't turn around, just bowed his head slightly and asked, "Why?"

"Because she *didn't* kill herself. I'm sure of it. And I *will* prove it."

If possible, Chang slumped a little further. Then he straightened and turned. "Are you staying in the city?"

Eddie narrowed his eyes and nodded.

"Do you know Chinatown?"

Eddie nodded again. Where the hell was Chang going with this?

"On Mulberry, near Canal. Find Wong Palace, my family's restaurant." He chomped his gum furiously and tucked the folder under his arm. He dug out his wallet from a back pocket and pulled out a business card. "You must visit. And order Siu Foon's favorite. If you forget, it translates to 'smile happy.'"

Eddie waited. The guy had barely said two words, and now he was drumming up business for his family's restaurant? From a grieving man who was trying to prove his wife had met with foul play? What was he up to?

"Warren is my brother. Tell him I sent you. And don't forget, you must order the Siu Foon." For the first time, Chang held his eyes. "It will be worth your while."

CHAPTER 5

EDDIE TURNED his face upward, relishing the cold rain as he marched up the short walk toward Miranda Hill's building. It was Saturday. And his precious appointment wasn't until Tuesday. But he needed answers—now. Besides the fact that the city was making him antsy, Kathleen had waited long enough for him to get his head out of his ass.

Eddie blinked, rain splatting his face, and raised an arm to wipe it with his sleeve. Wet was nothing. Frustration, however, ate at him, especially after the emotional visit—for little yield—with Kath's family. Her parents had initially been glad to see him, but became dismayed at his purpose. They insisted that if she'd had good news, she would have called them. They refused to question the cause of death—only their part in it. Kathleen's mother had cried and asked how they had managed to fail her so terribly. Why hadn't they spent more time in the city with her? Should they have brought her home? What might have made a difference? Eddie's father-in-law had become angry. Why was Eddie bringing this up now? What did he hope to gain?

Eddie shook his head. There was no gain for him. He wanted the truth for Kathleen's sake. He wanted to do right by the woman he'd once loved and married, the woman he'd left alone by heading overseas. It had seemed like the right thing at the time, and Kathleen had supported him in it… But if he hadn't—would she be here today?

He pushed hard on the electric buzzer for Apartment 1A, right next to 1B, with the same scenario for floors two and three. He wanted answers. Maybe Miranda Hill, of the slamming-door goodbye, was the one who had some. She was no angel, despite that heavenly face—that was for damn sure.

And the fact that she so obviously didn't really want to talk to him made him all that much more determined to pin her down.

"Yes?" came the crackle of the intercom.

Eddie darted a glance at his watch. "Your four o'clock's here."

Not true—but he was past playing nice. He'd looked at her hours online and knew from what she'd said on the phone, that she'd be booked full up. All he needed was five minutes, in person, so he could gauge her reactions.

A series of electronic clicks sounded. Eddie's lip curled in a half-smile at his luck, and he pushed open the door, even as he mentally shook his head at the woman's naïveté. Safety precautions were important, and she'd just blown it a second time. He and Aiden taught a self-defense series at the karate studio, and therefore heard lots of stories *after* the fact. Never failed to astound him the stupid things people did.

In the minuscule vestibule, he angled his shoulders from long-ago habit, so that he actually fit when he yanked open the inner door. Man, but he'd gotten used to the space he enjoyed in the Poconos. Still, just like jaywalking, the New Yorker in a person came right back.

He looked more closely than he had last time. The door to the right wasn't marked—in fact, it looked as if the number had been pried off the door at some point. At his left was 1A. Just as he stepped forward, it swung open.

The auburn-haired beauty's smile froze solid the second she saw him.

Man, but she was a sight. Thick, loose waves flowed to just past her shoulders and framed bright green eyes, ivory skin, and soft pink cheekbones that begged for his thumb. And God help his currently celibate self, because Hill had even pinker, softer lips—the plump curve of which made him ache with immediate need.

Didn't matter—he'd keep his distance. But Eddie couldn't deny the woman was a looker, and he'd been parched in the desert—literally—a long-ass time.

Her hand tightened on the edge of the door—unpainted fingernails showing white with the pressure.

"You again," she said, and stepped back to plant half her body behind the door even as she narrowed the opening. "Your appointment is Tuesday."

"I can't wait until then."

Her eyes flashed with annoyance, but he spotted guilt there, too.

"I only need a few minutes," he said. "I really need to speak with you." He recognized the hard edge in his own voice and tried again. He breathed slowly and spoke as softly as a man like him could manage. "Please."

Her gaze lifted to his and held. Besides beauty and intelligence, he saw...compassion, maybe? She'd have to have a fair amount of that, given her line of work.

"You're not the type to give up, are you?"

He couldn't help himself—he grinned, because he knew then that she'd fold. "Nope."

She practically glared at his smile before she moved aside. "Five minutes. I do have a four o'clock."

The room held a comfortable living area—both a loveseat

and a padded armchair. A side table sat between the two with a tiny vase of fresh flowers. Another antique-looking table with two straight-backed chairs was tucked into the room's corner and held an array of mismatched mugs, glasses, a pitcher of water, an electric teapot, and a box holding tea packets, sugars, and the like. Prominent was a black-and-white picture of an elderly woman laughing in a silver frame. Another, similar, but the woman was joined by another older woman and a younger one, probably about Miranda Hill's age. The walls held a series of photographs: family shots—brothers and parents, he assumed, given the similarities in looks—and some with groups of girlfriends. A nice touch, all the photographs, reminding visitors that family ties and friendships were the important stuff of life.

But the cozy feel was interrupted by a tripod with a large, mounted camcorder, and some odd-looking square lights on stands: the Goodbye Angel's studio.

Miranda bustled at the table, arranging things, then turned her head to meet his eyes. "I am sorry about the other day."

"Slamming the door in my face?"

She winced. "Yes." She angled her face away. "It was a really bad day. No excuse, though." She waved her hand.

"Apology accepted." Curious, though, that *his* arrival had set her off.

She took a deep breath and turned to face him. "I have strict rules about clients' privacy. That doesn't change when a client passes on." Did he detect a note of apology in her voice?

She crossed her arms over her chest, inadvertently, he was sure, pushing her breasts up inside the snug V-neck sweater. Eddie kept his eyes trained on her face—unfortunately, his peripheral vision was damn good. He felt like a shit for even noticing, but hell, he *was* a male, and she was so very beautifully female.

"So," she continued, "the only information I can share is the same stuff you surely saw on Kathleen's video."

"Then there is other information?"

She huffed. "I'm just telling you my rules."

"Look," he said, "I'm not trying to get you to go against your personal code here. I was away when Kathleen died. I'd been away for a long time, and the logistics made it hard for us to talk. So I'm just looking for…more." Their eyes connected, and Eddie said, "I just need…" He shrugged, not even sure himself. "More."

Miranda blew out a breath and gestured him to the armchair. She took the far end of the loveseat and rested her elbows on her knees, hands clasped, head bowed. "It's been quite a while, and I don't have a copy of her session to remind me."

He'd watched it enough for the both of them. Eddie sat, Kathleen's last medical report in his pocket crinkling. He took a deep breath. "She talked a lot about…regret. And forgiveness. The way life doesn't ever turn out the way you think. She said"—Eddie cleared his throat—"she still loved me."

Miranda smiled and nodded.

"You remember?"

"Honestly, nearly every client I have says those same things. When life is drawing to a close, and a person has the chance to look back, one tends to take off the blinders—and, well, it's always the same."

"That's just it. Kathleen's life wasn't over."

"Advanced cancer, wasn't it?"

"Yes, but she was fighting it. According to her doctor, they tried a new drug, and it was working, even better than they expected."

She sat up, frowning. "So she had hope."

"Yeah. She should've had hope—yet on the video she seemed...resigned."

"Maybe she hadn't gotten that news when she visited me. Maybe the drug stopped working."

"No. I've checked the dates, and I've talked with her oncologist. She would have had word that things were improving by the time she recorded with you. And by the time she died, she was officially cancer-free."

"I don't know, then. All I can tell you is that I am very sorry." Miranda's eyes had grown soft.

The intercom buzzed, shattering the quiet, and Miranda bolted to her feet.

He followed her to the box next to the door. "How did Kathleen find you?"

"A coworker."

"Who?"

He saw a tightening around her lush mouth—because he stood close enough to smell her shampoo? Or because she didn't like the question?

She pushed the button and asked through the speaker who was there.

"There's really nothing you can tell me?" He was crowding her, putting on the pressure. "Anything that I might not have known?" What he didn't want was to notice just how good that herbal shampoo smelled on *her*. Like a summer breeze in the middle of a dreary fall chill.

An elderly man's voice traveled over the wire, announcing a Mrs. Eleanor Durning, and Miranda turned away. Pushing buttons, throwing the bolt to keep the door from latching, and stepping into the hall.

Eddie blew out a breath and followed. "Why did you let me in if your next appointment was female?"

She bent, shoving a rubber wedge under both doors, then grabbed a folded metal piece, one of two, from the corner. "A lot of my clients come with caregivers."

Eddie grabbed the other piece—heavier than he expected, given that Miranda had lifted it without difficulty. "Did Kathleen come with anyone? A nurse or friend?"

She avoided his eye and ignored the question.

"Hello, I'm Miranda," she said to a frail woman in a wheelchair, and Eddie could hear the warm smile in her voice. "Just let me get this set up, and we'll get you out of this rain."

The woman, wrapped in a rain scarf and a stadium blanket, smiled. Her chair had an umbrella stand, but the old man who'd been pushing was wet from his cap to his galoshes.

Eddie set to work beside Miranda, unfolding the two tracks as quickly as possible and making sure they felt secure.

"May I?" Eddie asked the elderly gentleman as he gestured to the wheelchair.

"Yes, please come on in and get dry, Mr. Durning," Miranda urged him, as she slanted a look at Eddie. The man expressed his thanks and tromped up the steps.

Eddie followed and navigated the wheelchair up the ramp and all the way inside Miranda's apartment.

"Mrs. Durning, are you more comfortable in your own chair or would you prefer one of mine?"

"I'd love to get out of this contraption, but I'm tired today. Not sure I can manage it myself."

"I can help, ma'am," Eddie offered.

"Henry," she said, chuckling, "you've got competition."

"So I do. Are you sure, honey?"

"Why yes, it's not every day I have a handsome young man at my beck and call."

Eddie smiled and hoped—unreasonably—that Miranda had taken note of that comment. He found that Mrs. Durning really was weak, and ended up just lifting her into his arms.

"Oh my," she said.

He headed for the armchair, but she waved a bony hand. "The couch, please. Much as I'm enjoying this, I need my Henry to sit with me."

Eddie felt Miranda's eyes on him as he straightened, but by the time he'd turned, she was moving the wheelchair aside. He approached, squashing the insane urge to touch her. "Do you want me to stick around? Or come back, for after?" Jesus, he was a goddamn softy, when she'd been far less than helpful. He told himself he was offering for the older couple's sake.

She shook her head. "Mr. Durning and I can manage, and I expect this will be a long session."

He nodded to the couple now holding hands on the couch, then reached for the doorknob. Miranda stopped him with a hand on his arm, though she dropped those slender fingers just as fast.

"Thank you," she said.

He looked into her pretty face, feeling an odd pang of regret. When he saw her again, it'd be to push her hard for information—she knew more than she was saying, he'd bet on it—*not* to sweeten her up. Too bad—because the photographs on her walls didn't include a wedding portrait. No crayon drawings, either. She was obviously principled, hardworking, and compassionate—yeah, and hardheaded, too—all traits he normally valued. Couple that with the fact that he found her heat-seeking-missile-attractive?

Ooh-rah.

But she was keeping secrets from him. Eddie didn't want anything to do with a woman who wasn't truthful, one who couldn't be trusted across the board.

Even if that weren't the case, Eddie was investigating his wife's not-suicide. Granted, he and Kathleen hadn't exactly been singing Sinatra duets and penning mushy love letters the last few years, but he'd never pictured himself with anyone else.

He inclined his head once and walked out.

Suddenly Eddie wanted so much more than he'd ever considered.

That proverbial second chance.

He wouldn't. Not ever again.

But he *wanted*, nonetheless.

CHAPTER 6

MIRANDA HUSTLED INTO leggings, sports bra, a tank top, and a baggy sweatshirt, then sat to buckle up her rollerblades. Today's chill rain had quickly given way to sharp wind and a cloudy, but dry, sky. Puddles didn't scare her. And blades were a fast way to navigate the city—without being trapped in public transportation. Besides, she loved flying through Central Park, feeling the burn while soaking up all the soft green and curvy paths in the middle of a dense, right-angled world of concrete and steel.

Most of all, tonight she needed a release from the tension that had mounted ever since Eddie Mackey's visit. She sure hoped she'd done lovely Eleanor Durning justice despite being distracted.

After strapping on her helmet, she shoved her running shoes into her backpack—the exercise one. Already there was a flashlight, a utility knife, a roll of gaffer tape, and a small first-aid kit. She had two bottles of water, four granola bars, protein powder, and numerous packets of nuts. Her purse was much the same. And she'd lightened the amount of camera gear she carried in the compartments of her work backpack in order to fit food and extra water there. Video journalists—or shooters, for slang—pretty much went by the same motto as the Boy Scouts: always be prepared.

These days, however, she'd raised the bar to nearly psychotic. Whatever. She needed what she needed. That was all there was to it.

Miranda exited her Upper East Side building and set off toward the park. She needed to talk with her brother—something she damn well should have done long ago. She, of all people, knew better.

David hadn't responded to her repeated pleas to call her this evening, but if she left now, she'd easily hit his apartment and be back before dark. She was banking on the fact that he'd be home now. Likely gathering steam for a wild Saturday night—probably the only day of the week he let loose anymore.

Miranda hit the light just right and darted across Fifth Avenue. As soon as she entered the park, she stretched her legs and pushed hard. She'd do most of the Upper Loop—hopefully just enough to calm her—before exiting on the Upper West Side and laying into Davy. She nearly laughed. He was still Davy to her when he was in trouble, as if he automatically reverted to an overactive, hyper kid who was always pushing the envelope. Heck—historically, he'd shredded it.

She blew out a breath. David had come a long way, but he sure wasn't perfect. Still couldn't always be trusted to use his head first. Which brought her back around to Kathleen Mackey.

The woman's husband had a darn good point. Miranda herself had assumed that Kathleen's demeanor during her goodbye session had been a result of a losing battle with cancer. If Eddie Mackey had those dates correct—and he hardly seemed like a man prone to mistakes or misinformation—then his wife should have been gathering hope like one sucked in fresh air after being trapped under—

Miranda cut that thought off fast. The point was Kathleen would have been looking forward, daring to make plans. *Not* saying goodbye.

Before she knew it, Miranda had exited the park and navigated four blocks of pedestrians and vehicles. She leaned hard on the bell. David's roommate—a kid who took his young career a little too seriously, but was probably just the right kind of non-distraction for her trouble-loving brother—exited just then and told her to go on up.

"Thanks, Keith."

"He's sacked out. Pound loud."

Miranda entered the building and sank down on the steps to swap her blades for shoes. She could navigate steps with blades, but a fifth-floor walkup called for some traction.

After sliding her fingers between the boots and wheels and grasping one rollerblade upside down in each hand, she took the stairs fast and steady and didn't let up—might as well make it part of the workout. Puffing hard by the fourth flight, she considered Eddie Mackey, betting he could carry her up these stairs and not even suck wind. Prominent cheekbones and a chiseled jaw were surely just the icing on the cake—not that there was one extra calorie hiding on that particular dessert. She'd bet that under his leather jacket and T-shirt were some seriously defined pecs and abs.

Yikes—now she was really breathing hard. Miranda rolled her eyes at herself—but hey, every girl needed a fantasy man, especially when she'd basically given up dating.

Hitting the last landing, she walked to the end of the hall and banged on David and Keith's door.

"Oh, hey, sis," David said, half-asleep in gym clothes and rumpled hair. He had her curls, albeit far shorter, and his took instruction well. In fact, the couch must have ordered that mop to stand straight up on the left side.

"Oh, hey? That's it?"

"What?"

She shoved past him. "Why didn't you call me back?"

"Figured I'd call you later."

Miranda sucked in air. Nobody could annoy like a younger brother.

"Dork," he added, eyeing up her helmet.

She rolled her eyes. "Better a dork than dead," she said, and piled all her stuff, helmet included, on the floor by the door. The apartment was minimally furnished, but thankfully it wasn't a sty. She felt confident that no cockroaches would be hitching a ride home on her head.

"You want something?" David said.

"Water." She didn't want to use her stash if she didn't have to; she might need it later.

He got her a glass, then flopped on the couch beside her. "What's so important it couldn't wait until Monday?" They often saw each other at work in the mayor's office or his home. David had participated in a city jobs initiative for young people—one of the mayor's pet projects—and that, along with Miranda vouching for him, had landed him a position as one of the mayor's assistants. He was a glorified gofer, really, but it was a start. Miranda shot all the mayor's video. In a pinch, sometimes the photos, too.

She set her cup of water on the floor, shifted to face him, and crossed her arms. "We need to talk about Kathleen Mackey."

David's eyes darted to hers before he played innocent. "Kathleen? What about her?"

"I know about the affair."

His eyes widened, but he sat stock-still. "The affair?"

"Don't play dumb with me, Davy. I know your IQ."

"She's been dead for, what? Well over a year?" he asked.

She frowned at his callousness and shook her head. "Listen, it's one thing to hide an affair when the only person who an apology means something from has passed." Miranda rubbed her forehead. Cheating was plain wrong, and yet she'd heard peace and joy in Kathleen's voice, seen it in her eyes. "If the relationship gave her comfort, then who I am to say? But it's more complicated than that now."

David was looking at her as if she had two heads.

"Her husband paid me a visit," she explained.

"You *didn't* tell him about her infidelity."

"Of course not. It's not mine to tell, and it's pointless to hurt him like that after the fact. But that's what I'm trying to say: it's bigger than that now."

"No, it's not. She's gone, so it's over and done with."

Miranda pressed her lips together. "Eddie Mackey doesn't believe Kathleen committed suicide."

David just stared. Either he was processing, or he just wasn't getting it. "But she was ill. Dying. She—"

"Apparently not. He believes she was responding well to a new, promising cancer treatment."

"An accident, then? Maybe she took too many pills. Maybe—"

She shook her head. "If Kathleen was…" God, she could barely think it, let alone say it. She gulped. "…*murdered*. Then her husband will find out. And if he does…"

"Murdered?" His voice was little more than a whisper.

She reached for David's hand and gripped it tight. "I'm scared. Fingers will point to you."

"Me?"

He sounded horrified. Davy was not known to make the best choices, and an affair with a married woman certainly qualified as shitty, but he wasn't a truly bad person. Except it wouldn't matter. Eddie Mackey—and the authorities—would be suspicious of "the other man." In this day and age of media insanity, suspicion alone was enough to ruin a person.

"Yes."

"Why? Why in the world would anyone think I'd murder Kathleen Mackey?" David's expression had tightened. "And back up. How do you even know she was unfaithful?"

"She came and made another video."

"She *what*?" Any color left in David's face leached out. "Another goodbye video?"

Miranda bit her lip. "More like a confession video."

"What?" He jumped up and ran both hands through his hair. "No. No way. No, no, no."

Miranda had known Kathleen, but only professionally. The first time she'd come to film, David had escorted her. In fact, he'd been the one to set up the afternoon appointment. He'd been so sweet, comforting her after the emotional session. Miranda had been touched, but had wondered.

The second time, the woman contacted Miranda directly, and showed up alone for an evening session. To confess. And then, given what Kathleen had said that night, Miranda had known for sure. Her brother was in the midst of an affair with a married woman who was—or maybe not, it seemed now—dying of cancer.

Miranda had never breathed a word of it. "I think she needed to come clean...before she died."

"Oh, this is bad, bad, bad," David said. He spun to face her. "If you've got any copies of that confession—get rid of it."

"I don't."

"So it's at Kathleen's? With her husband? He's seen it?"

She thought back to both her sessions with Kathleen and pondered Eddie's demeanor. "She implied that the goal was only to get it off her chest, not to share it. I have no idea where it is now, but Eddie Mackey certainly didn't act as if he'd seen it."

"Good." David shut his eyes and heaved out his breath. "Wait, you always keep a copy. Why not this time?"

Miranda scowled. "Remember when my keys went missing and I thought someone had been in my apartment, but I didn't think anything had been stolen?"

"Shit," David said, and sank like a stone to the couch.

"Yeah, I didn't even realize at first that it was gone. Not until later in the week when Kathleen called"—she gulped—"and told me to destroy it."

Eddie had gotten himself a decent room in a chain hotel north and west of Times Square. Tight but clean, with all the modern amenities. This was day three in the city, and he was feeling antsy. Yet there wasn't a whole helluva lot he could do toward unraveling Kathleen's death on a Sunday.

Early this morning, he'd hit a playground to use the bars, then ran while it was still quiet. He'd walked the city streets, killing time. Nudged old watering holes out of his memory, took note of some favorite eateries that must have gone under, avoided the jazz festival on Fifty-second Street. Kathleen had always enjoyed street festivals of any kind. Dragging him along, insisting they'd find bargains or unique items or new music.

The smell from the festival's food vendors brought those days crashing back, and his stomach had turned. Eddie had turned west. Then south. Eventually, he'd found himself at Ground Zero.

He hadn't gone into the museum, just stood there, looking at all the gleaming, tidy, new surfaces, and remembered the area as it had been. He and Kathleen had lived only a few blocks south, in a funky, renovated loft in Tribeca—all hard angles and industrial materials.

They'd been too close, living the aftermath every day. He remembered Kathleen, coming home daily, covered in…it. He'd felt caged, watching her. Full of rage, feeling impotent with nowhere to go—his office gone, the neighborhood like a war zone. He'd come to dread her leaving—holding tight in the early hours of the morning, making love as if the weight of his body could keep her from returning to that place. Dreaded even more her coming home. Her face, her clothes, her hair. Dull, wet eyes, her spirit deflated.

Hot showers didn't really wash it off. It infected your heart, your soul…in her case, her very cells.

Eddie realized he'd been standing with his eyes shut, and forced them open to look out the window of his hotel room. Gleaming glass. Smooth concrete. Upright buildings. Flat ground. Whole people.

Eddie sucked in air. And turned away.

No one could predict the future, gauge how our actions would affect our loved ones.

Kathleen had done what she'd needed to. And so had he.

Eddie scrubbed his hair in frustration—nowhere to go in this damn cube—and snatched his leather jacket off the chair. He bust out of the room, down the tiny stairwell, and back out onto the street.

He walked a few blocks then chose a pub that was likely to show Sunday football on some big screens. Sure enough, he caught the first half of the Eagles game, ate a burger despite little appetite, and nursed a couple of beers during the second half.

Back in the hotel room, Eddie did a few stretches as he halfheartedly flipped channels on the tube, checking on the evening games.

Loose of limb, but still tense, he was at a loss for what to do next. The trip downtown had sent him into a funk that hadn't yet eased. Plus, he missed all the green and the quiet he'd gotten so used to in the Poconos…the open rooms in his house, the peaceful views. Not to mention his pal Stripes. This claustrophobic feeling, however, was surely more an issue of circumstance than space.

He was missing something, caught in a loop of endless questions. But it was awfully hard to find what you didn't know you were looking for.

Eddie settled on the bed with a bottle of water and rolled his ankles, popping them. Here he was in his old stomping grounds and he was hiding out in a tiny hotel room. Charise had invited him out to her and Frank's house, but he'd said no. He probably should be attempting to meet up with other old friends—okay, acquaintances at this point, given his years in the military and then the abrupt move to Pennsylvania after burying Kathleen.

Except he didn't give a shit, not really. He'd come to the city for answers, not social hour. And he wanted Kathleen.

Aww, fuck, Eddie thought, rubbing a hand over his face, then the stubble of his buzzcut.

If he was being truthful, he wanted the *idea* of Kathleen. He wanted marriage, a real home, kids. He wanted what he'd robbed them of, what she'd given up on. Someone with whom to cook dinner or spend a lazy morning drinking too many cups of coffee, to tag-team kissing boo-boos and getting ice packs, hell—even to argue with. He hadn't had that with Kathleen for years, not since he'd signed on to officer candidate school.

She was more ghost to him than anything now—more past hope than clear memory, the edges blurry, the features fading. It was why he'd stopped to buy that external DVD drive to connect to his laptop. He needed to reset her in his mind. Especially because he kept thinking of the woman he'd seen again today.

Miranda Hill.

She wasn't fuzzy. She was all taut skin and toned muscles. Crisp colors and warm scents, like hot cider. Tall, maybe five ten, given that he would only have had to dip his head to kiss her. He shut his eyes as he imagined sliding a hand into those glorious waves of auburn hair and pulling her to him. The heat of her rosy mouth, the press of her perfect breasts, her soft curves against his—

Fuck.

Eddie shoved the DVD into the drive and waited, settling the laptop on his thighs and propping pillows behind him.

He knew exactly how the session started. Kathleen looking worn out, too thin, and wearing a sad smile. Self-consciously, she reached up to smooth her blond hair, cut much shorter than she usually wore it. He imagined it must have been easier to take care of. Then "I'm not going to say hello, Eddie, because this is more of a goodbye."

Eddie hit play and his wife filled the screen, saying it just as he remembered.

"I feel pretty good right now. But there's no sure bet with

cancer…and I wanted to leave you with something, in case. I know how angry you'll be when you get this, if I'm gone. I know you won't really understand why I didn't ask you to file a dependency discharge. It's complicated. I hope I'll be able to explain, at least to some degree." Kath's eyes darted away, then she looked back toward the camera and nodded.

"Remember when we met? God—way back in school. That cheesy pick-up line you used that made me laugh so hard I cried?" She smiled, then looked wistful. "And later you said that was the moment you fell in love… And how you wanted to go beat up my summer boss at that awful temp agency? How you encouraged me to follow my dreams and become a first responder?"

Kathleen went on for some time. Then she rubbed pale hands over her jeans—baggy because she'd lost so much weight—before looking directly at the camera. "We had so many good times, Eddie. I remember them all. More fondly than ever now. And that's what I want for you to do—remember our early years, when we were in love and so confident about our careers and our future together. Focus on the little things—a good laugh, a tender moment, good sex"—she waved her hand—"whatever. But forget the guilt trips, the fights, the tears…" She sighed.

"I'm sorry. Life doesn't usually turn out like we think." Kathleen pressed her hand high on her chest, over a little gold necklace. Not one he recognized. Probably costume jewelry, as she'd never been big on fancy or expensive stuff. She seemed to draw inward, then after a long moment, she continued. "I struggled with that, I blamed you for changing the plan. I was hurt, angry, lonely…scared for you, and for me. But I under-stand now that it wasn't fair of me. Circumstances change; life happens. We are who we are. I loved who you were, and I still do. I ended up okay—better than okay—even with what I've been dealing with. And you will, too."

Kathleen nodded, and the video ended. Eddie drew a ragged breath.

Twenty-two minutes and three seconds. Too much sometimes, and not nearly enough. Eddie watched it over and over, wishing for answers, staring hard at his wife, listening intently for clues in her language, her voice. Eventually he turned off the TV and set the laptop almost at the foot of the bed. Drowsy now, he bunched up a pillow and stretched out diagonally, listening more than watching, only half paying attention as he finally began to drift off.

That was when he saw it—a movement at the side of the screen. Something he hadn't noticed when he'd been focused on Kathleen, the center image. Eddie levered up and rubbed his eyes. What had he seen? Something out of place? Or had he been dreaming?

He snatched up the laptop and dragged the slider back.

Yes, there. Just a flash of dark fabric.

Kathleen had glanced in that direction a few times, but he'd assumed that the person recording—Miranda—had moved about the room, the camera mounted steady on a tripod.

He zoomed in, hit play again. The figure wasn't Miranda. Not female, and surely not a caregiver, either. Not in a dark suit, a hint of a white shirt cuff.

A man.

Eddie's body temperature skyrocketed and he clenched his fists. *Goddamn it.*

How had he not seen it before? A man was present in the room during Kathleen's tender catalogue of her marriage.

Obviously, he was someone she trusted. Someone she felt

comfortable with. Close enough to her to be well acquainted with her history, her feelings, and her present situation. Involved enough in her life that she'd invited him to this emotionally difficult session. Someone who would give her support and comfort...

Or someone who controlled her, held sway over her in some way...

Eddie tried to keep the thought at bay, but it burned like a blister that'd ruptured in a stiff pair of boots. This man had probably been fucking his wife, too.

CHAPTER 7

EDDIE PRESSED long and hard on the buzzer to Miranda's apartment despite the early Monday morning hour, because the Goodbye Angel undoubtedly knew the answer to the question that still clung to his thoughts like singed rubber: who the hell was the man in Kathleen's video?

He waited, jaw set, boots planted, arms crossed.

No answer. Was it possible that this address was solely an office, rather than her home, and she wasn't in·yet? Or maybe she'd headed out early for that other job she'd mentioned.

He couldn't wait much longer. He had that appointment downtown at city hall with Annette Thompson.

Goddammit. He *would* return and get his answer.

He wasn't going to like it—that he was sure of. Because if it had been a nobody, a non-issue, Miranda would have had no reason not to tell him.

And if it'd just been a...best friend? A confidant? No— if she'd had a "just friends" bud, surely Kathleen would have mentioned the guy at some point.

No, this was someone she'd kept from him. Someone secret. Important. Trusted. A lover. Again and again, Eddie came to that likely conclusion.

He gritted his teeth and laid on Hill's buzzer, not wanting to believe it of Kathleen. Nor did he care to think of the ramifications. Because if she was involved with someone else, her death was that much more complicated. That man was key. He would have been close to her, would have had both knowledge and access. Would he have been passionate enough, motivated enough for some reason, to commit murder? And if so, why? The medical examiner determined suicide—no red flags pointed to a crime of passion committed in anger. Perhaps to cover up an affair? To keep some other secret?

Or maybe the guy had called it quits. And after Eddie "leaving" her for the military, that additional rejection was one too many? Making suicide—shit, he'd been so damn sure she wouldn't have—a possibility.

Eddie shook out his hands and rolled his neck. Today, he'd get answers. He glared at Miranda Hill's door one last time, then spun and headed for the street.

New York City subways at rush hour, doubly so on a Monday morning, sucked. He'd forgotten how much. People everywhere acting like small bulls, heads down and determined to rush their own little red flag—that stairwell, those dinging doors, that sliver of a spot in the car. He had to call back up the skill it took to remain encased in your own bubble while bodies pressed all around you. It was a long ride, Upper East Side to city hall, but at least it was a straight shot, no transfers.

Historical and beautiful, city hall seemed an oddly small building for such a big city. But Eddie remembered articles he'd read. Though not the original building, city hall boasted some seriously cool history, like George Washington's inauguration. Back then, the plaza had been a regular gathering spot intended to promote democracy, but these days people had to actually schedule a protest or gathering. Case in point: Eddie was required to pass through an outdoor security hut, set up just like screening at the airport, before he could cross the plaza and take the steps into city hall.

Straight ahead was a rotunda with a stairway that split in two to curve up to the second floor. Just before that, hallways stretched perpendicularly. To the right were city council offices. Eddie headed left toward the office of the mayor, and stopped at a security desk that had been erected in the middle of the hallway.

Security made a quick call, then said, "Just a moment, sir."

Eddie chose to stand to wait, rather than sit on the available benches. Shortly, a young woman with black-framed glasses bustled from around a corner in the offices, heels clicking, and approached him.

"I'm sorry, sir," she said, "but Mrs. Thompson has been asked to join her husband for an impromptu press conference. Would you like to reschedule?"

"No, I'll wait."

The security guy seemed focused on his phone.

Kathleen used to say he could charm the wings off a fly when he wanted to, so he chatted the blonde up a bit, then asked, "Did you know my wife, Kathleen Mackey?"

She smoothed the ponytail that lay over one shoulder, a nervous habit probably, but her expression was earnest. "I did, and I should have said: I'm so sorry, Mr. Mackey."

"Thanks, but call me Eddie."

She glanced behind her. "I'm not allowed."

"Gotcha. So how long did you and Kathleen work together?"

"A while, but we didn't work together that often. She was already sick when I started. That's why they hired me—to fill in for her. If she was up to it, she would come to work, and if she wasn't, she didn't have to worry about it." The young woman smiled. "Your wife was very nice. Said she was grateful I'd shown up, so she could focus on getting well. Even offered her number in case I had questions. Said not to hesitate."

Eddie heard more clicking footsteps, and the aide glanced behind her and stood a little straighter.

"Mrs. Thompson," the girl said, just as Eddie stepped to the side to make room.

Annette Thompson looked younger than she did on TV, Eddie thought, partly because the heavy makeup and long, overly coiffed hair was deceiving, and partly because she looked so unsure. Maybe even uncomfortable. Given how Kathleen had raved about the woman, Eddie had imagined someone dynamic. But with circles under her eyes to match the deep purple suit she was practically swimming in, she came off as weak and inconsequential.

"You must be Mr. Mackey." Annette surged forward as if she'd been kick-started, and took his outstretched hand in both of her own. "I'm so very sorry for your loss. I know you must miss Kathleen, still. I certainly do." She gulped, and Eddie wondered if she was a consummate actor or perhaps just one of those extremely emotional people.

"Thank you, ma'am, and thank you for seeing me on short notice."

"It's no problem at all. Despite being an employee, Kathleen was a dear friend." Her voice broke. She turned. "Tara, would you escort Mr. Mackey into my office? Bring some coffee, please." To him, she said, "I'll join you in a moment."

After they'd settled in, Eddie said, "I wanted to thank you for coming to Kathleen's funeral."

Annette set down her coffee, the cup rattling against the saucer. "I needed to be there. Even though she'd been unwell, she'd seemed to be doing okay. So, it just...well, her passing came as such a shock."

Eddie nodded. It'd sure as hell been a shock to him. She hadn't even told him she'd been diagnosed with cancer. A fact that still burned him. Didn't she know he would have come? Dropped it all and taken the first flight home? He would have been there to ease her fear, deal with the doctors, hold her hand, and make sure she wasn't alone at night... But surely that was the point. She purposely kept him in the dark, made sure he hadn't come home...because she hadn't been alone.

"I know you were abroad."

Eddie refrained from snorting. That made combat sound like vacation. As if he were riding the rails on a student visa, painting nudes in Paris, or dining his way through Italy. "Active duty in the Middle East."

"Kathleen was very proud of you."

He raised an eyebrow, and Annette smiled—a sympathetic turn of the mouth that seemed to him the first genuine reaction he'd seen from her. Today, anyway. Her sobs as dirt hit Anne's coffin had been heartfelt. She'd been inconsolable, Eddie remembered, and was escorted to a waiting limousine. Definitely the emotional sort.

"I know she didn't want you to go," Annette said, "but that doesn't mean she wasn't proud that you did."

Eddie cleared his throat. "You two were close?"

Annette sat back in her chair and looked off into space. "Yes...she and I spent a lot of time together." She reached for her necklace, sliding the gold piece—sort of a tube with an infinity symbol—back and forth over the chain. She blinked. "One becomes quite close to personal staff."

"Maybe you're the one who can help me, then."

"What is it you need, Mr. Mackey?"

"Eddie."

She nodded. "Then call me Annette."

No way could he ask straight out if Kathleen had had an affair. It was too fucking humiliating. Eddie cleared his throat, tamping down a swift surge of anger. "I wonder if there were things going on with her that I might not have known about."

Annette's face paled and stiffened, the powder she'd caked on standing out in stark relief. "Like?"

"I don't know." He grimaced. "If you were close, then you must know... Well, maybe it was harder on her than I thought when I was gone."

"Yes," she said.

"I don't..." Did he even blame her? No...and yes. "I'd like to know about her last months, even if it's hard to hear."

Annette didn't quite nod.

Eddie said, "Maybe she made some bad choices..."

"That would be unlikely." Her tone was brisk. "Here? In the mayor's office, where everyone is doubly concerned with reputation?"

"Where, then?"

Annette shook her head. "We were close," she said, "but not confidantes."

But she talked to you about me and my decisions, huh? Eddie thought, and swallowed the dregs of his coffee—still better cold than the hot swill he'd had overseas. This sideways questioning was getting him nowhere. Setting down the mug, he said, "Did Kathleen tell you that she entered a drug trial for the cancer?"

"Yes, initially, but I never heard much about it in the long run."

"The drug was working."

"Working?"

"Her numbers were improving—drastically. She was beating the cancer."

Her fair skin dropped to another level of pale. "But..."

"Yeah. That's the thing. That *but*."

"She'd mentioned she had news. The day before she died." She crinkled her forehead. "But then, well, she was gone."

She didn't say anything for a long while, her hand returning to that necklace. She murmured, "It doesn't make sense."

"No, it sure as hell doesn't."

She snapped out of it and speared him with alert eyes, those perfectly drawn lips pressed tight. "Many things don't, Mr. Mackey, especially accidents."

Interesting. "What if it wasn't an accident?"

She stood. "I've always believed Kathleen overdosed accidentally. What I wasn't able to reconcile was suicide."

Eddie rose and faced her. He said, "There is another possibility."

"No, Mr. Mackey, there isn't. But I am glad you stopped by," she said.

"I'd like to meet your husband and the rest of Kathleen's coworkers."

"I'm sure, but now isn't the ideal time."

"I'll schedule an appointment, then."

"That's best." She hit a button and moved to the door. By the time she opened it, Tara was there. "Thank you again for calling on us."

Eddie followed Tara and decided to see if he'd loosened her wings any. "Mrs. Thompson suggested I try to see her husband today, given that I'm only in the city for a brief stay. Could you check for me whether that might be possible? I'd only need a few minutes. Want to express my gratitude for all they did for Kathleen."

Tara pushed her eyeglasses up on her nose and made the phone call.

"Okay, since you only need a quick meet-and-greet, the mayor has agreed to see you now."

Eddie gave her a big smile, deciding she had fairy wings instead of fly ones.

Unlike his wife, Mayor Thompson aged in person. Not that he wasn't a decent-looking guy, but the slick business attire and pomaded salt-and-pepper hair looked less forced on camera.

"Mr. Mackey." The mayor pumped his hand in a firm shake. "My sincerest condolences. Kathleen was an amazing woman—such an integral part of this office, like family, really."

Family, huh? How close had this greasy politician gotten to his wife?

"Thank you, Mr. Mayor. Sorry to show up—"

"Please." He held out a hand. "I'm glad you're here. Can we get you anything?"

When Eddie declined, Mayor Thompson nodded at Tara, who slipped out of the room. He gestured to one of the two chairs facing the desk. The room itself was gorgeous, but the framed diplomas, awards, and handshake photographs swamped the walls. Total overkill.

"I know you're busy," Eddie said.

"I've got time for Kathleen's husband," the mayor said.

Eddie *didn't* have time for roundabout. But he couldn't make himself come right out and ask if Kathleen had had an affair, or if there was any possibility she'd been murdered.

"Well—" Eddie scratched his neck, letting his discomfort, at least, show. "I can't accept that Kathleen committed suicide. I'd hoped you could shed some light on her last months, her state of mind and her choices—maybe some bad ones?"

"Quite frankly, I can't imagine Kathleen making poor choices," the mayor said. "She was one of the finest women I've known."

Smooth, Eddie thought. No telling facial reaction, no give-away in his tone, just one hundred percent slick. "You didn't catch a whiff of anything unusual going on—maybe a difficult situation socially with a friend or coworker?" *Like yourself?* Eddie worked hard to keep a bland expression—his gut really didn't like this guy. Too polished, too even, too perfectly presented.

"No, nothing. Kathleen was a hard worker—organized, caring, and dedicated. In her steady way, she was as heroic in this job as she was as a first responder."

The mayor continued, "It wouldn't have done for her to..." He waved a hand. "She knew her position here was bigger than her actual job."

Eddie remembered what Annette had said. "Meaning the staff in public office is held to the highest standards?"

"Beyond that. Surely, she told you why I hired her?"

Kathleen had—the mayor's whole rewarding-heroic-New-Yorkers thing to fulfill his campaign promises—but Eddie hadn't understood her excitement about it. To him, it seemed so...staged. Kath had helped at Ground Zero because it'd been her job, and because she'd felt compelled to serve. Period. Was the whole dog-and-pony show really necessary? Besides, it also had seemed like something from another world—so removed from the combat situation he'd been living. Obviously, he should have listened more, paid better attention.

Eddie only inclined his head—somewhat of a non-answer.

Thompson said, "Your wife gave her all as a first responder, especially in disaster relief. I promised to help the families who lost loved ones, the survivors, and the heroes who charged in. I take that task very seriously. And so did Kathleen."

"I thought your wife had recommended her. That they'd been friends in college."

Thompson steepled his hands. "That's true, but on paper Kathleen wasn't exactly qualified for the job. She hadn't worked in an office for a long time. But one's actions are the best résumé. I agreed to hire her because she was a hero, a true New Yorker. In thanks and support. Something I wish I could do for every person who was involved in these kinds of travesties."

Eddie pressed on. Information was the goal—the only way he'd make sense of Kath's death. "She was in your employ for, what? About two years?"

"Closer to three, I think."

"Did she tell you right away when she was diagnosed?"

"I believe she kept it quiet for some time," Thompson said. "Cancer is a terrible trial. All the more so when it strikes a hero like your wife. It might comfort you to know that there is a silver lining. Kathleen's tragedy did do our cause some good. Because she was willing to speak up about her struggle, we got the funding we'd been fighting for."

She spoke out? How? To whom? Him?

So he'd definitely *used* her—as an illustration, a story, a marketing tool? Not only for the first responder thing, but again, after she'd been diagnosed with cancer? Not once, but twice? *What the hell?*

Eddie clenched his teeth and his fists as his stomach twisted. He fought to convince himself that ending up in jail for decking this fucker wasn't worth it. He didn't care how many people that money helped—slick Bernie here had exploited his wife. At possibly the lowest point of her life.

And where had Eddie been? When he should have been protecting her from assholes like these?

Fighting terrorists. To protect people, yeah. But *other* people. People he didn't know, would never know.

He shut his eyes and sucked in air, nostrils flaring. When he looked up, Thompson was smiling, a goddamn half curve of patronization and pity.

"It must be hard, all this talk of your wife, even now after so much time."

Eddie grimaced—let Thompson think what he would.

A short rap on the door and a young man entered. "Mr. Mayor?"

"David, please get Mr. Mackey a cold glass of water."

The kid—late twenties at most—stalled and stared for a few seconds, then crossed hastily to a sideboard. He looked vaguely familiar, but Eddie decided that was only because he looked just like practically every other young man he'd encountered in the military: medium height, clean cut, clean shaven, and *young*.

"I believe I have a taping any minute. Have they both arrived?"

"Yes, sir," David said as he set the water down on a coaster near him, then retreated behind Eddie.

Mayor Thompson rose, moved around the desk, and bull-shat his way through some pleasantries. Eddie's jaw was practically locked shut, but he managed a brief thanks.

Not a second later, as he left the mayor's inner sanctum, the smoldering fuse of his anger collided with propellant.

Miranda Hill—wearing a sturdy backpack with gear hanging off the side and gripping an oversized purse and what looked to be another smaller camera bag.

The Goodbye Angel stood right in front of him. Startled,

eyes gone wide. *Here*, past security in the mayor's inner sanctum, looking like she belonged—where Eddie's wife had worked.

She'd lied to him. Omitted the fact that she knew Kathleen as a coworker, avoided his question about who brought Kathleen to her studio.

Which meant that, at the least, oh yeah, she knew something he could use.

At most, she knew friggin' *everything*.

That pretty face, the soft skin and hair, the full mouth, and those eyes that reminded him of lush Pocono summer grass—his idea of a sexy angel—hid a lying devil, with a soul as tainted as hell.

He should have known. She was a videographer, a photojournalist, a visual storyteller, a reporter—didn't matter which specifically. Always cataloging, always looking for an angle. Probably stirring up trouble, creating drama, exposing everyone's bloody guts to the world. As bad as politicians—and here in city hall, there were both, in collusion.

"You work here?" Eddie asked. He let every ounce of disgust show on his face. She flinched.

She was dressed more formally today. Pressed blouse and classy slacks that still managed to showcase her figure. The layers of thick hair he'd lusted after were smoothed into a tight bun at her nape. A serious look for a dirty job.

"Yes." Miranda's voice was barely audible. Her eyes flicked past his shoulder and back, then she pasted on a little smile. "Got to pay the bills." She didn't quite pull off a flip tone.

Yeah, he just bet that combined apartment she called an office—1A *and* 1B—cost a hefty penny. Did they pay her a bonus to keep secrets, too?

"Oh, you're acquainted—excellent." The mayor appeared

at Eddie's shoulder with that David kid trailing him. "How is it that you know each other?"

"We don't. Not really," she said.

"Right," Eddie said, "she's not at all who I thought she was."

Miranda stared at him and swallowed visibly—like she was trying to get a grenade past the lump in her throat. Eddie felt a sick satisfaction.

Miranda's eyes locked on to the mayor. "We're getting a late start. I'm going to go set up." She brushed past, the pack she wore bumping Eddie.

"Enjoy our city, Mr. Mackey," Thompson said, following her.

David shot Eddie a look before disappearing into the office after them. What the fuck was that? Had the little twerp just shot him a back-off-my-property warning?

Either David was protective of his boss, or he had laid claim to Miranda Hill. Or maybe...Eddie's very own wife.

CHAPTER 8

MIRANDA HAD BEEN pushing around the takeout Asian fusion on her plate, when she suddenly realized that the room had grown dead quiet. She looked up to find three sets of crossed arms and raised eyebrows around the cozy round table. Cora and Aggie, short for Cordelia and Agnes, sisters who'd essentially claimed Miranda as one of their own, and Max, Miranda's bestie who was Aggie's blood granddaughter, and, of course, Cora's grand-niece. Miranda and Max had dubbed the elderly pair the Wise Ones. Every Monday, they all gathered here at Aggie's place, a Fifth Avenue penthouse overlooking Central Park, for takeout. A multigenerational version of girls' night out held, well, in.

Miranda slumped back in her chair. "What?"

"What do you mean, what? Max told us about the other night," Aggie said, her New York accent both accusatory—*you can't keep anything from us, sweetie*—and sympathetic.

Cora, who knew Miranda even better than Aggie, because she'd lived across the hall from her for many years before moving in here with her sister, reached over, her bony hand gentle and loving as she patted Miranda's. "You'll get there, but you obviously need help."

Miranda blew out a breath. She *should* be worrying over her damn phobia. Instead, she'd been obsessing over Eddie

Mackey's furious face ever since that horrid encounter this morning. "I'll find a new therapist, promise."

"I told you," Aggie said, "call Dr. Feinstein. He knows what he's doing. He cured me of that wretched gas."

Miranda and Max shared a smile. Feinstein was an internist, and he'd suggested she stop eating broccoli seven days a week.

"Shush, Aggie," Cora said. "She needs a psychologist, maybe a psychiatrist."

Miranda groaned. "I really don't think drugs are going to help in this case. I'm fine until it comes to actually going underground."

"I don't know," Max said. "The anxiety is more pervasive than that. Your two-ton purse—" she pointed an accusatory finger at the oversized bag sitting on the cherry credenza in the foyer—"is a prime example."

Miranda cringed. Like her backpack, her purse was loaded. She'd even added a protein shake and another fresh pack of batteries today.

Max didn't let up. "And you are definitely acting out of character."

"You are not helping here."

"I'm trying to," Max said.

Miranda sighed and shook her head. "I know."

"What do you mean, Max? She seems the same as always. Maybe a little moody," Aggie said, and nudged Cora, "but these gals still get their monthlies."

Max rolled her eyes at Miranda and said to Aggie, "She slammed a door in some guy's face. A client, no less."

"You are such a tattletale!" Miranda said.

Cora looked truly concerned. "Why ever would you do such a thing?"

"He must have been coming on to her," Aggie answered.

He hadn't, actually. Miranda had been the one who'd eyed Eddie up like the dessert case at Sadie's Corner Bakery—best in New York, in her book. The memory—damn her pale skin—warmed her cheeks.

"Did he?" Cora asked, and Miranda noted that each woman's eyes positively sparkled with excitement.

"No. Don't get ahead of yourselves," Miranda warned them. "It was nothing, and there's no chance of a relationship." She twisted her fork in her food, then set it down. "But I will admit, when a guy like him shows up on your doorstep, you start to think."

She gave Max a wry look. "It's one of the reasons I was so adamant about not letting another year pass before I made myself go underground." She huffed in disgust. Colossal failure, that. "I'm not living a full life." She swallowed hard. That was so damn hard to admit. "I'm tucked up safe, yeah, but what if I'm missing out? On my future? Right now?"

For once Aggie had no smart-aleck reply, and even Max was uncharacteristically quiet.

Cora leaned in, propped her chin in her hand, and broke the heavy silence. "A guy like him? Do tell, bubeleh." She grinned, all the beautiful age lines in her face creasing, while the term of endearment eased Miranda.

They all burst out laughing. Attention-seeking Aggie was always cracking jokes, but quieter Cora could blow you away at the most unexpected moments.

"Oh, Lord," somebody said after they'd finally calmed down, and passed napkins to dab their eyes with. God, the Wise Ones were in rare form tonight.

"You're not getting out of it, you know." Max smirked and

tapped one perfectly manicured nail—now dark red—on the table.

"You most certainly are not," Aggie said.

Cora just shrugged, a small smile playing about her lips.

Miranda rolled her eyes. "He showed up at my door on Friday, and then again on Saturday."

Max asked, "You found time in the schedule for him after all?"

"Nope, he tricked me into letting him in."

"He's a stalker!" Aggie said.

"He's not after *me*," Miranda said. "He just wants information."

Max's eyebrows rose. "Obnoxious or charming?"

"Determined."

"Brown hair or black?"

"Blond."

"Eyes?"

"Jeez. You want every detail?"

A chorus of yeses answered that.

"Fine." Miranda laughed. "Gorgeous, darkish blue eyes, great smile. He's smart…" She paused. *Sexy* came to mind, but she was hesitant to give them too much ammunition. "Nice."

"Nice is boring," Aggie said.

"All right, amend that to caring," Miranda said. "Because trust me, I doubt there's a boring bone in this man's body."

"Stop holding back," Max demanded. "How hot is this guy?"

"Smokin'."

Squeals erupted, and Miranda laughed. "Seriously, I might have drooled. He's military—way fit. Sexy voice and a smile that could melt your clothes right off. And he was a doll with my client—sweet, thoughtful—"

"Did you jump him?"

Miranda knew Max's question was largely staged to get a rise out of her grandmother, though it would have been seriously posed if they'd been alone. Sure enough, she received a swat on the arm.

"Who is he? What kind of information does he want?" Cora asked.

"That's why I said not to get excited. Remember that woman from work in the ads for Mayor Thompson? The one that committed suicide? He's her husband, Eddie Mackey."

"Her *widower*," Aggie corrected. "What's the problem?"

"I don't get it." Max frowned. "There's something you're not telling us." She and Miranda went all the way back to college—in fact, they'd ended up roommates through much of their twenties in the apartment opposite Cora.

"I can't share the details."

"Of course you can," Aggie said.

Max narrowed her eyes, and Miranda knew she'd draw all kinds of conclusions, right or wrong. She also knew she could trust these women with anything.

Still, in her charity work, confidentiality was everything. No good could come of sharing the details of Kathleen Mackey's life—because she'd left people behind. People who would undoubtedly be better off if Miranda let sleeping dogs lie. Eddie Mackey, for one. Her own brother, David, for another.

She rubbed her forehead. "I won't talk about Kathleen, nor anything she told me in confidence. It doesn't matter that she's gone. She trusted me."

"Can you tell us why Eddie is asking questions?"

"He aims to prove that Kathleen did not commit suicide." Miranda saw their faces and held up a hand. "I have no idea if she did or didn't. And yes, I've thought about what it could mean if she didn't."

Aggie said, "I don't see why that should keep you two from getting it on."

"Gram!" Max scolded, while Cora reminded her, "He's just been widowed."

"It's been well over a year," Aggie said, crossing her arms defiantly. "Back in my day, a man would be married again in half as much time."

Miranda looked for a hangnail, raising her hand to her mouth.

"He was interested, wasn't he?" Max said, giving her the eagle eye. "What'd you do, sabotage it?

"The door slamming? Bah," Aggie said. "Men like women who play hard to get."

Damn. If Miranda were ever going to manage to get out of this conversation, she'd have to come clean to some degree.

"I hadn't told him that I knew Kathleen before the video, that I worked with her, so when he discovered me at the office today..." She grimaced.

"So he thinks you're a total shit," said Max, and "Oh, I see," said Cora.

Miranda shoved her plate away, knowing she wouldn't be able to eat now.

"Why in the world would you have hidden that from him?" Max asked. "That's public knowledge."

Miranda waved a hand—she couldn't tell them she'd been protecting David, or it'd all end up out on the table. "At the time, it didn't seem pertinent."

Cora tsked at the uneaten food, but pushed a bowl of M&M's toward her. "You were hoping he'd just go away."

Miranda took a handful of the ever-present, comforting

treat—M&M's representing Max and Miranda—and nodded.

"Let me guess," Max said, "this guy is not the walking-away type."

A man who obviously still loved his wife, who still wore his wedding band? Who suspected—possibly with good reason—that something about her death was off? A man who'd already proven he didn't play by the rules, at least not for long? A total alpha male, one willing to do battle—a warrior by career?

Uh, yeah, Max had pegged it. No way in hell was Eddie going to let this lie. Miranda hugged her arms to herself to suppress a shiver. Without a doubt, she'd inadvertently put herself at the top of his takedown list.

———

Eddie waited across the street, in view of the security hut and plaza at city hall. Mrs. Thompson's assistant, Tara, departed well after 1800, but there was still no sign of David Hill.

Yes, Hill. As in the brother of Miranda Hill.

The Office of the Mayor of New York City had a very thorough website with profiles of all their employees. *We serve the mayor, but more importantly, we serve you*, each page said, and listed contact information.

No wonder the twerp had looked familiar—Eddie had seen photographs on the walls at Miranda's, and they had similar features and coloring, although the kid's hair was more brown than red, hers more red than brown.

Fine—she and her brother both worked with the mayor. So had Kathleen. Why not just say so? Why the cover-up?

A dead giveaway that something wasn't right, that there

was something Miranda didn't want him to know. Was she protecting her brother? Their jobs? The mayor himself? Or someone else in that place that Eddie hadn't even come across yet?

He had a hard time picturing Kathleen and David together. A little boy toy? Christ—the thought made Eddie want to retch. Kathleen wasn't a loose woman. She'd had to have really *needed* someone. He grimaced. Companionship, caring, attention—the things she lacked from Eddie, but also hadn't fought for, hadn't even bothered to ask from him, he'd realized. She'd have chosen someone established, he thought. Someone secure and settled and steady. He'd lay odds on Mayor Thompson over the peewee.

But Jesus, a married man? One whose wife she worked for?

He shook his head and pressed his shoulders into the building at his back, pedestrians crossing every which way in front of him. Hell, until last night, he would have staked his life that Kathleen wouldn't have had an affair, period. He hoped he was wrong, but apparently when it came to his own wife, it seemed Eddie didn't know jack shit.

And the fact that he was now trying to picture her with one man or another was a total mind fuck. He clenched his hands in his pockets.

Could he blame her, though? With each additional tour he'd done, the more the emotional distance between them matched the physical distance. His assignments hadn't exactly lent themselves to requesting frequent leave or regular communication, and the longer he did the job, the less easily he shed it when he was stateside. But it wasn't all his fault.

The last time he'd taken leave, he'd only been able to take a few days. It started out okay—visiting both sides of the family and hitting a favorite restaurant for a good American meal. Even a drink with dinner hadn't made conversation flow any easier, but Eddie assumed once they got physical, they'd connect.

But Kath had balked. One minute he'd been kissing her, sliding his hands up her shirt—and the next she pulled away, a look of horror on her face.

"I can't."

Probably his eyes had bugged out—who knew now?—and she'd started yammering. "It doesn't feel right. Let's take some time to reconnect first."

He couldn't help it—he'd been looking forward to bedding his wife for months and he didn't have much time, so he was pissed. He said, "Far as I'm concerned, sex is a damn good way to reconnect."

"I feel like I barely know you anymore," she said, as she frantically stuffed her shirt into her pants.

"I'm not a stranger, Kath. Christ, you married me."

"You aren't the same guy I married. That guy wouldn't have left me!"

"You told me to go!"

"Well"—she slashed the air with a hand—"it changed too much for us. I'm not the same person now either."

The tears had started then, and it'd been an off-and-on monsoon for the rest of his leave. The only breaks were the fights—yelling things they both knew they'd regret, saying things he knew neither of them really meant.

Eddie scrubbed his hands over his hair. He'd realized later that she must have been only recently diagnosed and started treatment before his visit.

Now, of course, he had to wonder if she'd already been having an affair. He had no proof on that score yet.

She'd also been coughing during that visit. He'd urged her to get a checkup, and later, she told him she was better, that the cough was nothing serious. She'd missed their Skype sessions, claiming she had to work or the computer connection had failed. He hadn't put all the pieces together at the time, but later, he'd added things up. Excuses and lies. She'd been hiding symptoms, avoiding making a slip.

He'd been struggling this past year to reconcile her choice to keep him in the dark, to keep him away... That part he did blame her for. Because even if it'd been her way of protecting him, by allowing him to keep serving? It wasn't fair. When she'd found out that she might only have a little time left on this earth?

She should have called *him*. He was her *husband*. He would have gotten his fucking priorities in order and taken emergency leave. Hell, he would have retired, and gladly, to have been with her.

Christ, no good would come of rehashing it. He never got anywhere, only went around and around.

Eddie forcibly dragged his thoughts away to the other things he'd learned today in the hours to kill before he expected Hill would get off work. Thanks to the Internet, he'd easily found some old articles on the mayor's platform when he ran for office. A lot of it was pure political bull—

David Hill. He was out, and passing through security.

Hill headed east toward St. Paul's Chapel, and Eddie, wearing a ball cap to hide his face some, followed from across Broadway. The kid checked his phone, slowing as he did so, then picked up his pace again. Eddie had already bought a MetroCard—good thing, since it looked like the kid was headed for the A, C, E line. Eddie preferred not to confront Hill at the workplace or on public transportation. If, however, he could get him relatively alone, Eddie might convince him to talk.

He followed Hill onto the subway and hovered near the doors at the opposite end of the car. Hill exited at Fourteenth Street and walked south and west, and Eddie trailed. The kid was clueless.

Hill peeled off his suit jacket, then pulled open a non-marked door in the Meatpacking District. The area had largely turned over to clubs, bars, and restaurants. Sometimes legit, sometimes underground. Eddie counted off a minute before yanking open the door to a chorus of male banter.

"Hey, Hilly! What the fuck, man?"

"Dude, where you been?"

Hill's friends slapped him on the back and ordered a round of draft beers. Not one paid any attention to Eddie, who took a seat at the other end of the bar.

David downed a shot and a full beer in the first five minutes.

Eddie heard him mutter, "God, I needed this," and knew he was in for a long haul of watching this baby shithead get drunk. But maybe he'd get lucky, and the alcohol would loosen Hill's tongue.

Eventually, Eddie scoped out the shitter—a single with a working deadbolt—knowing Hill wouldn't leave when he'd just ordered another round for him and his pals. And when Hill finally had to go take a whiz—what was the kid, part camel?—Eddie followed. He closed the distance fast in the back hallway, and just as David attempted to shut the door, he shouldered his way in.

"Hey, what the—"

Eddie flipped the lock and had the kid pinned against the

wall next to the urinal by his neck in a second flat. He twisted Hill's dominant wrist (he drank with his right) at a painful angle. The twerp's eyes bulged with panic as his other hand ineffectually sought for purchase on Eddie's back. Eddie's knee was bent as he leaned in, shoulder pressed into Hill's chest, hip pressed into his groin. Baby face was stuck.

Surely all kinds of alarming scenarios flipped through Hill's mind. Brutal rape, or maybe robbery and a wicked beating—either of which could feasibly be life-threatening. Eddie grinned, good and nasty, letting the kid's imagination do all the work.

"I already don't like you," Eddie growled, and saw the shock on David's face the second he realized exactly who had him pinned. "But you talk to me, and you'll at least walk out of the head on your own two feet."

David's face had turned red, but he nodded.

Eddie let him go and stood to his full height.

"Jesus." David glared and rubbed his neck. "What the hell is wrong with you?"

Eddie sneered. "Me? You want to know what's wrong with me?" He let all the anger of a wronged husband show on his face. "When you're the one who had your pin-sized prick in my wife?"

David's eyes widened again as his mouth dropped open. "I didn't! I never touched her!"

Fuck. It looked like he was telling the truth.

"You knew her."

"I *worked* with her. You know that already, right?"

As far as Eddie was concerned, there were only two options. And an accident wasn't one of them. That left murder—and what a fucking hornets' nest that would be—or suicide. And if she was beating the cancer, the only other thing he could fathom was maybe a crime of passion—a love affair gone wrong.

"Did you date her?"

"No."

"Lead her on?"

"No."

"Reject her?"

"No! Why the hell does everybody assume it was me sleeping with your wife?"

Bull's-eye. "Who?"

"Nobody."

"Now I know you're lying."

Pounding erupted on the door, and David jumped.

"Let us in! What the fuck's going on in there?"

So the kid's buddies had seen Eddie force his way into the bathroom. David looked relieved, except Eddie wasn't at all concerned about those jokers. He'd taken their measure, and he'd counted their drinks.

Eddie shook his head, and Hill's eyes widened again.

More pounding, so Eddie raised his voice. "Who was my wife sleeping with?"

"Nobody. As far as I know."

Eddie slammed him against the wall. "You think I'm stupid? Or are you? You just told me *somebody* was sleeping with Kathleen."

"I didn't say that."

It hurt, knowing he was right, that Kathleen had... Fuck. He'd think about it later—he couldn't pummel this kid. It wasn't his fault.

Eddie wrapped his hand around David's arm and dug his thumb into the pressure point just above his elbow.

David grimaced as he buckled. "Fuck! Stop!"

"Your boss, maybe?" The kid writhed in pain but kept his mouth shut. "Is that why you're afraid to tell me? Big scandal if it's the mayor—you'd lose your job."

David shook his head furiously.

"Maybe if your sis isn't protecting you, she's protecting the mayor. Is she sleeping with him, too?"

"Leave Miranda out of it!"

The shouting and door rattling continued outside. "Okay, maybe you'd rather talk about who murdered Kathleen? The pair of them—your sister and the mayor."

Now Eddie read total freak-out in Hill's eyes. "You're crazy, man!"

"Maybe you had a hand in it," Eddie said.

"She committed suicide! She committed suicide!" He yelled it like a mantra, then closed his eyes as if he could shut Eddie out. He drew a ragged breath and his voice shook. "The cancer… Everyone thought…"

Eddie released David's arm. He was damn tired of this same conversation. "She was beating it. I have proof. My wife *did not* kill herself."

The melee outside suddenly quieted. Somebody had likely tracked down a key.

"This isn't over," Eddie warned, and spun just as the door flew open.

He lowered his shoulder and barreled into the first guy, who flew back into two others. One recovered and advanced. Eddie uppercut him, snapping the guy's head back before he even got his fists up. Peripheral vision told him he was about to get rushed from the left and had somebody reaching for him on the right. He kicked left at waist height, and as soon as he set his foot down, he shot out a fist his toward the other guy's gut. Both doubled over.

Eddie had noted the fire exit to his right. He shoved the guy in his path, even as he swept out his feet. He fell hard on his ass, and Eddie leapt over.

He hit the door running, the bumpy cobblestone alley blurring under his feet. He reached the corner before Hill's pals even spilled out the door. Another street, and he was sure they'd given up. They knew they couldn't take him, and besides, they were probably already busy harassing their buddy for answers.

Eddie laughed. Finally slugging somebody had him feeling nearly happy.

He could charm old ladies and kids and soften a sexy woman—no chore, that. And being military, uniforms—with or without rank—posed no problem. But it had been a long time since he'd dealt with suits and their head games. Even when he'd actually carried a briefcase, Eddie had never really related. He'd certainly been out of his element today at the mayor's office—but this, the physical?

Damn, but he finally felt right at home.

Until he realized he didn't know where to take this investigation next. He could say with near certainty that David Hill hadn't had an affair with Kathleen. Surely the kid couldn't pull off a slick murder, either. Which left Eddie where, exactly?

He scowled. Back to square one. Miranda Hill.

CHAPTER 9

MIRANDA HAD SPENT the day trailing the mayor through Brooklyn, recording both the dedication of a community playground and some meet-and-greets with numerous shop owners in a couple of different neighborhoods. She'd needed a day like that—too occupied to stew. And she'd been relieved, too, because being off site meant there'd be little chance Eddie Mackey could track her down.

She simply couldn't imagine that someone would have murdered Kathleen. The woman didn't have the kind of personality to attract trouble. She was a heads-down hard worker, and had a warm smile when she did look up. Honestly, Miranda had been shocked the woman had cheated—she didn't seem the type. But in Miranda's line of work, she'd learned not to judge.

But if Eddie pursued that line of questioning—and given that he'd been at city hall yesterday, he seemed to be—the guy would be taking another slam to the heart. Surely, he wasn't going to find a killer, but he might just unearth that affair.

Damn. She'd thought her days of apologizing for David's behavior were over.

The mayor's motorcade pulled up to city hall, and most of the staff, including David, would go inside to continue the workday. Miranda would head home to edit footage.

"Make me look good, Miss Hill," the mayor called over his shoulder.

"You've got that covered, sir."

Midway between a joke and a serious request, it was their usual parting. Though sometimes she wondered if he meant good attractive, or good at his job. Probably both.

She waved to David as well, and turned toward the street to hail a cab. One spotted her, swerved to the curb, and squealed to halt.

From long practice, Miranda heaved her various bags to lay next to her on the seat. She refused to use the trunk—she needed access to her things, in case, God forbid—

No, Miranda, stop while you're ahead. Don't think.

She slid in and told the cabbie, "Eighty-fourth and York."

Before the driver could even put on a blinker, the rear door opposite her flew open. A man's lower half appeared—long legs in worn jeans, trim torso, broad chest clad in a soft, faded T-shirt and leather jacket—ducking into her cab. Whoo-ee, but still indisputably *her* cab.

"Hey—I was here first," she said, then froze as the man's head cleared the opening. Oh, he was good-looking, all right, but the stormy blue eyes leveled her way belonged to none other than Eddie Mackey. The set of his jaw and grim, flat line of his lips told her he was none too happy to see her, despite the fact that he'd invaded her space. Again.

"You can't just—"

"I'm headed your way, and we know each other. Saves gas, saves money."

She narrowed her eyes. "I thought you said you didn't know me at all."

A horn blew behind them—another cab.

"Lady?" the cabbie asked.

Eddie crossed his arms and leaned back.

"It's okay, just go," she told the cabbie. Due to daylight, or maybe anger, Eddie's eyes looked darker now, a gray blue, like the small lake that skirted her family's property in Minnesota.

Miranda looked away to stare straight ahead and clenched her jaw. She'd known he'd try to talk to her again, but she'd already explained her position. She'd never broken trust with a client, and she wasn't about to start now just because the client was dead. Plus, she really didn't appreciate his tactics.

"What do you want?" she said, thinking that Eddie could ruin a lot for David. The mayor liked her brother, seemed pleased with his job performance—thankfully, since she'd recommended him—but David would be screwed if Thompson learned he'd engaged in an affair with a coworker—a married one, no less. She'd lose face, too, and she liked this job. It wasn't nine-to-five, yet still paid well.

"Why didn't you tell me your brother worked there? That you worked there?" Eddie's eyes were hard. "That the mayor's office is one big happy fucking family?"

Miranda breathed in slowly, trying not to answer anger with anger. "Only my brother and I are related."

"I came to you asking for the simplest bit of information—"

"You came implying that someone *murdered* your wife!" Crap. So much for keeping calm.

"Someone did."

"That is a serious stretch."

"You didn't think I'd figure out that you were all connected? That you were coworkers, for Christ's sake? What's so secret about that?"

"Nothing! For all I knew, you already knew that."

"You are seriously ticking me off." He shook his head. Disgust rolled off him—seemed to be his most common setting.

"I could say the same about you."

Eddie's nostrils flared. "How can you not even consider the possibility? Are you that sold on your boss's bullshit?"

"Stop," she said. "Mayor Thompson is a good guy."

Eddie's eyes slid toward the cabbie, and Miranda realized maybe she shouldn't have named him, even as her ire rose and her mouth opened. "He's doing a lot for this city, righting wrongs, compensating people that should have been taken care of in the first place. You should know, given who your wife was."

Eddie's gaze bored into her, more like hard steel than fluid lake now. "What do you mean who my wife was?"

She threw out her hand in exasperation. "You know, the Face of New York."

Eddie scowled and turned to her, bracing his forearms against the seat behind and the divider in front, leaning over her equipment. "*That* again. Was it that big a deal?"

The cabbie chimed in, "Yes, yes, everybody know Face of New York."

"It *was* a pretty big deal," Miranda said. "Did you two never communicate?" A flash of something she couldn't quite decipher crossed his eyes. "It wasn't just about her. As the Face of New York, she represented so many, all the men and women who serve the people—you know, everyday heroes. Firefighters, police, emergency services, and even good Samaritans. Kathleen, as a first responder, certainly qualified. Though she wasn't the only one who ended up rewarded."

"She was only doing her job."

"Of course. But she did more than that. She spent weeks after, you know…" Like many New Yorkers, the various horrors of that day flashed through her mind. She pushed them away, refused to say the words. "Then during the…E-Train Disaster…" That one she forced herself to say. She swallowed hard. Less loss of life, but harder for her personally to talk about. "Kathleen became a sort of liaison between the recovery teams and the mayor's office. And then, during his re-election campaign, things kind of came full circle because of her illness. By sharing her story publicly, she helped him accomplish the campaign promise he ran on."

"Which was?"

"Compensation for the folks who became ill because they'd spent so much time at Ground Zero. The victims and families had it. He vowed that responders would have funds for medical care as well."

If possible, Eddie's scowl deepened, the creases on his face as pronounced as fissures in the sidewalk. A muscle ticked repeatedly below his cheekbone. Ruggedly handsome when he smiled or cajoled, she realized he could also look quite fierce when he was leashing his anger, like the combat soldier she suspected he was. Miranda forced herself not to lean away. She wouldn't let him intimidate her.

He cocked his head. "And you?"

"He hired me because of some filming I did."

"Something *heroic*?" He said the word as if it was poison.

She shrugged and looked out the window. She didn't consider it so, but the mayor had. It had gotten her this job. One she'd never aspired to, yet it had been a godsend after that day, allowing her to feel safe and secure, to control both her schedule and her commute. And that was not something she was inclined to share with a belligerent, suspicious widower who was bound and determined to malign people who'd tossed her a lifeline—in more ways than one.

"You headed all the way home?" he asked. She nodded, then saw him look at the cabbie's meter and shake his head. "Gonna be a helluva fare."

Oh goody, she thought, more disgust. What would a day be without a heavy dose of disdain from this obnoxious, intrusive, abrasive—

"Let me guess," he said. "You get to expense it."

She opened her mouth, wanting to say *I don't* and *It's worth every penny* and, most of all, *Fuck You*, but he'd shoved open the door and disappeared before the light turned green. Only a twenty-dollar bill remained where his very fine ass—unfortunately attached to the rest of him—had sat.

Miranda bit her lip, cursing because she felt like crying. Not because he was an asshole, but because somehow she wished he knew, wished she could tell him. She wasn't all the things he thought she was. She'd made the choices she'd needed to, was still making them. Dealing with the honking horns, jerky stops, never-ending traffic, and hefty fares because she *had* to.

Every stupid day that fear ruled her.

Every goddamn day she couldn't make herself whole again.

———

Eddie had tapped the hotel's Internet connection—which, incidentally, sucked—for all it was worth. He'd found what he thought were all of Kathleen's ads for the mayor. He couldn't wrap his mind around it. Kathleen—the Kath he knew, anyway—wasn't the type to care much about politics, let alone influence them, nor air her personal life. But she had. Apparently willingly.

He'd thought the Face of New York thing had died down, that once she'd been "rewarded" with a job, it was over. The guys on his team had teased him about having a famous wife, but even they'd tired of it.

Yeah, he'd been worlds away, and apparently hadn't been paying enough attention. He didn't realize there were more ads with a different angle. But she hadn't *told* him, either. Because if she wasn't sharing about being diagnosed with cancer, how the heck could she explain the whole political spin of helping the mayor win an election by airing the details of her health?

Part of making a relationship work was sharing shit. *Communicating.*

He'd trusted the commitment they'd made, trusted that she'd taken her vows as seriously as he had. He'd also believed that they had time enough to sort things out, that they'd be able to reconnect when he came home.

Obviously not. His temper spiked every time he tried to reconcile the Kathleen that would lie and cheat with the Kath he'd thought he'd known, so he made himself set it aside and focus on the screen.

She looked tired, perhaps born of worry or of treatments—he didn't know—but still relatively strong. She'd been dressed simply. A blouse, a necklace, her hair done and still hers. Her EMS uniform stood on a mannequin behind her, and at one point she held up a picture of him in combat gear, stating that he'd been moved to serve in his way, too. They focused on her service to the city, to the families. And what had she gotten for her efforts? A deadly disease, and jack shit from the city.

Eddie's words, not hers.

He rubbed his hands hard over his face. Kathleen had been gracious, serene, and accepting—except for the part that the city could do more for people like her, that they could no longer deny the link between toxic disaster sites and resulting illnesses. Then, leaning toward the camera, looking right into it, she urged the listeners to let their voices be heard. "*Help right a wrong. Elect Bernard Thompson. He's working for me, for you, for all the true heroes of New York.*"

Despite feeling like she'd been exploited, Eddie could see how the viewing public would have been moved. And yeah, Kathleen herself had definitely seemed willing. He was shocked at how comfortable she was on camera. Her eyes had strayed often, just beyond the lens, seeming to talk with a person, making the ads feel intimate. Surely the videographer, Eddie thought. Probably Miranda. He'd seen her work with that older couple. She had a soothing voice, a face you felt you could trust.

Uh-huh. Miranda Hill—involved in this up to her eyeballs.

How had she gotten the job with the mayor? What had she filmed? It was yet more she hadn't shared.

Eddie started a new Internet search.

Seemed she'd been on staff for one of the big news stations for several years, Channel 8 WNYN. Trailing reporters into the crime scene or tragedy of the day, shoving her video camera into people's faces when they were dazed or stunned or sobbing. Eddie shook his head in disgust. This was how the world worked. He knew it was a job, like any other, but to him there was something so distasteful about that work, so intrusive and callous.

Her name popped up, a whole list of video's, news links, and clips, all related to the catastrophe on the E-train at the

Fifty-third and Lexington Avenue station, which the press had dubbed the E-Train Disaster and often shortened to ETD. A tragedy initially suspected of being a terrorist act, but eventually determined a natural gas explosion. Even Eddie, overseas, had kept tabs on this event. Miranda, it seemed, had filmed some of the footage.

Eddie gritted his teeth, hit a link, and crossed his arms over his chest as he leaned back in the hotel chair.

She'd been trapped with a subway car full of other New Yorkers—thankfully, it hadn't been jam-packed, as it wasn't rush hour. But that line ran deep. He'd been in that station. The escalator took you at least four stories underground.

Smoke filled the tilted car; people moaned from injuries where they'd been thrown; others cried or prayed. Miranda had narrated, taking everyone's names, dictating the time and the route. Two people in her car had died on impact. She turned off the camera, but found their wallets and read the names as she zoomed in on their IDs, her voice shaky.

She filmed in bits. There were, apparently, hours in between. Eventually, the emergency lights failed and the only light was from people's phones, and her camera, which she used sparingly. What little food and drink people had, they shared. Men bashed out windows—but the rubble outside allowed no exit. The doors were bent to hell and wouldn't open. No one had service. Everyone coughed from smoke and dust. Another woman died…just expired.

People began to record goodbye messages on their phones—no service, so the calls wouldn't go out. But they likely figured someone would find the phone eventually, hopefully give it to their loved ones. Those who didn't have phones or power came to Miranda. She comforted them when they broke down. Promised that everything would be all right—though by then, they all must have believed they wouldn't be found in time. Swore if she made it, she'd find their relatives, share their messages.

The Goodbye Angel, Eddie thought, realizing that she hadn't named herself, but had been dubbed by others as a result of this incident.

When rubble shifted, the car would too, terrifying everyone all over again. One passenger, a black man maybe in his fifties, had a heart attack and lost consciousness. The camera thudded to the floor, filming nothing, but the sound was captured. Miranda was giving CPR, counting under her breath, giving orders—*I need light, he's not flat enough, help me.* When the man breathed and his pulse steadied, claps and sobs burst forth from all directions.

"Jesus, Chuck," Miranda said in a muffled voice. "You scared the shit out of me."

Eddie imagined her with her head bowed to Chuck's chest, or maybe burying her face in her arm. And something in the region of his chest began to thaw.

He'd wanted to believe Miranda was a cold, calculating bitch. But she hadn't weaseled her way into this; she'd found herself there. She hadn't exploited the disaster, simply documented it. Counted heads, taken names, used her head, kept her cool, and doled out compassion the whole way—despite the fact that she was obviously just as scared as the rest of them.

She'd forgotten about the camera. It had run until it petered out.

The rescue, Eddie learned, had been an excruciating process of leading people from car to car and eventually hoisting them one by one, up through smoke-filled elevator shafts, despite continued risk. Everyone was aware that a sudden shift of debris, additional explosion, or pop-up fire could halt the process and claim more lives. The wounded, children, and elderly were evacuated first. Miranda had refused comment afterward, but the witnesses had claimed she'd tucked the digital memory card into Chuck's shirt pocket with a note that read: *Contains names of every car 7256 occupant, just in case.*

Despite the fact that they'd said their goodbyes, car 7256 happened to have the most survivors, by one.

CHAPTER 10

"WHAT DO YOU MEAN, you got nothing?" Eddie asked Wik over the phone. The whole reason his unit had nicknamed the guy was because, fingers flying, he was like an Internet encyclopedia—only better. Not that you could list his methods on a bibliography.

"I mean the guy's clean. Squeaky, even."

"Which means he's dirty somehow," Eddie said.

"Hell yes," Wik said. "Nobody's that clean. Every politician out there has slick shoes and greasy palms. Precisely why they slide right on into the next elected position."

Eddie rubbed a hand over his jaw. "What about the wife?"

"Now she's got a couple-a stains. Some blowups with the press. You know, gettin' a little physical with the paparazzi."

"No way," Eddie said. "She looks as weak as a matchstick."

"It's that sulfuric top you got to watch, though."

Maybe so, Eddie thought. She'd been a sobbing mess at Kathleen's funeral. When he'd pressed her at the office, soft and fragile swung to cold and stiff. What kind of force did it take to ignite her? The paparazzi? Photographs? A husband's infidelity?

"What about Miranda Hill? Find anything linking her and the mayor?"

"Not even a whiff of a sexual relationship. No personal

or social crossover," Wik said. "But in addition to her salary, there's a subsidy to her charity."

Of course there was. She'd said as much herself. The mayor was big on rewarding "true heroes." Still, it didn't mean much. Could be perfectly legit.

Wik agreed, and they signed off.

Eddie stood at the window staring at the hopping street below with his arms crossed over his chest.

He'd been counting on Wik to unearth something useful. Ideally a honking X that read *dig here* or a fat arrow that said *this way*. He wasn't a private investigator or a detective. He wasn't remotely qualified for all this.

Well then, he decided as he blew out a long breath, he'd just have to be a dog with a bone, and thought of Stripes. That mutt could gnaw a chew toy to bits.

He pulled his phone from his pocket and dialed Wik back.

"Is it possible to find *previous* employees of Thompson and his wife? Names, addresses, phone numbers, date of termination."

"Somebody disgruntled?"

"Bull's-eye. Find me somebody the mayor fired."

———

Miranda slowed and hovered behind another skater, debating. Of all places to see Eddie Mackey—Central Park on a gorgeous fall afternoon. Despite the fact that it was a weekday, it was crazy mobbed. Schools had resumed weeks ago, weekend beach-goers had settled back into routine, and city dwellers from every neighborhood seemed to be out soaking up the beautiful weather while it lasted. She'd skate until snow blanketed the ground, but most wouldn't.

On her second full loop, she was well into her routine, warm and relaxed, so she hadn't been paying attention specifically to the people around her, just to body language. *Anticipating which way that skater would go around the slow jogger* kind of attention, but Eddie, keeping up a fast clip on foot, had caught her eye in the pedestrian lane. The height, breadth, and build of this man was somehow—ridiculously—already familiar to her. Even the back of his neck, strong and tanned, with a super-close crop of light blond hair that curved to a small V at the nape. She couldn't help herself, ogling the play of his muscles under the T-shirt, the narrow waist, the rear end shaping up oh-so-perfectly under long workout shorts, and the muscular legs—all power in a long, smooth gait. He wasn't one of those awkward runners—no, Eddie Mackey was about as physically perfect as they came, making the most of a body that was meant for all things physical. Miranda felt herself tingle at the thought.

Man oh Manischewitz, as the Wise Ones would say, but he was hot. She shook her head at herself. Angry, suddenly. No point in looking. The guy despised her, despite the fact that he barely knew her.

Well, she wasn't going to let him ruin her afternoon. Miranda shifted her shoulders, slipping off one backpack strap, so the bag swung forward. Unzipped the small pocket and snagged her sunglasses. Settled again, and slightly more incognito, she passed the man she'd been hiding behind. She pushed hard, immediately gaining speed. With no cars on the loop at this hour, she could zoom well away from Eddie in the far traffic lane.

Inexplicably, she held her breath as she passed him. Something about this man thrilled her—on an elemental level. Pulling ahead, she wondered at herself, pushing hard with her legs to get ahead, though surely he wouldn't spot her. Even if he did, he'd never catch her.

Unbelievably attractive, charming when he wanted to be, smart, and principled, she could have been tempted to pull a Max and invite the man into her bed until he moved on. So unlike her, but so tempting.

Therefore, a very good thing that he didn't care for her character.

Needing to pass again, Miranda used the opportunity to check and see how much distance she'd put between her and Eddie.

Crap. He was far closer than she'd imagined. Had he sped up? On purpose? His eyes hidden behind reflective shades, she couldn't judge whether he'd spotted her or not.

Miranda skated on, then decided to cut over Seventy-second Street toward the skate circle earlier than normal. Easy enough to get lost in the crowd there.

She smiled as the dance music hit her ears. Sounded like DJ Big Bobbie today—a regular for the Central Park Dance Skaters Association. Miranda slowed considerably to weave through the circle of onlookers and slipped into the circle. Like a small outdoor skating rink, you just went around and around, grooving to the beat, either on blades or skates. One of her happy places, she'd loved this crazy mix of people and styles the first moment she'd seen it, years ago. Enzo was here. Older than the park itself, it seemed, and dressed in vintage disco clothes. Chubby Maude too, who always wore rhinestone glasses and a leotard with sweat pants. The young black girls, twins, who knew every line dance perfectly but couldn't sing for anything.

God, she loved it. As always, the energy infused her, and she couldn't resist moving to the music.

Miranda scanned past the crowd in search of Eddie. All clear. She'd lost him.

———

Eddie had been running Central Park's lower loop—waiting on Wik and killing time in the city while he figured out his next move—when his peripheral vision had caught her. Definitely Miranda Hill. Same lithe form, same grace, no matter that she was on wheels. Most of all, he'd recognized that hair. Such a rich color, streaming out from under a helmet to float behind her. Next thing he knew, his legs were pumping harder, his breathing adjusting in accordance, so he could keep up. She'd been flying, and he found he had to run fairly hard. Might have lost her eventually on a downhill; however, he'd seen her break off and followed on a whim—an impulse he'd given in to before he'd even blinked. Yeah, he needed information he suspected she had. But this wasn't about that. He was just…curious.

Eddie halted a ways back, just watching, intrigued. Had considered that maybe she'd was simply cutting across the park to the West Side, or maybe she'd sack out with a book in the Sheep's Meadow. Never would he have pegged her destination as that dance circle, though. Should have, maybe—she was graceful and fit. But it was so…hell, so Woodstock for the disco crowd. Anything went. Saggy pants, fake camo, bling, cleavage, skintight jeans, bell-bottoms, even a tutu—all of it on old, young, fat, skinny, and everything in between.

He'd only ever seen Miranda Hill hard-core uptight, or sweet but strait-laced. Until now. He shoved his shades up to get a better look.

Arms waving over her head, her helmet in one hand and

her hair loose, Miranda skated backward and forward, looping and weaving with the music. Shaking that luscious ass,
too?

Eddie hopped up on a bench to see over the crowd.

Uh-huh. Tight T-shirt and leggings. Pert breasts and sweet
cheeks, long, firm legs. If he wasn't so parched from the run,
he'd salivate.

Miranda high-fived the DJ as she went by, and they
exchanged a few animated words. *I'll be damned*, Eddie
thought, *she's a regular*. Between the subway footage he'd
watched earlier and now this, all his preconceived notions
about her were getting shaken and stirred.

He zeroed in again. The wide smile, the sexy curves, the
looseness in her movements. Yowza, if he didn't stop watching
those swinging hips, he'd be fighting some serious wood right
here above the crowd. Around again she went, but this time
her head snapped back—eyes locked with his.

For a second, Eddie would have sworn he saw desire
there, and an answering heat surged in his own body. Except
Miranda went straight, hands planted on her hips, as she
glided backward on her skates. She held his stare, like a challenge, and if her look was hot at all, it was like an angry flame-
thrower, not a sexy sizzle.

Caught staring. At the enemy, no less.

She spun, breaking the connection, and called out to
the DJ, who threw up his hands in a hey-where-you-going
motion. She yelled something to him before dashing between
onlookers at the far side.

Eddie dropped from his perch to the pavement and delib-
erately turned in the opposite direction.

He'd see her tonight anyway—1900 sharp for his hard-
won appointment.

But by the time Eddie got back to the hotel after his run—with just enough time to shower and shave and get back uptown—Miranda had left a voice message.

"Don't come tonight. I've canceled your appointment."

First he swore a blue streak and kicked the bed. Then he dialed her repeatedly, to no answer.

He considered going up there anyway, but knew she'd refuse to let him in, or simply wouldn't be home. She might have gone as far as rescheduling all her evening appointments.

That little witch.

Eddie was furious. And yet her determination *not* to see him was impressive.

And interesting.

Little did she know, she wasn't off the hook. Not until he had answers.

————

Chinatown at night was as hopping as any club. Canal Street was always lit up, pulsing, and jammed with bodies. People returning from work, stopping at fish markets to pick up dinner, heading for restaurants, or looking for bargains.

Even Eddie got solicited for the last. Older Asian women and young black men spoke a mile a minute as he passed: jewelry-perfume-purse-for-your-girlfriend. Same refrain every twenty steps, like a chant.

Music blared from various places, and Eddie thought again of Miranda skating to the beat in Central Park. He was still annoyed that she'd killed his appointment tonight, but at least it'd left him free for other things. According to Winston Chang, things that would be worth his while. Eddie snorted.

He doubted it—and yet he couldn't afford not to check it out when something about the meeting with Chang kept bothering him.

Eddie found Wong Palace easily, despite the fact that it looked like a hole in the wall—or, more accurately, in the basement. The place was small and the patrons were all Asian, save him. The walls were bright yellow, the tables were small and tight, but each had fake yellow flowers in miniature red vases and a full lineup of condiments. A man in a boxy, patterned short-sleeved shirt came forward. With a thick accent, he asked how many.

"One," Eddie said, and was waved to a small table for four. He squeezed into the chair he could see most of the place from.

There was no liquor license here, apparently, so he ordered water. He scoured the menu but didn't see the dish Winston Chang had suggested. He asked for Siu Foon's favorite anyway.

The waiter froze for a moment. Then he turned and went to talk to another guy near the door to the kitchen. Heads together, they both watched Eddie as they spoke. The second guy came to Eddie's table.

"What did you order?" He was tall and thin, with a shock of dark hair that hung over a very suspicious expression. He also wore a short-sleeved button-down, but it was solid black, and his accent was far more Americanized.

"Siu Foon. Maybe my pronunciation is off?" Eddie lifted his hands, palms up, to show he meant no harm. "Smile happy?"

"Who said?"

"Winston Chang. Said to ask for Warren and order that dish."

The man just stared at him. Then he spun and headed for the back. He pulled a cell phone out of his pocket, said something to the initial waiter, and disappeared. That waiter leaned against the wall, crossed his arms, and kept a steady eye on Eddie.

In no time, Eddie had been served what looked like ground beef, peas, and some rectangular white chunks—tofu, he guessed—in some kind of sauce with rice. He nodded his thanks and dug in—*delicious*—as his mind raced. Why the hell was he here? Why the wary looks?

He was nearly done when the tall man appeared with a bottle of Tsingtao beer. He set that down, but held on to a little plate of fortune cookies.

Eddie squinted up at the guy but couldn't see any telling resemblance. "Are you Warren?"

"Yes."

Eddie sat back in his chair.

"Who is Siu Foon?"

"Our sister. She was murdered many years ago."

"I'm sorry," Eddie said. "The guy who did it?"

"Still free."

Ah, Eddie thought even as he grimaced in sympathy, that explained…well, maybe why Winston Chang had chosen to go into forensic science, but not much more. He shifted in his chair and pulled out his wallet from his back pocket.

Warren shook his head. "It's on Winston."

Eddie nodded his thanks. "Why did your brother send me down here?"

Warren's mouth pulled tight with displeasure. He set down the plate and walked away. Rolled up between the cookies was a small piece of white paper, about the width of a cash register receipt.

Eddie took a hefty swig of beer to calm the buzz that suddenly raced through him. He plucked the tiny paper from between the plastic-wrapped fortunes and unrolled it, knowing this would hold a far more important insight. It said:

There may be proof, if you succeed.

CHAPTER 11

EDDIE WAS HEADED for Miranda's apartment bright and early Wednesday, when he saw her crossing the street about a block ahead, wearing that backpack again. She traveled west, away from her apartment, and he considered it pure luck he'd spotted her. He stabbed buttons on his cell. She dug in her bag, glanced at the screen, and said, "Hello?"

She must not have programmed his number into her cell. No surprise there—the woman was definitely hoping never to hear from him again.

"It's Eddie Mackey," he said, "Don't hang up."

"Oh my God." She'd halted abruptly, one hand on a hip, but all that frustration was evident in her voice as well. "You again?" She resumed walking again, this time at a brisker pace, pulling a luggage cart of tidy equipment.

Eddie followed half a block behind, keeping her in his sights. In case she hung up on him, or because—masochist that he was—he couldn't get enough of looking at her? The swing of those just-right hips, this time under a fitted skirt? *Nice.*

"Had you been straight with me from the get go," he said, "you wouldn't have heard from me more than once."

"Leave me alone," she said.

"No can do."

She huffed in frustration, the sound audible even through the street noise. Eddie had to smile. He got a kick out of riling her up—she deserved it.

Eddie said, "You didn't tell me you're in the guy's pocket."

"Assuming you mean Mayor Thompson, he's my employer, and my situation is none of your business."

"Damn well is. The man probably killed my wife."

"Enough, okay?" She was shaking her head. "He's a good man. There's no way."

"Of course you're going that route," Eddie said. "Not only does he employ you, he funds the Goodbye work."

"He doesn't fund it."

"Subsidizes—no difference."

"Big difference," she said, stopping at the top of the stairwell to the subway. "There is a *small* subsidy covered under the mayor's fund. It went through all the usual checks and balances and was approved. Yes, the mayor spearheaded it, and yes, his connections do help when it comes to private contributions." Her voice had gotten thin.

Eddie hung back but could see that her hand gripped the railing as people flowed around her. He said, "You're so naïve."

She didn't answer right away, and he saw her stretch out a foot. It hovered and then returned firmly to the cement. She scooted back a bit, flatfooted.

"And what?" she asked, voice shaking, "What happened to you to make you believe there's no good in anyone, that everyone has an ulterior motive?"

He snorted, the question hardly answerable.

She was peering down the stairwell, then bowed her head to her chest. "Never mind," she said, "I don't care."

All at once, Eddie put together the change in her voice, her posture, her delay. She wasn't reluctant to lose the cell phone connection by entering the station—she couldn't make herself go down into the subway.

Did she go through this routine regularly, walking to the subway entrance, trying to work up the nerve to go down into the station? Every day since the ETD?

Miranda backed away in increments, apparently loath to turn her back on what must look to her like a gaping tunnel ready to swallow her whole. Once her arm had stretched to its full length, she let go and spun toward the cross street. Her hand shot out to hail a cab, and Eddie snapped into gear, because he had information she needed to hear. Wik had come through—sort of.

"I found out something you will care about—or should."

"Oh, you didn't call to harass me about my work?"

He smiled, appreciating a woman with spunk—evident despite the shaky quality to her voice—though this was no laughing matter. "Did you know that two members of the campaign finance board have died in the last few years? One ruled a heart attack, the other a stroke. But there seem to be no autopsy reports, and no warning signs or ongoing health issues."

"How exactly are you getting this information?" Miranda asked.

He plowed on. "A man serving on the CCPC, the Commission to Combat Police Corruption, was the victim of a hit-and-run, the driver never found."

"People do die, Eddie," Miranda said.

"They do. They die. Whatever they might have said silenced permanently."

"Oh, come on," Miranda said with exasperation.

"If you think about it," Eddie said, "there seem to be an abnormally high number of deaths connected to the mayor's office. Interestingly, nobody seems to get fired." He let that sink in.

Because she was facing traffic to scan for a cab, he saw her bite her lip.

"Here's one you'll especially like," he said. "The mayor's last assistant, young man by the name of Jeremy Rashorn, only twenty-four years old, first job out of college, died while in the mayor's employ. Jumped by somebody late at night and killed with a blow to the head."

Miranda's head dropped and her hand fell to her side, even as a taxi slowed and then continued past her. Either she'd given up on transportation, or he'd finally gotten through to her.

Eddie decided to give her one more good push. "Do you want to share that tidbit with your brother, or should I?"

———

Miranda was filming a fluff piece highlighting Gracie Mansion, the official residence of the mayor. Annette Thompson led the tour, with appearances by the mayor and various key household staff. Miranda had only logged about an hour at the office, then they'd all come up here and had been at it ever since.

Miranda had been gnawing over Eddie's little bombshell that long, too. The minute David went to the buffet table in the formal dining room, Miranda sidled up to him.

She murmured, "I really need to talk to you."

"No you don't," he said.

She leveled him a questioning glance.

Under his breath, David said, "Mackey cornered me this morning."

"I should have known." God, the man was pushy.

David shushed her. "Forget it."

"But—"

"Not now. Not here."

Miranda scowled. "When then?"

"Sis, I mean it," David said. "Forget every word he's said." Louder, he said, "Try the buffalo mozzarella. It's from Sal's." Then he lowered his voice again. "I might need you to help cover for me later." He grabbed silverware and walked away.

She dumped food on her plate, barely noticing what she'd chosen. Cover for him? Why? What the hell was he up to now, when he'd just ordered her to keep her own nose down? When all her questions stemmed from *his* screw-up.

Miranda gritted her teeth and chose the biggest hard roll there was, along with a generous helping of butter. Whatever it was, he'd better not get caught.

After the lunch break, the mayor was to share a bit about the history of the house.

David approached them in the yellow sitting room, opulently furnished in the Federal Period, phone between his palms. "I'm sorry, Mayor Thompson. Should I have the police commissioner call back or...?"

Apparently, the mayor was all too happy to have real work to discuss, because he took the phone and waltzed right out of the room. David, looking smug, slipped out of the room via another door, catching her eye as he went, sticking his finger in his ear.

She rolled her eyes at the throwback from their childhood: the old pinky-digging-for-earwax signal. As children, they'd nearly always erupted in giggles, ruining the stealth they'd been aiming for. Now she only felt a ball of worry congealing in the pit of her stomach. *Please*, she thought, *let him be sneaking off to call a girl or grab a smoke.*

Miranda turned and smiled at the mayor's wife.

"Just you and me, I guess," she said.

Annette smiled. "Yes, just us girls." She sighed and sank into an embroidered chair, before slipping off her shoes.

With quick, efficient movements, Miranda dismantled the boom mic and monopod from her camcorder and laid each carefully into the padded compartments in her backpack. She'd never have a better opportunity. Crossing to the other paired chair, she sat and drew in a deep breath.

"Annette, did you know Jeremy Rashorn?"

The mayor's wife's head snapped toward Miranda, her face pale. She blinked, then said, "Of course. Why do you ask?"

"Someone mentioned"—Miranda fumbled—"that it's bad luck to work in the mayor's office."

"Surely, you aren't the superstitious sort?"

Miranda smiled, but shook her head. "I heard it was a tragic death."

Annette's eyes strayed. "It was. He was young, and brutally beaten during a mugging." She shook her head. "My husband was horrified. His own assistant, killed on our city's streets."

"Was he the assistant before David?"

The lines between Annette's brows creased further. "I believe so," she said. "How long has David been with us?"

"Two years, maybe?"

Annette nodded.

"Can I ask you a question?"

"Sure," Annette said, and rubbed her neck with her eyes

closed. When she relaxed, the mayor's wife looked much younger than the near forty she was.

"You spent more time with Kathleen than any of us," Miranda began. Annette frowned, but Miranda forged on. "I've been bothered by what her husband said. About her... health...and her death."

Annette sat up, now rigid, and narrowed her eyes. "What are you asking me?"

"What do you think? Would she have really committed suicide, if she'd been getting well? If she knew—" She broke off when she saw Annette flinch.

"I can't imagine," Annette said, "and it's pointless to wonder now."

"But what if—"

"I don't know, and I don't care to think about it," Annette snapped, even as her eyes darted to the doorway.

"Sorry," Miranda said, wondering who she was more worried about overhearing. David as the illicit lover, or the mayor as the employer—or something far more sinister? "I just can't seem to get the idea that she may not have committed suicide out of my head."

"You must," Annette said as her fingers closed over Miranda's forearm in a fierce grip. Then she seemed to realize that she'd overreacted, smiled uncomfortably, and removed her hand to smooth nonexistent wrinkles from her pencil skirt.

"We simply have to accept that she's gone," Annette said in a soft voice. Then she rested her head and eyes again. Her hand went to the necklace she wore and slid the piece back and forth across the chain.

Miranda sat quietly, mulling over the conversation as unease curdled the food in her gut. She'd hoped for some insight, some reassurance. Instead, she'd been shut down by both David and Annette, raising even more questions in her mind.

She wasn't stupid and didn't care to stick her nose where it didn't belong, but she was beginning to get *very* concerned for her brother. Something wasn't right.

She bit her lip. But there was no way to tell yet if the trouble was of David's own making or not.

The mayor burst back into the room. "Sorry about that." He looked around, a hard look flashing quickly over his features. "Where is David?"

Miranda faltered, suddenly afraid, despite the fact that she'd known this man for some time, any semblance of words sticking in her throat.

"Nature called," Annette said, slipping her shoes back on.

"I was just there."

"There are eight bathrooms in this behemoth, Bernard," Annette retorted, before turning to Miranda. "Maybe we should put that tidbit in the video." She laughed.

Miranda, suddenly very glad Annette Thompson knew how to handle her husband, chuckled too, hoping it sounded natural.

Where the hell *was* David?

———

Max had insisted on going out for drinks after dinner with the Wise Ones, despite Miranda's melancholy mood. She said it'd be just the thing to lift her spirits, get her mind off things…

It wasn't. O'Donnell's Pub was more crowded than usual, and they'd had to yell, making it hard to talk. But Max had her eye on some new guy, so Miranda stayed far longer than she would have preferred.

Miranda walked the last few blocks home, distracted, the late night streets relatively quiet. Her thin jacket flapped open with each step. Her cross-body purse was stuffed and heavy.

Out of nowhere came a sudden whoosh of air, a presence practically on top of her and a flash of movement from her peripheral vision on both the left and right—hands and forearms—reaching around her face.

"Stop!" someone shouted before she even had time to gasp.

A muffled curse near her ear—and in an instant the body that had surrounded her vanished. A split second's respite only as she twisted instinctually—

A sharp pain seared her side and the perpetual weight of her bag on her shoulder disappeared. Then she was shoved hard from behind. Knees, elbows, and palms slammed the pavement and she cried out.

My purse, she thought. *The bastard took my purse.*

She registered the pounding of soles on the pavement, a shadow fleeing into the street.

"Thief!" she yelled weakly. She vaguely realized the inanity of worrying over her things when she was hurt, but was unable to stop herself from focusing on it.

Then she registered more rapid footfalls—this set approaching.

"Help!" she yelled, louder this time, immediately terrified of another attack. She tried to push up, but gasped instead as the pain near her waist suddenly felt like fire.

"Miranda! Jesus! Let me see you."

Strong but gentle hands turned her. Eddie Mackey. Why—

"Christ, you're bleeding."

He peeled off his jacket and bundled it under her head. He peered closely at the wound, using the light of his phone. She looked too, and—

Miranda groaned, nearly passing out. She *hated* the sight of her own blood.

"Uh-huh. Look at me. Miranda—do you hear me?"

Miranda looked at him, only to find him stripping off his T-shirt.

Bare chest. Yep, seriously defined muscles. She was right.

"Ssssst," she breathed, as he pressed his shirt to her side.

"A woman's been stabbed, corner of Eighty-forth and York. Hurry," Eddie said, phone pressed to his ear. "Conscious but bleeding." A pause, then, "No, but about as long as my finger, and I can see subcutaneous fat."

Miranda grimaced. She *wasn't* fat. Longer than his finger? She pictured blood coming out of her from a gash four or five inches long, and her eyes started to roll back in her head again.

"Miranda," Eddie said sharply.

She focused back on him. He craned his head toward the street.

"Fuck this," she heard him say, then a shrill whistle as he left her side.

The squeal of brakes, and he was lifting her in his arms, sliding into a cab.

"Nearest hospital, fast," he barked as he slammed the door.

He didn't lay her on the bench seat, but on his lap. She was propped against him, his arm supporting her while his hand curved to press the T-shirt against her wound. She felt oddly safe despite it all.

"ER?" the cabbie asked. "You want Lenox Hill."

"Go," Eddie said.

She bit back a moan.

"Sorry," he said, a gentle finger trailing down her check.

"Not you," she managed. "The bumps."

"Typical New York cab ride."

She smiled, best she was able.

"You are so pale," he said, frowning.

"Don't do well with blood." She shuddered.

"Or shock."

She nodded, figuring she probably *was* in shock—because she was cold, even in Eddie's arms, the bare skin of his torso flush against her left side. Frozen against a hot military man—Max wouldn't believe it.

Even over the hum of the engine and the street noise, Miranda could hear the operator. "Sir, sir?" Somehow Eddie still had the phone between his ear and his shoulder.

"I'm here," he said in reply.

Max, Cora, Aggie. God, she hoped she'd see them again.

"No, forget that. I'm taking her to the hospital myself." A pause. "The police are welcome to take a report *at* Lenox Hill."

Miranda concentrated on Eddie, afraid to shut her eyes. Flashes of light and shadow flickered across his face as they flew by storefronts, streetlights, headlights, and the dark gaps between. Strong jaw, stubble tonight. Tight lips. Eyes that searched out hers—gauging her well-being. So serious now.

"Is it that bad, then?" she whispered.

"No. You'll be fine." Her skepticism must have showed, because he held her eyes and said, "For real. I promise."

"Oh, good," she murmured.

"How are you with needles? 'Cause you're going to need a tetanus shot if you haven't had one lately."

She groaned. "If this is your grand plan to distract me, it sucks."

Eddie chuckled, and she felt a bit better.

The cabbie swerved and laid on the horn. "Two blocks more."

"You'll be in good hands soon," Eddie said.

"In good hands now," Miranda whispered, and winked. Because Max would want her to. Because *she* wanted to. Because she was damn glad he was here.

He shook his head, yet a smile crinkled his eyes as he pulled her even tighter against him.

Apparently, she'd already died and gone to heaven.

CHAPTER 12

"OUT!" EDDIE ORDERED, blocking the three women who'd converged on the door of Miranda's temporary hospital room. They were waiting for the doctor to clear her and hand over a prescription for antibiotics and pain pills, and Miranda had just dozed off.

He'd lost patience hours ago. The initial relief of arriving at the hospital had dissipated somewhere between the intake paperwork (he knew none of her information, and she was so rattled she couldn't remember the name of her healthcare provider at first), the lame-ass police report (they'd stick with the random mugging theory, he could tell), and the seemingly endless hours of waiting at every stage of the visit. Yeah, he'd pretty much had it.

Thank God he'd been right. The wound had needed a fair number of stitches, but was technically superficial. He hadn't meant to scare her out there on the street by overreacting, throwing her in a cab like she was going to bleed out or something.

He'd just freaked a bit—because it wasn't one of his teammates; it was *Miranda*. And seeing her nearly get her neck snapped like a twig had loosened a tidal wave of fear in him. That bore thinking about later, but not now.

The younger woman, Max, short for Maxine, whom

Miranda insisted he call earlier, reacted to the order. "Who the hell put you in charge?"

"I did."

"You only met her last weekend."

"And I saved her life today. Out. Now."

"I am not going anywhere until I see for myself that—"

"And you are not coming in until the three of you"—he glared at all the women in turn—"can get a hold of yourselves. She needs rest, not a circus."

One of the older women swatted them both with a surprisingly firm hand. "Shush up, you two. Look." She pointed a gnarled finger at the bed.

Miranda was awake and trying to get their attention by waving. "It's okay." Her voice was a little weak. "I could use a good show right about now."

Eddie glared. "Behave."

The trio rushed forward and surrounded the bed, with a riot of clucking and exclamations of relief. Each of the women laid a hand on Miranda's cheek, hand, or arm.

She was loved.

Eddie felt a lump rise in his throat and practically dove out of the room. Jesus, he must really be fried, he thought, rubbing his head and stalking off toward the water fountain he'd discovered down the hall.

A few minutes later, Max found him outside Miranda's room.

She stared at him, like she was trying to see what was behind his eyes.

He crossed his arms. Refused to apologize for trying to throw them out.

Her words surprised him. "Thank you," she said, then

shook her head. "To think what could have—" She pressed the back of her fist against her mouth.

Eddie nodded once. He got it—knew all too well, in fact, what was on the other side of that thought.

"Why were you there?"

"I was waiting on her stoop, to convince her to talk to me. Figured she'd have to come home sooner or later."

"She might have stayed out all night. Hooked up and gone home elsewhere."

Eddie tensed and felt a tic in his cheek. "She's not the type."

Max grinned, then sobered.

An instigator, this one, Eddie decided.

"She's fixated on her purse." Max frowned. "Insists it was a mugging. But it doesn't sound quite right."

He shook his head.

"You're sure?"

"Positive."

She blew out a breath, pushed at her black hair, and settled her hands on her hips. "Come on. Time for you and me to gang up."

Aggie and Cora had both taken chairs on the left side of the bed. Max and Eddie stood at the foot.

"Tell me what happened, what you saw," Miranda said, her eyes searching out his.

"I was sitting on your stoop."

She raised an eyebrow at that, but he ignored it.

"Saw you about a block and a half up." Well before the dark allowed him to see her face, he'd been sure it was her from the build, the outline of her hair, the way she moved. "I stood—didn't want to scare you." Christ, he thought, shaking his head. "A shape peeled out of nowhere and was on you, fast.

I yelled and took off running, but you were down in seconds."
Eddie flinched, wishing like hell he could change it.

"I never even heard him," Miranda whispered.

"He got in close and reached over your shoulders. As soon as I yelled, he changed tactics—slashed at the strap of your bag and shoved you. Took the purse and ran."

All over again, Eddie felt like he was going to explode. God how he'd wanted to chase down that fucker. Could have caught him easily—and would have fucking relished beating him to a pulp.

But Miranda had needed him.

Eddie realized the women were all staring. He forcibly unclenched his fists. "He must have been hidden for a while, because I never saw him. The street had been quiet. From the angle he wouldn't have been able to see me once I sat down. Probably figured I'd gone inside."

"Did you get a good look at the guy?"

"Dark jeans, dark hoodie, dark boots. About my height and lean. Couldn't see his face at all. It was too dark in the spot he chose, between the streetlights."

"A gang member?" one of the older women asked, but Eddie was watching Miranda.

"Highly doubt it. He didn't move like a kid or a street thug."

"No matter that we feel safe most of the time, we do live in New York," Miranda said, her fingers twisting the bed sheet. "Muggings happen all the time."

Eddie hated to upset her, but it had to be said. "This wasn't your average purse snatching. That was only a cover-up—and your side just got in the way."

Max elbowed him.

"I'm trained. I know…things. And this guy did, too. The way he came in, the hold he was going for—he intended much worse."

He snapped his jaw shut before he went too far. A seasoned soldier was not only trained in the art of killing, he didn't hesitate. The instinct lurked inside somewhere, ready to be called up when a situation became life or death. Self-preservation. Him or me. Which often meant attack first, inflict as much damage as possible, as quickly as possible.

And this guy had planned ahead. He was primed and ready to kill Miranda. There wasn't a shred of doubt in Eddie's mind.

Miranda stared at him and said, "That's ridiculous."

Caught up in Miranda's big green eyes, he searched desperately for words he could use, without terrifying her completely.

Max turned and nodded at Eddie. "Tell her about the *much worse*. She needs to hear it."

Eddie rubbed his palms over the top of his head. Damn, Max was right. No matter how hard this would be to hear, Miranda *needed* to know.

He slid behind Max, and in a split second had his left palm against her forehead, his right hand cupping her chin. Max had tensed. He didn't blame her. He'd moved fast, and instinctively a person knew this was a bad position to be in.

He lifted his hands just off her skin to demonstrate the motion, twisting his hands in tandem. Chin up and right, forehead pulled left.

He stepped back, giving Max some space, and heard her breath whoosh out in relief.

Miranda looked pale, and he knew she was remembering the feel of that bastard's hands snaking toward her face.

He said, "It's not foolproof. But with the element of surprise, the strength, and the training—it's possible to snap someone's neck and kill them instantly."

Cora gasped. "He might have paralyzed her instead."

Eddie nodded. "There's no guarantee someone will die when you shoot or stab them, either. But this guy wouldn't have tried this tactic unless he was pretty sure he'd be successful."

The fucker definitely knew what the hell he was doing. And he almost got away with it. If Eddie hadn't been there, hadn't realized what was coming, hadn't shouted immediately...

Miranda's eyebrows lowered, but she held his eyes, no tears, just a firm set to her lips.

Max said to Miranda, "This has gone way beyond protecting whatever code of silence you've sworn to. You should talk to Eddie—about whatever it is."

"You can't be trusted right now," Miranda said to her friend, "You've always had a thing for a guy in scrubs."

Eddie glanced down. He'd forgotten that a nurse had handed him a hospital shirt to wear, since his own T-shirt had gotten bloody.

Miranda rolled her eyes, but he could see the jab at her friend was a tactic to buy time. Eddie wondered—would she come clean finally? He wanted to like her, wanted to trust her, but if she lied to him again...

Max said, "Shut up. I'm serious. Don't you think it's a little coincidental that the minute this one"—she jerked her thumb at Eddie—"shows up and starts asking you questions about his wife, you're nearly killed?"

Eddie scowled. *He'd* certainly considered that all his prodding had gotten Miranda hurt. Ran it around like his brain was a hopped-up hamster on a wheel, in fact. He said, "I asked questions of the the mayor and his wife, too." And her brother.

"Me too—of Annette, I mean, not the mayor," Miranda admitted. "I was fishing—trying to see if she had any doubts about Kathleen's suicide. Just yesterday, but it seems like ages ago now." She rubbed her forehead. "She really didn't want to talk about it—shut me down pretty fast."

"See?" Max said. "Maybe if everything is right out on the table, this can all get cleared up. Sooner rather than later. Because I don't like it one bit."

"But—"

"Stop." Max moved alongside the bed and squeezed Miranda's hand. Miranda's eyes darted to Eddie's.

"Jeremy Rashorn," he said to her.

"What?" said one of the older women, as they all looked around. Miranda paled.

Max asked, "Who's Jeremy Rashorn?"

Miranda frowned, obviously considering what to tell this crew. "He used to work at the mayor's office. Nice kid. Ate Chinese leftovers for lunch every single day. He and I joked about it once. But that's all I know about him." She fiddled with the sheet, pulling it up and tucking it around her. "He's not…what we need to talk about right now. Help me sit up some." When she was settled, she took a ragged breath and raised her face to Eddie's.

"I'm sorry. I lied to you—or at least didn't tell you everything." She shut her eyes. "I thought I was protecting my brother."

"David?" Cora said, while Aggie asked, "What's he got to do with anything?"

Max said, "Oh, shit."

But Miranda ignored the peanut gallery and kept her gaze

trained on Eddie. "I thought if you knew, it'd come out and"—
she waved a hand—"I don't know. I imagined the worst."

Then she back-pedaled in a hurry. "I don't mean about
David—he's a softy; there's no way he'd hurt someone. Big mistakes and stupid moves, he's the king of those, but he'd never…"

The other women murmured in agreement.

Eddie motioned for her to go on. He knew enough about
her brother. But he still needed to know if he could trust
Miranda.

Miranda took a breath. "David was the one who brought
Kathleen to her taping with me. They seemed close. He comforted her. It made me wonder." She shook her head. "Later I
found out for sure—David had an affair with your wife."

Eddie felt a margin of tension drop from his shoulders. She
was being honest—or at least she *thought* she was. She looked
both upset and sympathetic, but rushed on. "Kathleen came
to me again—for a second session—alone. She confessed on
video—to you—that she'd been having an affair. That's how I
knew what David had done. I was sick over it, couldn't believe
he'd sleep with a married woman, let alone one who was so
closely connected to his job and his boss. God." She shook her
head, hard. "I intended to confront him, but wanted to do it in
person. He'd been away, and—whatever. She died soon after,
and then it seemed best to just let—"

"Where's that video?" he demanded.

"It's gone. My place was broken into and—" Her eyes
jerked back to his. "Oh God, it *is* all related, isn't it?"

He nodded, lips pressed tight.

"I'm sorry," Miranda said. "David can be such an idiot. But
he'd never hurt a woman, never." The horror on her face gave
it all away. She thought he'd try to pin Kathleen's murder on
David. "He doesn't have a violent bone in him. He—"

"Your brother didn't sleep with Kathleen." Eddie kept his eyes pinned to Miranda.

"I know it's hard to hear—"

"Someone did," Eddie said, "but it wasn't David."

All eyes swung to him, and he clenched his jaw tight. Damn, it sucked having this conversation with an audience.

"What?" Miranda tried to sit up, pain flashing over her face as her hand shot to her bandages. Eddie had to fight to keep his feet in place—too many people hovering over her already.

"Are you sure? How do you know?" she asked.

"I tracked him down. He's adamant that he wasn't sleeping with my wife."

"You believe him?"

She looked like Stripes waiting for a treat, all big eyes and hope.

"Yeah, he's an open book under pressure."

Miranda's eyes narrowed. "What did you do to him?"

"After tonight, you think I would've hurt your little bro?"

"No. Sorry." She sank into the pillows. "God, what a relief." Her brow creased. "Now that I think about it, Kathleen never named him. And he never actually admitted anything. I just assumed… But David was upset. He knew *about* an affair. Wait—"

Her head snapped up. "It doesn't matter that he wasn't the one having an affair. Same as me, he knows enough to be in danger." Her eyes—filled with far more fear for her brother than she'd shown for herself only minutes ago—collided with Eddie's.

"I have to talk to David. *Now.*"

David wasn't answering his cell and he had no landline, nor did Miranda have his roommate's number—a fact Eddie could tell she was now kicking herself over. Tara, at the mayor's office, was horrified to hear that Miranda had been mugged (they left it at that), but hadn't seen David yet today—and it was now past noon. Apparently, the mayor had been asking for him, and was annoyed that he hadn't even called in sick.

Miranda's friends reminded her that David wasn't always all that reliable. She defended him, claiming he'd been so steady lately, had canned the partying, had turned over a new leaf. They were all visibly worried, however.

And Eddie had a *bad* feeling.

The minute Miranda was released from the hospital, Aggie insisted on having her driver take the lot of them to David's apartment on West Ninety-eighth Street. Miranda insisted she was well enough to climb five flights. Eddie, already having serious reservations about her safety, felt he should go alone. But Miranda and Max, the Ms, as the older ladies called them, overruled him. They believed David would be more comfortable with Miranda there. Probably true, given the shakedown Eddie had given the kid in the john—not that he was sharing the details of that with this protective pack.

Pounding on the door yielded nothing except a neighbor who claimed it'd been quiet all night. Bound in a robe and clutching a box of tissues, the girl said she hadn't heard David or Keith at all since sometime around nine p.m., and she'd have known because "the walls in this dump were built out of rice paper."

"I'm his sister. If you do see them, tell them to call me right away." Miranda provided her landline number, since her cell had been stolen.

Eddie tried the door handle—whaddya know, it was

unlocked. Not good. Nobody left their place wide open in the city.

"Give me a sec," he told Miranda. From the hallway, he pushed the door open, wishing like hell he had a weapon on him. He had a concealed carry permit, and it had seemed wise to bring his Glock to New York, given that he was intent on proving that not-suicide could well mean murder. Unfortunately, the handgun was tucked safely away in his hotel room, because he'd never expected he'd actually need it.

Eddie slid through the place in seconds. Small two-bedroom apartment, furnished minimally. Unmade beds, piles of laundry on the floor, dirty dishes in the sink. Typical bachelor pad.

Definitely empty, and therefore safe. Relieved, he called Miranda in to see the interesting part.

The big-screen TV was on. The tail end of a burrito on top of its takeout wrapper sat on the coffee table along with an open can of soda. A pair of men's dress shoes underneath.

No big deal, probably, except for the cell phone, sitting on the far end of a deep windowsill. What twenty-something left their phone behind anymore?

Miranda snatched it up and scrolled through text messages and calls.

"Anything interesting? Calls?" Eddie asked.

She looked up, frowning. She shrugged. "I don't know all of David's friends. There are a lot of 'where the hell are you' texts. Apparently, David missed some fun last night."

"Could've bagged? Met other friends."

"And left his cell phone here? And didn't show for work?"

"If he ditched the guys for a girl, it's possible they could have stayed in bed—her bed."

"I guess," Miranda admitted.

Eddie blew out a breath. He didn't like it himself. "Without any evidence to prove otherwise, I don't think the cops are going to think much of a guy missing for"—he checked his watch—"maybe sixteen hours."

Miranda's shoulders sagged. Eddie had the craziest urge to gather her into his arms and tell her everything would be okay. But it probably wouldn't. He said, "Why don't you see if anything else seems unusual?"

Nothing did, and they tromped back down the stairs much more slowly than they'd ascended them. Miranda's energy seemed to be flagging—or perhaps it was simply disappointment weighing on her.

Yet, as soon as they'd climbed back into the limo and updated Max, Aggie, and Cora, Miranda set to work, attempting to reach David's friends, asking if he'd ever showed last night.

When she slammed the phone on her thigh and then gasped at the movement, Eddie shoved the bag of meds from the hospital at her.

She glared at him. "I don't need those. They called it a surface wound."

"Doesn't mean it's not deep enough to hurt like hell," Eddie said. "You won't need them for long, but they'll help for now."

"They'll make me sleepy."

Eddie could only hope. He was all too aware of her whole right side, shoulder to knee, pressed against him, her warm, sweet scent still teasing him under the lingering odor of fear, blood, and antiseptic. He suspected the older women had orchestrated the seating, though he could have told them it was pointless to matchmake.

Despite his instincts on that score, the whole ride, he'd been fighting the urge to put his arm around Miranda and tuck her into him—just like inside David's apartment.

"You need to rest," Cora insisted.

"I need to find David," Miranda said, her voice tight.

Aggie pulled a water bottle from the car's tiny minibar. "Here," she said. "Drink. You'll do him no good if you're a disaster."

"Give me his phone," Eddie said. "I'll try the roommate, and I'll field return calls if you fall asleep." When she handed it over, he knew Miranda must really be hurting—or maybe she was just completely exhausted from the ordeal. "I'll wake you if there's anything important."

"I hate to be the one to say it," Cora said, and patted Miranda's knee, "but it is feasible, isn't it, that David's just out having a good old time?"

Miranda flinched. "I know it's not out of the realm of possibility, but he's been so responsible, even steady, for such a long stretch."

"I know, bubeleh," Cora said, but Aggie pursed her lips and shook her head.

Eddie ignored all that subtext for now, and scrolled for roommate Keith's number.

The guy actually answered. "Dude, I'm trying to work here."

Eddie explained who he was, and why he was on David's phone.

"Oh, man. Sorry. I stayed at my girlfriend's last night. Never stopped home."

He had no helpful information, but took Eddie's number and promised to call if David turned up.

Miranda had fought the pull of the painkiller and the lull

of the limo during the conversation, but fell asleep moments after he'd relayed the information. Hardly surprising. They'd only snatched bits of sleep at the hospital. And between the shock of being attacked and the worry over her bro, she must be emotionally fried as well.

Eddie didn't like the odds on this situation. Too damn coincidental that David went MIA the same night Miranda was attacked. But David wasn't his priority. Miranda was.

How the hell had that happened?

He tapped the kid's phone against his thigh as the blocks slid by outside. Was it because he'd blown up the status quo, inadvertently putting her in harm's way? Or maybe because he'd saved her life, he felt...not just attracted to her, but attached somehow?

Miranda's head slumped onto his shoulder, fine strands of her hair catching in his scruff and tickling him. He smoothed it down, refusing to look at the ladies, despite the weight of their eagle eyes.

Resolutely, he squashed the urge to turn and press a kiss to the crown of her head. No fucking way.

His nostrils flared, and he yanked his gaze to the window.

Whatever. Miranda, likely only because Kathleen had confided in her, was involved in his wife's mess, warranted or not. And like the first punch of a newly opened can, he'd only let the pressure escape. Eddie figured they had to pry up the lid before they'd find out what kind of rancid shit was inside. The process was bound to be dicey, sharp edges everywhere.

He'd already determined to be a dog with a bone, and he for damn sure wasn't done digging up dirt. But recent developments changed things considerably. He'd have to add guard dog to his résumé.

By the time Aggie's driver double-parked in front of her building, Miranda had crashed but good.

The women looked at each other. "We'll have to wake her," Cora said, and pulled out her keys.

Eddie shook his head. No time like the present to get started, he thought, as he scooped Miranda into his arms.

CHAPTER 13

MIRANDA WOKE GROGGY and disoriented. The clock read six p.m.; however, she'd been so totally zonked, she wouldn't have been surprised if it was morning. Hearing noises from the kitchen, she levered herself gingerly out of bed. God, she didn't even remember climbing in. She was still wearing the loose button-down and yoga pants Max had brought to the hospital. Better than yesterday's bloody clothes, she thought, suppressing a shiver, but she'd just love a shower. Then she made a face when she remembered that she wasn't to get her bandage wet. Dang—a sponge bath, then.

As soon as she opened the door, an incredible aroma woke her stomach.

As she made her way down the hall, Miranda started unbuttoning her shirt and called to Max, "Can you help me wash my hair in the sink, so I feel human when we eat?"

"Love to," came a distinctly male voice.

She froze. Holy moly.

Eddie's eyes surveyed the valley between her breasts, before he looked up, eyes glinting as a slow, teasing smile curved his lips. Heat billowed from her toes right on up her to her face, as if she'd stepped onto a sidewalk grate over a subway platform in the middle of August.

She gripped the cotton over her chest together in a tight fist. "I expected Max."

"I figured." He winked. "Hungry? You barely ate that breakfast your friends brought to the hospital."

She nodded. "Yes, but I'm feeling kind of…gross."

"I'm sure. You've been through the wringer."

She blinked. She should feel uncomfortable right about now, but she didn't. Eddie had saved her life, held her while she bled, stayed through the night at the hospital…he'd already seen her at her worst.

"Any news on David?"

Eddie shook his head. "No. All the guys called. David never showed or got in touch with them."

Miranda pressed her lips together. She'd expected as much, but God, she'd hoped…

"I'm sorry," Eddie said. She ached to go to him for a hug, but chalked it up to feeling fragile after such an ordeal. Though truly, she couldn't think of another man she'd consider burrowing into for comfort. For some reason—only this one. Of all people.

Stepping into the kitchen, Miranda peered over his forearm at the stovetop.

"Chicken, mushrooms, sun-dried tomatoes, onions. Cooking outta your fridge. Couldn't deal with another round of takeout."

"Smells better than anything in my fridge."

"It's all in the spices. You don't cook?"

She shrugged. "Sure, but it's usually just me, so I keep it pretty simple. I like to bake, though, for my clients."

He smiled—a big, genuine grin that showed sexy white teeth and blue eyes—lighter now than she'd seen; not so haunted.

"What?" She narrowed her eyes. Was he happy about the "just me" part or did he have a sweet tooth?

"Want a taste?" Eddie blew on a spoonful of the vegetable mixture. He'd changed his clothes, lost the scruff, and smelled like soap and aftershave and garlic.

He raised the spoon to her lips.

"Wow. Delicious." That earned her a smile. "You seem… different," she said, and cocked her head to the side. "Not so serious. Did we get some good news I don't know about?"

"I'm"—he shrugged—"compartmentalizing. Something I learned in combat." He stirred the food. "There's nothing I can do tonight to right things for Kathleen or for your brother, so I'm concentrating on the moment. The fact that it feels damn good to be out of that hotel room, cooking real food, sharing it with—"

Miranda caught a sheepish grin before he turned back to the skillet, but she supplied the words *she* wanted to hear. *With a beautiful woman, with you…*

She was reading too much into this. Or—oh, no. Had she developed a savior complex? Jumping straight to the white dress because this hot soldier had saved her life?

Complex or not, if she was being honest, she could admit she had been attracted to him from the get-go.

She felt a blush coming on and tucked her head—which was when she realized he was cooking barefoot. Maybe someday she'd request that he cook in her kitchen bare-chested—

Whoa. Don't go there. He's only here because… Why *was* he here? "Where's Max?"

"Can we eat first," he said, turning off the stove, "while it's hot? And then I'll help you with your hair."

Panicked bubbled. "*Where* is Max?"

"She was here for a couple of hours while I took care of a few things."

"And she's coming back when, exactly?"

He grabbed plates from the cupboard, snatched up forks from the drawer, and divvied up the chicken like he'd operated in her space a hundred times before. "Don't know," he said, and ushered her to the barstools. "There's brown rice, too."

He sat next to her, and despite the fact that there was a stool between them, suddenly her counter felt tight for even two.

Starving or no, she refused to eat until she knew the deal. "Why are you here?"

"Because you need someone to watch over you," he said.

"I have plenty of someones, and they aren't *you*," she said, nostrils flaring, reacting probably more to the fact that she was a hot mess of conflicting emotions around him than anything else.

Eddie set his fork down carefully, and she noted the tense line of his jaw. "Need me to spell it out? Doesn't matter how much your women friends love you; their presence alone isn't enough to keep you safe. I'm trained, and I'm no stranger to violence."

"Surely, you don't think—"

"Yeah, Miranda, I *do* think."

She gulped. "Tell me *exactly* what you think." She'd been worrying over David, hardly pausing to think about herself.

He raised an eyebrow, doubtful.

She nodded, ready.

"The attack on you convinced me. Kathleen *was* murdered. You nearly were. And your brother..." His head moved in the barest of shakes, but he held her gaze, challenging her to face facts.

She could scarcely draw breath, but she made herself say it. "You think he's dead."

He blew out a long breath. "I think he's met with trouble. Whether he's alive or hurt or unconscious or being held somewhere or running scared. Whatever it is, I doubt he just happens to be out partying."

Miranda's face felt like stone, her hands cold as ice in her lap.

"I'm also concerned that you are not safe in your own home. Safer with me here, yeah, but I still don't like it."

"You're planning on staying here, then? Overnight?"

He nodded and attacked his chicken. Miranda stuck her hands between her thighs, trying to warm them, and forced herself to breathe—four counts in, eight out. And again. A strategy she'd learned from the counseling that actually helped a bit sometimes.

She looked around her apartment. Would someone try to break in? She had the whole floor thanks to Cora and Aggie, so the place was big by city standards. More places for thugs to hide. She shuddered.

Or they could set a fire to flush her out. As brawny, tough, and capable as Eddie appeared, he couldn't save her from fire, could he? Or a bullet through the window? Miranda shot a glance over her shoulder toward the windows that faced the street.

Eddie must have shut the blinds. Yet she still felt exposed. Uncomfortable and uneasy. Eddie would be lucky if she didn't crawl right up into his shirt.

Her pulse quickened as the skin-to-skin image popped into her head and words tumbled out of her mouth. "I only have one bed."

———

Eddie wasn't sure whether that had been a pass or an apology. Nonetheless, he enjoyed the flush that stole over Miranda's face, the racing pulse at her neck, and even her awkward delivery. She wasn't immune to him—far from it—but she was a nice girl, unaccustomed to extending bedroom invitations.

Which made him ache to put his hands on her, sink into her heat, hear his name from her lips on a moan. Christ— he shifted, hard as steel under the counter's overhang—he wanted her, badly, and he shouldn't. Yeah, he could give them both some relief, a diversion from the stress of the situation— that was about all he was capable of giving these days, which was probably not enough for Miranda. Besides, he didn't need the distraction.

"I'll take the couch or the floor. Whatever makes sense," he said. He didn't need to be deeper into this snake pit than he already was.

"Listen," he said, "I need to ask you about that other video Kathleen made. Any details you can think of that might be important."

Miranda considered. After a few moments, she shook her head. "I don't think there's anything. She didn't name anybody—obviously. She didn't say much about the affair itself. It was more about her coming clean to you—apologizing."

Eddie blew out a frustrated breath. "Keep thinking about it. If there's anything at all you remember—no matter how insignificant it seems—tell me."

"Okay," she said. Then, after a pause, "I'm going to call the police."

He nodded. "You should."

"Are you going to report your suspicions about Kathleen?"

"No. Not yet." Eddie took his plate to the sink. "They've got a report about your attack, and now they'll know about David."

"We're hampering them if we don't share all the information," Miranda said.

"We don't *have* any concrete information about Kathleen." He leaned against the sink, facing Miranda, gripping the countertop. "It won't matter that I believe she was murdered."

If only he could pin down that coroner, Winston Chang, as to the meaning of that damn note, maybe they would have something concrete. But Eddie had repeatedly tried the man's work, only to find out from the staff that he was away at a conference right on through the weekend. Wik came up with Chang's cell phone number, but the coroner wasn't answering. And Eddie doubted he'd return his call.

Because Wik had also dug up the circumstances surrounding Siu Foon's murder fifteen years ago, as well as her schooling, her extracurriculars, and her friends. And as far as they could tell, there was no connection between Chang's younger sister and Kathleen or any other staff from the mayor's office.

Was Chang just messing with him? Was there a connection he wasn't seeing?

Eddie stared into the sink as if it had answers. What he wouldn't give for one or two. There must be something Chang could tell him, some reason he'd bothered to hint that pursuing this was worth it. Eddie blasted the water over the dish, then turned off the faucet.

One thing he did know for sure: he'd be paying Chang a surprise visit on Monday.

When he turned back to Miranda, her lips were pressed tight in her pale face. "I want David found. The police need to know the whole score."

"I can only figure that my digging must have jump-started this shit show. But for now, the only connection between Kathleen, you, and David, is your place of employment." Eddie held her eyes. "The freaking Office of the Mayor of New York City. There is no way the cops are going to go parading in there on what we *don't* have."

Miranda looked as frustrated as he felt.

"For now," he said, "I'm letting things lie, so I can continue to poke and prod without a virtual fortress popping up around the guy."

She crossed her arms. "It might not be him, you know, the mayor."

"You're right. All I can say for sure is that it's not your brother. What about Annette Thompson? She prone to temper now and then?"

"Apparently. But I've never seen it firsthand. She's always been calm and polite in my presence."

"But if a loose cannon found out her husband was having an affair?"

"God, I don't know. What woman wouldn't erupt over that? How many actually murder the mistress, though? The numbers can't be that high." She shook her head. "And no way did she attack me; it was a man. You said so yourself. And David's not a big guy, but she couldn't have—"

"Anybody can hire a thug, Miranda. And anybody in a political position would. They wouldn't dirty their own hands."

"I know, I just… This is insane."

"We should ask Keith to report David missing."

She frowned. "But—"

"He'll tell them you've been trying to reach him, and they'll contact you, so you'll have your chance. But if it's not *you* who reports it, maybe the person responsible won't be so quick to come after you."

"Would they even know that?"

"I don't know, but I'm sure the police will be interviewing David's coworkers at city hall. And if they are saying *his room-mate* reported David missing, instead of his *sister* reported him missing…" Eddie shrugged.

"Let's call Keith, then. I don't want to wait a minute longer. I need someone out there looking for David—people who know what the hell they're doing. Because I don't."

Eddie retrieved David's phone for her, then leaned against the counter while she exacted promises from Keith. By the time she was done, he needed to reheat her meal.

"Sorry," she said, gesturing to the food.

"No big deal," he said, and it wasn't. Although she was still gnawing her lip with worry, he could see that she felt slightly better for taking some action. And he'd bet it'd make a big difference when Keith reported back, and she had the opportunity to speak with the police herself.

"So for the next twelve hours or so—unless I change my mind"—he cracked his neck—"we'll just let you rest. Eat, sleep, regain some equilibrium."

He had no intention of holing up indefinitely like sitting ducks—in fact, he planned to whisk her out of here tomorrow. Unless he got that feeling. The one he never ignored. Then they'd move out ASAP, no matter the hour. He'd already invaded her drawers and packed some of her things in his duffel while she'd slept. They were evac-ready—anytime.

She nodded and looked at her plate.

"So," Eddie said, in order to distract her, "tell me how you met your posse."

"My posse, huh?"

He pointed at her fork. She rolled her eyes, but took a bite.

"Max and I were roommates in college. We'd often spend weekends in the city at her grandma Aggie's, and I got to know her great-aunt Cora, too. They treated me as one of their own—doubly so once I moved in here. Back then, Cora lived here on this side, 1B, and helped Max and I get 1A. I couldn't believe my luck getting this great place *and* rooming with Max, but Cora was the icing on the cake. She's—well, she's like my own now."

"I wondered how you snagged such a big place."

"Eventually Max wanted some privacy and moved to her own place. Then Aggie's husband died, and since Aggie needs people, she asked Cora to move in there. With both of them getting older, it made sense. Cora gifted me her apartment, and Aggie paid for renovations to combine the two."

"Let me guess. A tax write-off. Charitable contribution to the Goodbye Angel," Eddie said. He was surprised to find he no longer felt any misgivings about her goodbye work.

She smiled. "If it had been just for me, I couldn't have accepted. But my work helps a lot of people, so…"

She pushed her hair away from her face. "What about you?"

"Let's see… I *don't* have a posse made up of eighty-year-old women and a ball-breaking thirty-something."

She laughed, and he felt his mouth curve. Crazy. Even in the middle of a shitstorm, he found himself smiling around this woman.

"Max and I," she said, "call them the Wise Ones. They call

me and Max the Ms." She smiled. "They do make an excellent posse. Not everyone is as lucky as me."

"True."

She raised her eyebrows, so he answered the question she'd originally asked. "As for family, my dad passed—he was never around much anyway. I've got two sisters and my mom. I don't see them as much as I probably should. Day to day, I'm mostly with my students; I own a karate studio in the Poconos with a friend."

"A good friend or an eh-friend?"

"Aiden's like a brother. Grew up training in the same dojo and played baseball together all through school. His dad contends that leprechauns spirited me away to another womb." He wiggled his fingers, aiming for a smile from Miranda. "Twins separated at birth with a little Irish magic thrown in." Aiden's pop was something. In fact, the Irishman could easily go head to head with Cora and Aggie. "Anyway, Aiden had recently moved out to Pennsylvania and I was really feeling...double-whammied. All at once, I lost Kathleen. Lost my team."

"They died?"

He gave a tight nod. "Some, yeah. Once I was out, I missed the others, too. I even missed..." He shook his head. Jesus, it seemed nuts to civilians, but a soldier could miss war. Not the threat of being killed or killing in turn, but the occasional adrenaline rush, the simplicity of purpose. Not the conditions, or isolation, but the connectedness a man felt with his unit, the understanding and acceptance, the solidity of a united goal. A man suddenly cut loose felt untethered, and— aw fuck, it was too complicated.

Miranda just sat, waiting. No judgment, no apparent need to press him.

He said, "I had to get out of New York."

Compassion filled her green eyes as she watched him, almost as if she'd heard what he hadn't been able to say. "It must have been hard, after," she said. "Contending all at once with Kathleen's passing and suddenly being Stateside again, and unemployed to boot."

"Yeah," he said. "It sucked."

When Miranda had eaten enough—which wasn't much—Eddie cleaned up, balancing dishes on her tiny wooden drying rack. Leaning against the sink, arms crossed, he considered her. She looked tired. And he wanted to move them along. "Ready?" He gestured to her hair.

Her eyes widened. "It's okay."

"It's no big deal, and you'll feel better."

"I can manage," she said.

He raised an eyebrow. "Reaching up over your head is bound to hurt, and the doc said not to pull on those stitches. Plus, your hands are a little scraped up still, aren't they?"

Her eyes traveled to his hands over his biceps. She cleared her throat. "It's gotta be the kitchen sink. I don't have a tub."

Eddie retrieved shampoo and towel from the bathroom, then scrubbed the sink down as he let the water warm.

"Okay," he said, turning to make room for her.

She leaned down and lifted her hands to her hair, but he saw her wince.

"Let me," he said, and slid a hand into her hair to push it forward. Damn, just as silky and soft as he'd imagined. Her knuckles turned white where she gripped the lip of the sink.

Eddie started spraying, and water sluiced down over her face.

He lifted a hank of wet hair and peered under. "Can you breathe?"

She nodded, eyes squeezed shut. Turning off the water, he grabbed the shampoo—citrus and tea tree oil, whatever that was—and spread it over her hair, pulling it through the long ends that lay in the sink. She relaxed, resting her chest on her forearms and drooping her head. Darker now, her hair, the red tone disappearing when wet. He began to massage her scalp with the pads of his fingers, the fresh scent wafting up. Mesmerized, he didn't realize that he'd stepped in—his groin pressed to her side—until she moaned and his cock twitched.

"God, that feels good," she mumbled into the metal basin.

Eddie granted himself another couple of minutes, fighting an erection the whole while as he soaked up the feel of her. Then, with the tap set to warm, he worked the bubbles out of her mane.

When he flubbed the attempt to wrap up her hair in a towel, she said, "I've got it."

She stretched her arms up gingerly, patted her face dry, gave the towel a quick twist, and then stood.

Holy shit. Eddie froze, dick straining, breath stalled.

Miranda's white cotton button-down was see-through wet, and the curve of her breasts above the edge of her bra tempted him like nobody's business. Damn pecker refused earlier orders to stand down but good.

Eddie dragged his eyes upward, and saw answering heat in her own.

He stepped forward.

Her eyes widened, lips parted. He reached for her hips.

For a split second, she leaned toward him. Then she blinked and skittered back, bumping into the refrigerator. She reached up to steady the towel on her head. The fabric of her shirt strained tighter, making him clear his throat.

"I'm...going to...go get the rest of me clean." And she

disappeared around the corner faster than he would have thought possible.

Eddie grasped the edge of the sink and hung his head. Fucking hell. Get a grip. What in the hell had he been thinking?

This mess was complicated enough. Miranda was linked to his wife's murder and remained a target. He had no intention of getting emotionally involved—with her or anyone. Not now, and not later. And Miranda didn't seem the kind to take sex lightly.

He had to concentrate on traversing this minefield, completing the mission. Figure out who murdered Kathleen, make them pay before anyone else got hurt, and get the hell out of this city and back to his dog.

And most of all, offering Miranda protection should mean keeping her safe, not showing up with a handful of condoms.

CHAPTER 14

THE PAIN OF her wound, residual shock, and continual worry about David had sapped Miranda's energy. Yet despite being all set in her pajamas and ready to crumble, she'd given one look at the bed and discarded the idea of climbing in. Her bedroom was only across the other side of the back of the U-shaped apartment, but she didn't want to be alone.

She padded over her creaky wood floors, newly refinished to that gorgeous light honey color she loved, past her laundry and storage area, to the office.

Leaning her head on the doorframe, she watched Eddie at her computer. Like her, he seemed desperate to *do* something, no matter how far-fetched a shot. He'd asked to see any video from the mayor's office that might show Kathleen or Annette Thompson.

Footage of the mayor would take days to slog through, and Miranda had explained that she didn't cover every event; sometimes they used other people. Plus, Eddie now knew it had been David's cuff, not the mayor's, in Kathleen's goodbye video. Eddie had said he suspected the mayor himself was too slick to be caught even looking sideways on video, although Miranda felt Eddie was unreasonably biased against him. She'd known the man for almost a year. Sure, he often acted with his agenda in mind—usually to both serve his constituents *and* further his career—and to that end, he placed high value on image. She simply couldn't imagine him risking any of that by having affairs and murdering people.

Still, they had to start somewhere.

"Hurting?" Eddie asked. He swiveled the chair to face her, then rotated his foot until his ankle made popping noises. "You're due."

Every time his eyes collided with hers, she got a little jolt. Was it just because he was so incredibly good-looking, and it'd been so long since she'd had a real, all-out relationship? Or was there a deeper connection between them, despite the fact that they barely knew each other? Perhaps the life-and-death situation they'd found themselves in worked like a fast-forward feature.

"Not enough to take something." She rubbed her arms. "If the police come to the door with news, or someone tries to barge in or—" Miranda shook her head, trying to stop before she really got wound up. "I need to be alert."

"It's late, and even just scanning, this is going to take all night," he said, bracing his hands on his thighs. "You can't stand over me that long. You're about to drop."

She bit her lip. She was scared. Plain and simple, petrified to be more than a few feet from her unexpected bodyguard. It was crazy, she knew, after all these years of living alone in New York. But last night had rocked her world in a big, bad, unsettling way.

Eddie got up, stood in front of her, and tipped her chin with his knuckles so she had to look at him. "What's going on?"

Drat; her eyes welled up with tears.

"Hey now," Eddie said. He pulled her into his broad chest, wrapping her in the thick bands of his arms. One large hand cupped her head. Miranda tucked her face into his neck, then shuddered as she gulped in his scent. She grabbed hold of his T-shirt in her fists and—to her horror—sobbed.

Eddie smoothed her hair and rubbed her back, murmuring *shhh* in a gentle rumble, until she calmed, snuffling. He felt as solid and steady as the sun-warmed boulders in Central Park. Like the city kids who all begged to climb those rocks, she wanted to be free to explore him, and maybe never leave. A dangerous spot this, and yet she slid her arms around him and held on for dear life.

He pulled away to snag a clump of tissues from a box on her desk. To her amazement, he gathered her right back up, pushing her hair out of her face.

"Sorry," she managed.

"Scared, huh?"

"Terrified." She looked at him, her eyes filling again.

"Don't cry," he said, and to her amazement, he leaned in and kissed her gently. Warmth shot through her.

He murmured, "You're killing me."

Miranda waited, on edge, worried he'd stop. Instead, he pulled her closer, flush against his front as he continued the sweet nibbling at her lips. Her nipples peaked instantly, for she could feel every inch of his erection. My God—Eddie *wanted* her, despite the surely blotchy face, red nose, and the still-tender nature of the kiss.

Her legs, wobbly only moments before, felt strong as she surged onto her toes to align their mouths. Eddie groaned and kissed her hard, angling her jaw with callused fingertips. When he sucked her bottom lip, she burst with heat.

Her hands slid into his hair—all soft bristle and hard skull, the cut was so short—as she tried to get closer, closer. Stretching up made her bandage pull, but she didn't care. Eddie's hands glided down her back to her ass, squeezing and lifting, pressing her against him. Miranda tilted her hips, rocking herself against his fly as he squeezed her rear in big palms. Lordy, but she wished they were already naked.

She shoved her hands under his T-shirt, the ridges of muscle clear in her mind, having seen him without his shirt last night as he held her.

"More," she demanded.

"Your cut," he said.

"I'll tell you if it hurts," she said. Sucking on his bottom lip, like he'd done hers, she murmured, "Promise."

Eddie groaned and pressed her up against the wall, hiking her up another couple of inches and pinning her hard with his groin. He curled his torso to go after her neck, then her breasts, unbuttoning her top as he went. It'd been the choice with the most coverage, but now she thanked her lucky stars for the easy access it provided.

"Oh God," she said as his teeth closed over a nipple. She tossed her head back and rocked hard against him. Her wound pulled a little with the movement, but she forgot all about it as she found her rhythm, the swirl of pleasure building fast as his mouth pleasured her breast.

She dug her fingers into his back, and her hips twitched as her inner muscles began to convulse.

"Yes, baby," he said, then tugged hard on her breast, sucking the nipple into his wet mouth. He gripped her hips, pushing her harder against him as she ground down and he pushed up, faster and harder, then—

She shattered, shuddered for long moments, and finally went limp. He held her secure against the wall, dipping his face into the skin of her neck, laying little kisses there, nibbling up under her ear. Both hot and sweet, this man was, and—

Entirely unsatisfied.

She roused, smoothing a hand down his chest, those amazing abs, and lower, trying to wiggle her fingers between their bodies. He stepped away, lowering her gently until her feet touched the floor, and she smiled, happy to have more room to maneuver. But when she went for the button on his jeans, he gripped her wrist and held it still.

"Just you tonight," he said, his voice low and gruff.

"But—"

He kissed her again, silencing her mouth but not her desire to touch him.

"You need sleep."

"I can't sleep. Come to my bed?"

"Miranda, don't." His eyes were liquid, all need and emotional intensity, but his face was chiseled into hard lines. "Not sure I can say no twice."

The sting of rejection was tempered by his words. He wanted her, too. She wanted so much more than what they'd just shared, and could, she thought, tempt him.

But he looked pained—and not just physically—so she nodded.

"Sleep really is going to be tough… Maybe if you're nearby?"

———

"Nearby" translated to Miranda's bed. Eddie sat propped against the headboard, because there wasn't a chair or even a stool in her bedroom.

Miranda slept next to him, her hair fanned out and stretching toward his hip. He kept wondering how it'd feel trailing his abdomen, and lower. Kept remembering the taste of her incredibly soft skin, the perfect curve of her breasts, those incredibly responsive nipples, the warm wet of her tongue. He'd ached like never before, she was so friggin' hot, so goddamned sexy.

He groaned—again—and dragged his gaze back to the current video. Another fundraiser. He'd seen absolutely nothing so far to give him pause, and he'd been at it for hours, using one of Miranda's camcorders to scan footage. He'd have to catch a few winks at some point, but he'd prefer to remain alert in the wee hours. If a threat occurred, that'd be the likely time frame. It killed him that she'd been harmed—and nearly snapped like a twig, for fuck's sake—essentially on his watch.

Eddie glanced at Miranda again, giving in to the odd urge to check on her, only to find her eyes open and watching him.

"Why are you really here?" she murmured, and tucked her arm under her head.

Christ, had she heard his groan, the raw need erupting from his throat?

"I mean, I know why you're here, but why are you here? I wasn't exactly honest with you. You shouldn't want to do me any favors."

He said, "You thought you were protecting David, probably figured I was wrong about Kathleen's death."

She picked at a thread on the coverlet. "True, on both counts. Also, I didn't see any point in hurting you. Suicide is…painful enough. To add another level of betrayal on top…" She shook her head.

Eddie pushed a chunk of hair off her face. "Is that why you do what you do, then? Filming goodbyes and stuff?"

"Yes."

He was surprised to find his hand had settled on her head, fingers threaded in her hair, thumb stroking her temple.

After some time, she said, "My older brother committed suicide. There was no warning, no note, no anything."

Years ago, he surmised, and yet the hurt still filled her green eyes.

"He was our idol, us kids. And my parents' shining star. It was brutal on everyone. It seemed to me that we should all learn from that, talk to each other, communicate even when it wasn't easy, but…"

"It didn't work that way, huh?" He leaned down and pressed a kiss to the crown of her head, just like he'd wanted to in the car ride from the hospital.

"No," she said. "My parents retreated even further—just shells of people. My younger brother, Will, already an over-achiever, became scarily perfect. So rigid and, in his own way, just as empty. David, who is youngest, went the opposite route. All about living life to the fullest and taking nothing seriously. But really, the constant people and partying kept him numb. He was over the top—totaled the car once, ended up getting his stomach pumped another time." She shut her eyes, as if to block that out.

"And you?"

"For a long time, I kept pushing. I was hurting, and I needed so much from them." A soft sigh. "Eventually I realized I'd never fix any of us. The Goodbye Angel stuff came later—by accident. My own family turned out to be a lost cause, but every time I film somebody's history, or even the really hard stuff, goodbyes like Kathleen's, I've helped somebody communicate with a loved one. And I feel just a little bit more whole."

Miranda looked up at him. "You never answered my question. Why are you here?"

Because he owed it to Kath? Because Miranda had been

attacked? Because he'd been working to eradicate evil for so long he couldn't let this wrong lie? And because a marine never gave up until a mission was complete?

Eddie wasn't entirely sure himself—it was all a snarled mess—except for one thing. He shrugged. "This is where I need to be."

CHAPTER 15

AROUND NINE A.M., Miranda woke to Eddie's gentle hand smoothing her hair out of her face—it was surprising how natural seeing him first thing felt. When he handed over her cell phone and explained that it was the police calling about David, she became instantly alert.

She spoke with Detective Iocavelli for a good half an hour, telling him everything she could think of that might help. He promised he'd do all he could to find her brother. The relief of knowing the police were taking David's disappearance seriously was huge. She went back to bed and finally slept deeply—right past lunch.

She'd already called off work. Still, she lamented the lost time. The minute she'd eaten and freshened up, she'd begun scanning her address book for anybody she hadn't thought of whom David might have talked to. Then she'd moved to his various social media accounts. She'd come up with zilch and was trying hard not to cry. Falling apart wouldn't help him.

The intercom buzzed, and Eddie slid past Miranda's office toward the front windows in the interview room, as stealthy and focused as a jungle cat. A jungle cat with a gun.

"Whoa—"

"You need a video monitor," he growled.

"I have all new locks and a new intercom system," she said, because she'd replaced them after somebody had entered with her lost keys and taken Kathleen's video. "But this is a client, and I have an appointment. Five o'clock."

He glared. "You didn't think to tell me this?"

"I've been a little out of it," she snapped.

"Tell them you'll have to reschedule." He flattened himself against the wall and aligned his eye along the edge of the blinds.

"I'm well enough to handle a taping."

"There was an attempt on your life and you want to throw open your doors? Invite anybody and everybody in?"

"This isn't just anybody." She flapped her arms in exasperation. "She's a repeat client. I'm sure of it—I just checked my calendar, and she confirmed early this week."

He crossed the room in two strides and got in her face. "How am I going to keep you safe if you don't let me?"

Miranda lifted her chin. She'd admit she was out of her element with all this, but she'd never let a client down before, and she wasn't about to start. "Go check it out. I'll stay here until you're comfortable."

He scowled and made a rude noise in his throat. "Lock the door after me. Then stand over there, out of the line of sight." He pointed to the corner near the windows.

She frowned.

"Miranda, blinds don't block bullets." He leaned in and pressed his lips to hers in a quick but intense kiss. "And I don't ever want to see you bleed again."

Stunned, she nodded. The moment the door swung shut behind him, she slid the bolt and the chain home. He cared for her—at least to some degree. Or was it just his nature? Big, bad protector of the weak?

How did she feel about him? Attracted, definitely—what his smile did to her insides, what his touch had done to her body in seconds flat...and hoowee, what she'd have liked to do to him, if only he'd let her. Her emotions certainly tugged whenever she thought of what he'd been through...and what kind of danger he might face by staying here with her.

Pressed into the corner, her heart began to pound.

The doorbell should be her client, but there could be another threat. Maybe somebody would jump Eddie, and he'd be hurt out there. Or maybe there was a gunman on a rooftop, and God forbid, he was killed. Or—

The intercom snapped, and she darted over to press the button. "Yes?"

"All clear. Let us in," Eddie said.

Miranda lowered her forehead to the wall and fought to breathe normally as she pressed her eye to the peephole, then opened the door.

She hugged her client, a sixty-ish soon-to-be grandmother who was determined to document her stories of growing up on a working farm—from being butted by a bad-ass billy goat to a midnight rendezvous with the neighbor boy, who became her husband of forty-some years—as a gift for her daughter and baby granddaughter.

"Before I leave," Eddie said into her ear as he entered, "I'm rigging you with a monitor and alarms and the whole bit."

His intensity—or maybe his mouth at her ear—rocked a shiver down her spine. She nodded, then he turned to her client with the charm turned back up to full melt and promised to let them be.

———

Eddie let his smile drop the second he left the room. Why he'd kissed Miranda again, he couldn't fathom. He'd promised himself as he watched her sleep that he'd steer clear, that he'd refrain from touching her at all costs. Except that inferno of an encounter last night had screwed him. He knew now how she tasted, how she felt—and face it, he wanted more. He wanted to throw her down, block out the world, and bury himself inside her. He wanted her hot and begging, then limp and sated, and then he wanted it all over again.

So many times he'd pushed himself to the limit. Forced himself to do or not do, to overcome, to hold his ground at any cost.

Yet here was this one woman, this one sexy, compassionate, headstrong redhead—and he'd lost his edge so entirely that he was nothing but a friggin' puddle. What an ass.

Eddie flipped on the TV in Miranda's living room to a news channel and set the volume low. He figured it'd give Miranda and her client a sense of privacy if he at least pretended to be focused on something else. He scrubbed his hands over his head in frustration, then dropped to the floor. He didn't count pushups, just dipped his nose to the hardwood over and over, well past the burn. Switched to jump crunches, wishing he had weights or an inverted bench. He'd moved to a series of kicks when he caught Miranda's name out of the blather on TV. He swiveled, leg frozen at head height, and swore when he saw her face flash on the screen, before it retreated behind the news anchor's head.

"...attacked outside her home Wednesday evening."

Eddie lunged for the controller and stabbed the volume button. Miranda was the lead story on the six o'clock news.

"Many will remember Hill's footage from the E-Train Disaster, where she saved a man's life and was dubbed the Goodbye Angel. The attack is believed to be a mugging, the suspect still at large. Hill is reported to be recovering at her Upper East Side home."

"Christ," Eddie muttered, and stalked to the front of the apartment.

Now Miranda really was a sitting duck. Wounded and pinpointed on the map.

And little did Eddie know, but Miranda's client was a two-hour appointment and chatty.

He tried, but there'd been no rushing the woman out the door.

———

"It's even worse than the last time I checked," Eddie said.

He'd been tense for hours, and Miranda was feeling increasingly uneasy. So obviously trapped, even though she was at home, and not underground. She'd already rummaged through the kitchen tallying the canned goods and dry foods. Two people. Water wouldn't be a problem, thankfully.

But how long would they be stuck here?

Miranda peeked around the blinds and cringed.

It was sweet, but…weird. The stoop was already covered in stuff. Get-well cards, flowers, stuffed bears, even poster board signs, which she couldn't read, since they all faced out. While some people had dropped items and left, a few had stayed and gathered in a clump, talking amongst themselves with worried looks at her door. Surely, she thought, there must be a better use of their time.

There were a couple of news photographers, too, though they'd taken their shots and retreated to the other side of the street with coffee, thank God.

"We've gotta get you outta here," Eddie said. "I put some of your stuff in my bag, but we can take time to do a better job of it, if you want."

Miranda blinked. "You what?" She was torn: half pissed and half turned on. The pushy, invasive jerk had been in her drawers. Yet, God help her, the thought of those large, capable, tanned hands gripping her dainties…

"Sorry," he said, though he looked anything but. "Needed you to be ready to decamp fast, in case."

"Oh." She looked away. "Listen, it's not like I'm Beyoncé. These people won't stay. It was like this for a bit after…" She waved her hand, hoping she looked more nonchalant than she felt. "They'll go soon."

"Not soon enough."

He scooped up his duffel, which had been poised for escape alongside the front door, and advanced until he was crowding her. His face remained hard, however, and when she didn't budge, he took her by the shoulders, spun her around, and herded her toward her bedroom.

"Where exactly are you thinking of going?"

"To my place."

"Your place." Uh-huh. That felt too…intimate. Somehow more intimate than midnight conversations in her own bed, more personal than that delicious head massage over her sink. "In the Poconos?"

"Yeah. It's got a security system. Not to mention my dog."

Of course he had a dog. He'd have needed some company after poor Kathleen…and Miranda loved dogs. She'd fall in love with a dog.

"Aren't the people out there"—she gestured toward the street as she entered her bedroom—"good insurance? It's less likely that an intruder—"

"You got a duffel? Something easy to carry?"

He was already reaching up into her closet and dragging down a small bag. Then he tossed both duffels on her bed.

She blew out a frustrated breath as he unzipped his bag and started switching her stuff. "Stop that. I'm not going anywhere."

"See what else you want, or I'm keeping it here in one bag."

She grabbed for his next transfer only to find herself in a tug of war with a handful of panties and bras.

He raised an eyebrow and smirked.

She felt her face heat, but kept her hold. "Don't you dare rip those."

He shrugged and let go, sending her off balance for a second.

He grinned. "Okay by me if you prefer commando." The remark was teasing, but the glint in his eye spoke of something deeper—almost dangerous. Miranda's blood rushed and her brain stalled.

She stomped to the dresser, yanked open the top drawer, and shoved the handful of intimates in. Of course she was freaked out a little, but...so many buts. "I can't just take off. I have clients booked up. Some don't have a lot of time left."

"They'll understand."

"I have a job."

He scoffed, "Yeah, smack in the center of the hornets' nest."

"You don't know that." She crossed her arms and glared.

He gave her another lifted brow, but this time it conveyed a whole different message, like *Really, little girl? You still believe that?*

"Don't you want some answers? If I'm there, maybe I can—"

"Get yourself killed?" His face looked like a thundercloud. "No."

"If I act like I have no suspicions, like it really was a random mugging..."

"I said no."

One stride, and he snatched her unmentionables back out of the drawer.

"Aarrgh!" was all she could manage at first. But when he turned his back on her again, grabbing a small stack of T-shirts from the drawer, her anger found its legs. "You are the pushiest, most stubborn, obnoxious—"

The grating buzz of her doorbell had him glancing sharply at her.

"Another client?"

"No, that was it for tonight."

He slid past her, focused and fierce. She checked, almost involuntarily, for the bulge in the back of his waistband. The gun was there. Her heart thudded with dread, as she was suddenly reminded of exactly why they were arguing, of what might be at stake. Her life? Eddie's? David's?

"Probably a reporter," she called to the empty hallway, faking calm.

She heard him grumble. "If you had eyes in this place, you wouldn't have to guess." A video monitor, he meant, she realized as she made her way to the front of the apartment.

The buzzer sounded again, making Miranda jump.

"Don't answer it," he said. "I can't see jack shit. No visual from here to the front door. People still hanging around the stoop." He looked at her. "There's a limo. The mayor?"

Miranda angled in to see, all too aware, even in this tense situation, about the proximity of his strong body behind her. "That's Annette's driver."

"Looks like the hornets' nest has come to you. Leaving right now is shot." He tilted her chin up to watch her eyes. "Might be a good chance to feel her out. You up for it?"

CHAPTER 16

EDDIE WATCHED ANNETTE Thompson pick her way up the stoop, weaving among the medley of donations. She wore sunglasses, despite the fact that the light was waning. Between the limo and the signature blond coif, however, she was hardly incognito. Her suit jacket and skirt were both perfectly fitted. She wasn't carrying on her person—at least not in a place she could access quickly.

She did, however, have a big purse looped over the crook of one arm and a grocery bag clutched in her other. He'd relieve her of both pronto.

The buzzer sounded, and he intercepted Miranda at the keypad. "Don't hit that until I get to the outer door."

Miranda nodded. She looked a little pale. He wasn't thrilled himself. But she'd been right about one thing—they needed information, somehow. Besides, *nothing* was going to happen to Angel Face during his watch.

He unbolted the locks and stepped into the hall. The outer doors had glass insets. Annette had her back turned, probably eyeballing the chaos outside. Eddie took the time to do a bit of surveillance, glad for the chance to see from another angle. Reporters had crossed the street to get to Annette though, and abruptly, she faced forward.

Eddie heard the buzz and simultaneous click of the lock, and Annette came through. He hung back out of site of the gawkers.

Annette gasped when she saw him, mouth frozen in a tight O. Likely she expected to get all the way to Miranda's door before encountering anyone. And she certainly wouldn't have expected to see *him* at Miranda's apartment. Damn shades—would've been helpful to see her eyes.

"Mr. Mackey," she said, having recovered.

He made sure the door latched behind her. "Mrs. Thompson," he said. "Let me take your things."

"Sorry." She shook her head and smiled slightly. "We'd decided on first names, hadn't we?" She handed over the brown bag, then startled when he slipped the straps of her bag off her arm. Again, not exactly telling. Socially speaking, it *was* an odd thing for him to do.

He rapped on Miranda's apartment door, and she swung it wide.

"Oh, Miranda, thank goodness!" Annette said, and gathered Miranda, who looked rather surprised, into a tight embrace.

Just as quickly, Annette pulled away and said, "I had to see for myself you were all right. You *are*, aren't you?" She held fast to Miranda's hands.

"I am, or will be soon."

Annette put a hand to her chest and shut her eyes for a moment.

Eddie moved to the table in the corner where Miranda kept the supplies for her clients. He used his body to block their view from his sweep of her things, but kept an eye on Annette.

"I'm sorry to show up unexpectedly," Annette said. "I tried to call, but couldn't get through on your business line or your cell."

Miranda grimaced. "I had to unplug the phone." She

gestured to the windows. "And my cell was in my bag when I got mugged, so it's gone."

"Oh, of course. Bernard is very worried about you. He'll be so glad to hear."

"Why don't you sit down," Eddie said to them.

They moved to the couch, but Annette jumped up almost as soon as her rear hit the cushion. "Oh, I brought some soup and savories from Sal's. A light meal that only needs reheating seemed ideal."

Eddie had just finished running a hand through her purse and poking through the bag. Soup and savories was an understatement: three varieties of soup, a medley of hearty deli salads, some hummus, olives, two kinds of cheese, and a bag of rolls. His stomach growled. Miranda's fridge hadn't had eggs or breakfast meats. The healthy cereal and milk he'd found felt like eating air. And there'd been nothing but butter to put on the box of pasta he'd scarfed for lunch.

He held up the bag. "Looks fantastic."

Miranda thanked her. Annette sat again, obviously not sure what to make of Eddie being there, but too polite to ask. Eddie smiled and leaned against the far wall, pretending to check his phone, yet attuned to Thompson's every twitch.

"Is there anything I can do for you? Anything you need?" Annette asked Miranda.

"I'm fine, really. In good hands," Miranda said, shooting a half-smile in Eddie's direction. "But I do want to ask, if the mayor hears anything from my brother, can you call me immediately?" Miranda had talked to Detective Iocavelli twice more today, and knew the mayor and his staff had been told that David was considered a missing person.

Annette blinked. "Yes, of course. But"—she glanced at Eddie—"I'm *sure* he's just fine. Out sowing some wild oats or something." She looked down at her lap. "Can I ask, Miranda, what happened to you?"

Miranda shifted further back on the couch. "I was nearly home when I was jumped from behind. I was flat on the ground before I could even process what had happened. I'd been cut because the man sliced the strap of my purse. Eh—"

Eddie shook his head at Miranda. Instinct told him they were better off if the Thompsons didn't know about Eddie's involvement.

She took the hint and said, "A good samaritan came to my aid."

"Did you see your attacker? Could you identify him?" Annette asked.

Miranda shook her head.

"Oh, that's just terrible. He'll probably never be caught then." Annette shuddered.

Miranda frowned. "The person who helped me saw him from the front. He might be caught."

"Good, good," Annette said, but seemed distracted.

The buzzer sounded again. "Grand friggin' Central," Eddie muttered. He crossed to the blinds again. "Flower delivery. Tell him to leave them on the stoop." No way was he going out there while Thompson was in here.

Miranda went to the buzzer.

"But I have to have a signature," the young kid insisted.

"Sorry, leave them or take them, but I can't come out right now."

"But, but..." the kid stammered.

Annette was standing now too, looking back and forth between Miranda and Eddie, her shoulders up around her ears. "You..." She waved a hand. "All this..." She turned to Eddie. "You don't think Miranda's mugging was random, do you?"

Eddie shrugged, and Annette wrapped her arms around herself. "I'd hoped…" She trailed off, then shook her head hard, the helmet hair moving as a solid unit. In a tight, bitter voice, she said, "Well, no one is going to hurt *me*. I'll sign for the flowers."

The minute the door closed, Miranda said, "She's acting really weird." Eddie read both concern and confusion in her expression.

"I hardly know her, but yeah, she's all over the map." Eddie redirected his attention to the stoop. Someone else, an older woman, set something on the stoop then turned to talk with the others. All kept an eye on the front door—probably waiting to catch a glimpse of Miranda accepting flowers.

In a minute, Annette returned and handed a big batch of yellow roses in a glass vase to Miranda, who set them on the table. They exclaimed over how pretty they were, and Miranda extracted the little florist's envelope.

"They're from Mayor Thompson."

Annette's fingers stilled where she'd been arranging the blooms.

Miranda smiled. "It says, 'I'm covered. Take care of you now.'"

Annette turned as if she was going to say something, then abruptly swung around with her hands out. The flowers flew off the table. Miranda jumped back, and Eddie surged forward, as the vase smashed onto the floor in a shower of glass shards and water.

"Oh, I'm sorry!" Annette said.

"It's okay, really," Miranda said, pressing a hand to her injured side and squatting slowly.

"No," Eddie said, grasping her elbow and pulling her standing.

Annette shooed them away. "Go sit and rest. I'll clean up."

Miranda mimed a what-in-the-world face at Eddie as he escorted her to the couch. He only shrugged and went to help.

"Please get me a garbage bag," Annette directed him without looking up.

"Under the sink." Miranda pointed. "Dust pan's there, too." Eddie retrieved paper towels as well, one eye on Annette the whole time. He picked up the bigger shards, while Annette knelt with the dustpan.

"There's another vase above the refrigerator," Miranda suggested, but Annette ignored her, tossing the roses into the bag after the glass, grabbing them by the tops, rather than the dangerous stems. By the time she stood, she was flushed and seemed heedless of the damp spots on the knees of her hose.

Eddie reached for the trash bag, but she shifted it so that it was nearly behind her. And suddenly her strange actions made some sense. He couldn't say if Annette was innocent or guilty, blame-free or evil incarnate, but one thing was clear—she wasn't entirely clueless. She knew *something*, at least.

She held Eddie's eyes. "You're headed home soon, I imagine," she said, but it wasn't a question. Her look was intense, like she was imparting a warning. "Safe travels." Then she scooped up her purse and turned.

"Leave that," Miranda said, gesturing to the trash.

"I'm going anyway," Annette said. She tottered over to the sofa and bent to kiss Miranda on the cheek. "Be careful with yourself, Miranda. Call me if you need anything. And don't worry about David. I just know he's okay."

And then she was gone, the tension in the room evaporating in a snap.

Eddie bolted the locks and then leaned against the door and regarded Miranda, who slumped on the couch.

Wide-eyed, she said, "That was like the *Twilight Zone*. I don't know what to make of it." Miranda pointed at the back table. "She purposely knocked the flowers over. Is she jealous? Does she think I'm having an affair with her husband? First Kathleen, now me?"

Eddie shook his head. "It's possible. I also think, however, she was trying to protect us—or maybe just herself."

That cute little worry wrinkle showed up between Miranda's eyes.

"Think about it," he said. "She knocked over the flowers then bagged it all up and took it out."

"Weird," Miranda said. "Why did she?"

"The flowers were bugged—or at least Annette suspected they were."

———

The intercom buzzed again, and Eddie said, "Christ, what now?"

Miranda couldn't help a groan herself. "Maybe Annette forgot something."

Already at the window, behind her, Eddie said, "It's Aggie and Cora."

Miranda smiled. "Past their bedtime, but I'm glad. I could use some friendly faces after that last."

Eddie shook his head. "I need to control the entry," he said, and came around to help her up, a look of concern on his face. "You holding up okay?"

Her heart gave a little thump. "I'll do." It had been a long time since a man had taken care of her. Or had one really? Ever?

"Back at your post, then."

Once the ladies were buzzed in, they exclaimed over how

worn she looked. Miranda admitted she was probably more emotionally fried than physically.

"Annette Thompson just left," Eddie told them.

"It was an odd visit. I just haven't had time to shake it off," Miranda added.

Aggie said, "Didn't you do your little ritual?"

In front of Eddie? *God no!* Miranda waved her off.

"Cora," Aggie said, "go get the spray stuff."

Miranda shook her head. "It's fine, Aggie, really. You're all here; that takes care of it."

"No, I'd like to see this," Eddie said, a smile playing about his lips.

Crap. She glared at him.

He crossed his arms over his chest, but a full-blown grin took over his tense, hard-edged bodyguard expression.

It made her happy—in that scary, thumping chest area—to see him smile. She liked seeing him looser and lighthearted— worse, she liked being the one responsible for it. Her body didn't seem to know or care that their lives might be at stake. That he was grieving a dead wife and intent on finding a killer. That she had a sickening suspicion that finding that killer was the best way to locate her brother. And last but not least, that she wasn't remotely worthy of a guy like Eddie—at least not until she did some serious fear-facing.

Cora pressed the spray can into Miranda's hands. She had a mischievous twinkle in her eye. Aggie—of all people—was the only one who was taking it seriously.

Miranda rolled her gaze upward, as if the ceiling understood her mortification, and shook the can.

"Stand back," she ordered. Then she took a deep breath, felt the heat of a wicked blush rise in her cheeks, and sprayed liberally as she moved about the room. She spent extra time over the scene of the smashed vase, because, hey, it couldn't hurt.

"There," she declared, marched over to the cupboard, stashed the spray, and slammed the door with finality.

"Say the words," Aggie demanded.

Miranda cursed herself. She'd only told the ladies in the first place to ease their worry about the icky clients. She'd thought they'd be comforted to know that she had a solution, or at least a ritual, no matter how silly. The ex-therapist had been big on visualization. So far it'd done squat for her ability to enter the underworld, but she had put it to good use here at home.

Eddie's brow was raised, his lips twitching. "Please."

Miranda gritted her teeth. "Begone, filth," she muttered. She waved an arm. "Room, you are restored to goodness and harmony."

Cora and Aggie looked satisfied, but Eddie, she could tell, was trying hard not to burst out in giant guffaws.

She shook her head—at the Wise Ones and at herself. She'd never felt so ridiculous in all her life, and embarrassment channeled into crankiness. "All right, you've seen for yourselves I'm still standing, and you've had your fun to boot." She hit on the perfect idea, one they'd never argue with. "Time to go. I need to rest."

Except they did.

"But—"

"Wait—"

Eddie's voice rose above the protestations. "Miranda's tired."

Cora shrugged at her sister. "Perfect. She can rest in the limo."

"Good idea," Aggie said. "You'll want to pack a bag, hon."

What? Were they all in cahoots? Miranda held up a hand

to halt them, imagining a repeat of the argument she'd had with Eddie—sans the panty tug of war.

"What's going on, ladies?" Eddie said, eyes narrowed.

"My housekeeper called," Aggie explained. Cora added, "The one from upstate." And Aggie continued, "It seems someone's been in the house."

Miranda felt the blood drain from her head and put a hand to her chest, feeling the shock of violation all over again. "Oh, Aggie."

"No, no, it's good." Cora patted her arm and led her to the sofa to sit.

Aggie said, "Nothing was smashed or taken—not even the art. Some food in the fridge disappeared."

She waited expectantly, but Miranda was too tired to follow.

Aggie threw her arms up. "Don't you see? We think it could have been David."

"He's been there to visit, of course," Cora said.

Miranda looked to Eddie, tears of premature relief gathering in her eyes. "To David, Aggie's Catskills house would seem safe—and yet nowhere anyone would know to look."

"When?" Eddie asked, his intensity back in place.

"Arlene's just returned from a couple of days off, so in that window of time," Aggie said.

"You get your wish." Miranda stood to face Eddie, taking a good look at his features. Clamped down on himself now, all playfulness gone, like cutting a whole sequence from film. Handsome, rugged, strong either way...

Miranda bit down on a sigh. She guessed this was it. Attraction be damned, their enforced togetherness was over. David would have the information they needed. And they'd all be safe.

"Meaning?" he asked.

"I'm getting out of town. Do not pass go, do not go to work, collect your brother on the way."

"Uh-huh."

"So, you're free of your bodyguard duties."

He cocked his head, considering her. "Did you conk your head on the pavement when you went down?"

Out of the corner of her eye, Miranda caught Aggie's elbow to Cora's ribs.

Eddie scratched his chin. "We'd only be making it easy on this guy by sending you out to some secluded country estate alone."

Her mouth dropped open. "You mean you're sticking around?" A little illicit thrill of pleasure shot through her.

"He means he's sticking to *you*," Aggie said.

Miranda turned away, embarrassed all over again, and hustled down the hall. Sometimes the Wise Ones didn't know when to quit. Well, Aggie, really. Cora was normally much more sensitive.

A warm hand grasped her shoulder, and she felt Eddie's heat behind her.

"What's up?"

She swiveled her head. He was close enough to kiss, but the grandmothers would *not* be getting that show. "I have to finish packing, so we can go."

She started forward, but he held fast and tugged her around to face him.

"Angel, it's too late tonight."

"What? I've been tortured waiting for some word of David. And you've been dying to get me out of here. Now you want me to hold off until morning?" She shook her head hard. "No."

"Aggie," he called. "How many hours' drive is your place?"

"Oh, about three and a half."

"There won't be any traffic at night," Miranda said. "It won't be nearly that long."

"You are in no shape to be arriving anywhere tonight, not this late," Eddie said, his mouth set in a firm line.

"I'm fine."

"Dear," Cora said, "I'm afraid he's right. Besides, there's no sense arriving at midnight. Arlene will be fast asleep, and it'll be too dark to see anything."

Miranda blew out a breath. "Like Aggie said, I can sleep in the car. I can't let this wait. If David is there…"

"Arlene says she's positive he's not there now," Aggie chimed in.

Oh my God, Miranda thought, frustration welling nearly to the snapping point. "Then why are you even tempting me with this?"

"We'll go up first thing in the morning," Eddie said. "Talk to Arlene when she's fresh. Take a look around." He squeezed her shoulders, and the tender move had her fighting tears.

"I promise," he said. "You know I want you out of Dodge anyway."

"If we miss him…"

"He's not there, honey," Eddie said, his voice gentle, his eyes way too full of sympathy.

Miranda wrenched out from under his hands and practically ran to her bedroom.

She needed to believe David was out there somewhere, needed desperately to hope. She wouldn't let any of them take that away.

CHAPTER 17

ANXIOUS TO LEAVE, sick with worry, and yes, still rather sore between her cut and her bruised knees and elbows, Miranda hadn't slept well. Up and packed early Saturday morning, they ate breakfast sandwiches at a deli on Second Avenue, before cabbing it to his truck. He insisted on taking his own vehicle, not Aggie's driver, to the Catskills. Miranda didn't blame him.

But her heart sank when they got out of the cab.

Of course his truck couldn't have been parked in one of those tiered parking garages where the cars were lifted and slid into an open-air, above-ground metal structure. Or one of those street-level lots, paved flat with a tiny hut for the valet who worked the grid like a sliding puzzle.

Nope, Eddie's garage was underground.

Where she couldn't go.

At the top of the ramp, irrational, but intense, fear hit her like collapsing scaffolding.

But she knew she had to try. Every day that had led up to seven hundred and thirty.

And now every day after—though she'd missed yesterday after her attack. Today was day seven hundred and thirty-eight.

She lowered her head and took a big breath, gripping her backpack tight in her already stiffening fingers.

And oh, Eddie. As pushy as he could be, that same determination meant that he'd saved her life, watched over her, and still now—if she read between the lines—meant to do whatever was in his power to do to keep her safe until this thing—whatever it was—was resolved.

What would he think?

She narrowed her vision to Eddie's feet. Maybe she could keep his pace. Chunky tan boots that somehow seemed—on him—as light as slippers. He didn't thud or clunk. And he was right here, within reach.

She managed—one, two, three steps.

Don't look up; don't look ahead to where it's dark.

But that fourth footfall hit a shadow, gray and sinister. Five brought deeper shadows, and she began to falter, her movements choppy as she tried, really tried, to make her legs go forward even as her head was screaming with increasing desperation to turn and run.

Six, seven—*no, full-on dark. No!*

She halted, fear seizing her chest in its tight grip. She tried without success to gulp for air. Worse, her feet wouldn't move at all now—not even backward to safety. It felt as if someone had nailed the soles of her shoes to the ground. She couldn't get free, couldn't move away from the dark.

Eddie's boots slowed, and he turned when he realized she was no longer with him. No, she thought, tears springing immediately to her eyes. Even if he could save her once more, she didn't want him to see her like this. Eyes probably bugging out, face undoubtedly white as a ghost, sweat beading fast, limbs that had frozen solid, petrified with terror.

"Miranda?" he said.

But, okay, his voice reminded her she wasn't alone. They weren't trapped, and they had air. There was an escape route—a wide one, totally unlike the narrow subway exits. She wasn't five, six, seven—not even *one* story underground...not yet. *Breathe, dammit,* she begged her lungs.

But she knew what was down there. From her old life, her old self, who'd never been scared of anything except losing another loved one. Who'd never thought twice about the subway system, parking garages, basements, elevator shafts...

"Miranda." Eddie's deep voice held firm command, and she obeyed, raising her chin and her gaze. Which helped to get a measure of oxygen down her throat.

His face was filled with understanding, sympathy.

How did he know? She didn't *want* him to know.

It was one thing to be embarrassed over a silly ritual because the Wise Ones put her up to it, or to need help because she physically couldn't wash her own hair without discomfort, but this, this was...

Something else entirely. Because he was so strong, so tough, so—and okay, she could admit it, she was falling for Eddie, hard and fast—and she hated for him to see how weak she was.

She tried to speak—to say what, she didn't even know—but only managed a squeak. She clamped her eyes and mouth shut. Trying to get a hold of herself. But her hands shook, her heart beat too fast, her breath came short—shit, breathing through her nose wasn't an option.

"Hey." Eddie's voice was soft and smooth and very near. "Open your eyes."

He'd dropped their bags in the middle of the ramp, and stood before her. Blue eyes full of concern, the tense planes of his face serious but calm. "Why don't you wait right here?"

Cautiously, she craned her head to look behind her. The street beckoned. Sunlight and air. Noise but no explosions, no shifting earth, twisting metal, screams, whimpering—just the regular cacophony of a busy city. Honking horns, accelerating cars, voices of all languages, clip-clops of dress shoes, and the rhythmic *flonk-flonk flonk* of some delivery cart's rickety wheel. Maybe a shipment of office supplies, or cases of beverages, or some large-scale laundry uniform service.

The norm. Safe and familiar. That was where she needed to be.

She shook her head frantically, which seemed to loosen her feet. She scooted backward just enough to draw slightly more breath.

Eddie reached out and settled his hands on her upper arms. Big hands, a gentle touch. "We need the car, and I can't let you go out there alone."

Panic flared. He must have seen it, because he rubbed her upper arms as if he was trying to warm her. Did he know how cold she was? Like an ice sculpture, frozen through and through. Even her perspiration felt cold. Damp and dark. Like the blackness before her, behind Eddie.

How many levels down? No, no…the valet would get the car; she wouldn't have to go any farther than that spot. Just there, where the attendant's glass-encased cube was. Where the drainage grate ran across the length of the ramp. She wouldn't drown—the rain couldn't swamp them. But that spot was a long way from here. How many steps? Too many. She wasn't even halfway there.

Eddie's hand slid down her arm to her clenched fist. His whole hand enveloped hers and his thumb rubbed back and forth over the back of her hand. The other hand cupped her cheek.

"Miranda, look at me."

She had a hard time pulling her eyes away from that grate. If he'd just let go, she could scoot back a little further.

"What if I hold you tight against me? We'll only go as far as there"—he pointed with his head—"because the valet will have to go get the car anyway."

Could she do it? With Eddie? She'd failed miserably when Max tried to help her at the subway stairs.

She had to try, right? That was the point…she had to keep fighting, so this debilitating phobia didn't swallow her whole, take over her life.

She squeezed his hand, signifying her yes. She wouldn't promise—couldn't speak, in fact—but she'd try. She had to. He pried her backpack strap from her hand and hung it over her shoulder.

He bent and reached for the bags, slung them both over his left shoulder, but before she knew it, he was back, pressed tight to her left side, his arm across her back and his hand looping up to squeeze her shoulder. His other reached for the hand nearest to him. She couldn't release her fist, and he didn't make her. Just enveloped that whole mass of cold, clammy tension in his big paw.

"Better?"

Was it? Maybe. She nodded, just barely.

"Okay, then." His voice was low and smooth. Compelling. "You can do this. One tiny step at a time."

With supreme effort, she managed a step.

"Breathe," he reminded her, and sucked in an exaggerated lungful himself. As if she was capable of even expanding her chest that much right now. But she tried.

"Again," he said, and she got one foot another half step further.

Maybe, she thought, if she didn't look at her feet…but no—bad move. Because Eddie's wide chest no longer blocked her view, his gaze wasn't there to pull her attention to him. Miranda's eyes fastened on the dim cavern in front of her.

She was unable to look away; the shadows became darker and deeper as she stared. The walls seemed to gape and bend. Like they'd swallow her whole if she stayed here one more second.

No, her whole body screamed. No!

There was no way she'd make her legs move forward now. Not with the underworld coming alive and reaching for her.

So what if someone shot her dead up on the street while she waited for Eddie? Right now, she didn't even care. Compared to this, this God-awful, sickening, horrible feeling that came over her every time she tried...

It was like trying to open a jar lid that wouldn't budge. No matter how much will and muscle she put behind the effort, she just wasn't strong enough.

"What do you need? What can I do?" he said in a pained but soft voice, squeezing her even tighter.

She shook her head, feeling ragged. "Unless you can turn that dark, awful hole into a big, wide, open-air stadium flooded with sunlight, nothing."

She made herself admit it to him. He should know just how damaged she was. "I can't do this. I just can't."

"Okay," he said.

Then he put his fingers in his mouth and gave a shrill whistle. She flinched.

"Sorry, I should have thought of it before," he muttered, as he backed them both up a few steps. "Here, put your back to the wall, and look to the street."

The valet came running and took the ticket and the bill Eddie offered.

"Bring it all the way up to the street," he told the guy.

Miranda sagged with relief as Eddie walked her up and out.

"I'm sorry," she whispered, as tears of shame spilled onto her cheeks.

———

Nearly out of the city, Miranda had just fallen asleep—emotionally exhausted, Eddie thought—when his phone rang.

It was the hotel, although he'd checked out yesterday. Probably some residual billing issue.

He answered it, aiming to let Miranda sleep, but she was already stirring.

"Mr. Mackey," a young female said, "an envelope for you was delivered early this morning. And sir, you have our apologies, because our staff member remembered you were a guest but neglected to check your status. I'll be glad to send it to your home address via overnight delivery."

What the hell? "What's the return address?"

"It doesn't say."

"Postmark?"

"There is none—it's a small manila envelope marked 'urgent,'" she explained. "It's got your name and the hotel's name written directly on the envelope."

"Listen, I'm in the car just leaving the city, but I need to know what's in there. Open it."

"Oh, I can't. We have strict rules about this kind of thing."

Frustration mounted, and Eddie scanned for somewhere to pull over. "Are you the manager?"

"Yes, but—"

"Amy? The pretty blonde?" He'd only seen two managers while he was there, and the other was a paunchy male with iron-gray hair.

Miranda rolled her eyes at him, and he grinned, even as the woman on the phone said, "Um, yes, thank you."

"So, Amy, you, as manager, have the authority to break the rules. Besides, I'm giving you express permission."

"Hold on," she said. "This better not come back to bite me," she muttered faintly.

He gave Miranda a thumbs-up and heard the distinct sound of a door clicking shut, some silence, then, "Mr. Mackey? I'm going to open the envelope now."

"Thank you, Amy."

He heard the noise of paper crinkling, just as Miranda pointed to a spot—half in the bus lane, but surely this convo wouldn't take long.

"It's just a piece of white paper folded in two," Amy said.

Silence.

"Amy?"

She cleared her throat. "It doesn't say much."

"Who is it from?

"No clue. It only says: *You are onto something. Please don't give up, but be very, very careful.*"

———

A short time later, hotel manager Amy left Eddie and Miranda alone in her office.

As it turned out, the words *VERY, VERY CAREFUL* were not only capitalized, but extra-large. And the "please" was underlined. Twice.

"A man wouldn't say please," Eddie pointed out.

Miranda made a face. "We're probably not talking about the kind of men you're used to."

"True. My guys wouldn't send sissy notes begging someone else to solve their problem. They'd be banging on doors and kicking ass."

Miranda flinched, and he threw the note on the desk.

"Shit. That was insensitive." He scrubbed a hand over his hair in frustration.

He knew she'd latched on to this little development with high hopes, just the same way she'd gotten all excited about going to Aggie's place, believing David would just be sitting there having a cup of tea or some shit. Eddie, however, figured the only thing they'd find of David was his dead body—right here, under their noses, somewhere in the city. And at this rate, sadly, Eddie would consider finding a body lucky. But damn, that would hurt her far more than crushed hopes.

"Does it look like David's handwriting?" he asked, shoving the note into her hands.

She frowned, brows pulled down in concentration, then shook her head.

"Mayor Thompson's? Annette's? Anybody from the office?"

"It looks like chicken scratch."

He nodded. "Purposely used their non-dominant hand."

She sighed. "They wanted to remain incognito."

She'd gotten that right.

As Amy had said, neither the paper nor the envelope held any indication of who'd sent it or from where. Since he'd been in New York, Eddie had scribbled down his cell number and hotel name for pretty much everyone he'd talked to, in case they'd thought of something he should know. *Anybody* could have sent that note.

The clerk, Damien, who'd accepted the delivery, knocked on the door and entered. He fidgeted nervously like a chubby-cheeked recruit. Eddie waved off his apology and asked for a description of the delivery guy.

"You know, what you'd expect," Damien said. With some coaxing, the details slowly emerged. The delivery man had been young and wore a knit cap and fingerless gloves. Also, a plain brown canvas messenger bag, cargo pants tucked into his socks, name-brand sneakers, hooded sweatshirt…

"What color? How tall was he?" Eddie asked, because the man who'd attacked Miranda had worn a hoodie. Not that it made any sense—why would the dude who tried to silence Miranda send a note? Still…

"Uh, he was white, Caucasian."

Eddie had meant the sweatshirt, but that was good info, too. That fit what Eddie had seen.

"Maybe five-nine?" Damien said. "He was a little shorter than me."

Eddie was sure their guy was taller, but the kid could be wrong. "Age?"

"Like, probably in college. Around my age."

That sure as hell didn't fit. Eddie would swear the man who attacked Miranda was seasoned. Focused, smart, and cold-blooded. Maybe not impossible, but definitely improbable, for a college-age person to be an experienced killer.

Miranda looked disappointed. Likely she'd hoped to hear a description that fit David, but it didn't match him either. In fact, she'd agreed to this detour, precisely because it might have led them to David. She'd be anxious now to get back on the road to Aggie's place. Eddie itched to touch her—a hug or even just a squeeze of her hand in reassurance—but didn't move.

She asked Damien, "What company was this kid from?"

"No idea," the clerk said. "I didn't see a company name on his shirt or bag or anywhere. So definitely not one of the big runners. They have"—he gestured to his head and chest—"like, a logo, usually."

Miranda bit her lip and turned to Eddie. "I can't think of anything else, can you?"

He shook his head. "If you see him again, call me. I need to know who sent him." Eddie peeled off a fifty. "There's more money in it for both of you."

The kid nodded eagerly and slipped out, but Eddie didn't hold out much hope.

Miranda wrapped her arms around herself, while Eddie paced in frustration. "That was a waste of time," he said.

"You gave him a pretty big tip for a waste of time."

"Seemed like good incentive."

"I'm sure. And who knows, he might just think of something, or the delivery guy might show up with another package," she said quietly.

He snorted. "This person took pains to remain anonymous. I highly doubt he or she just walked right up to our delivery kid. Probably there was a middle man or disguise or some other precautionary measures."

"Yes, but maybe he could supply something general, like whether he was hired by a man or woman. It'd be helpful to know something. Anything."

She sounded as frustrated as he felt.

"We do know something." Eddie looked her in the eye.

"What?" she said, that damn hopeful gleam back in her pretty green eyes, still red-rimmed from going through the wringer in the parking garage.

But she had to start coming to terms with the severity of

this situation—the unlikelihood that someone else in this deadly game wouldn't end up like her brother.

"Our pen pal is scared." Eddie watched, feeling her pain, as shadows dimmed her light. "Worried enough to take action. Yet unwilling—or unable—to come forward."

CHAPTER 18

PLEASE, PLEASE, PLEASE, Miranda thought as she squeezed her eyes shut and sent up a quick prayer, just as they made the turn for Aggie's country place. *Please let David be here. Safe and well. Help us get to the bottom of this mess quick, before anything else happens.*

Eddie let out a low whistle as the private drive finally broke through the tree line and displayed a magnificent view of the grounds. Miranda chuckled even as she leaned forward in hopeful anticipation. "The limo and driver didn't clue you in? Aggie's got some serious bucks."

"Yeah, well, she called it a *house.* This is…" He shook his head as he parked in front.

"I know." In fact, it'd taken Miranda years of visiting before she'd felt at home here. Not that it wasn't cozy inside, but the sheer size of the place was intimidating.

Aggie's housekeeper appeared at the front door, and Miranda waved. Like Damien's delivery man, Arlene was just about exactly what you'd expect. Slightly plump, a mop of curly gray hair, a friendly but sharp gaze, and a warm smile. She had the accent of a local, but ran the place like it was the White House. And she inevitably wore a house coat—where in the world did they still sell those, anyway?—over slacks and a blouse, plus a dishtowel over her shoulder.

Eddie came around to help as Miranda was scrambling

down from the high seat of his truck. Arlene met them in the drive, and wrapped Miranda in a firm hug. "Land sakes alive, I'm glad to see you safe and sound with my own two eyes."

Miranda introduced Eddie, who gave Arlene a charming smile. She narrowed her eyes, looked back and forth between them, and said, "Hmmph."

Miranda widened her eyes at Eddie, whose lips twitched with silent laughter. She suspected Aggie had been instructing the woman to matchmake. Not a task Arlene would likely undertake, until she'd made up her mind about Eddie for herself.

"Come in, come in." Arlene propelled them both by the elbow. "I've got lunch prepared. You must be starving."

Even as she scanned the trees—like her brother would just pop out or something—Miranda had to laugh at the older woman corralling a seasoned marine like he was a child.

"Thank you, Arlene," she said, "but I really need to know about David."

Arlene halted, hands on hips. "I told Agnes and Cora both that there was no proof that the intruder was David. Heck, it could have been one of the gardeners gone temporarily mad, or"—she waved a hand—"I don't know, some kid from town out playin' hooky from school."

But she looked unsettled, and turned to bustle off toward the back of the house.

"There is an alarm here, isn't there?" Eddie asked, craning his head back toward the front door.

"Yes," the housekeeper said without even turning her head, "and before you go asking, there was no sign of picked locks or cut wires or any of that other rigmarole."

They'd reached the kitchen, and she turned to face them, hands on hips. "I've been thinking on it, and all I can figure is that someone came in while I was here." A flash of anger passed over her features. "We don't use the alarm during the day—too much in and out, and Lord knows we've never had reason before. So I set it when I settle down for the evening, and a'course when I go for my days off."

"Arlene lives here most of the time," Miranda explained, "but goes home to her husband a couple of days a week."

"It's all I can take a'him." She pursed her lips and nodded briskly. "Works for everyone involved, I daresay."

"Why don't you think it was David?" Miranda asked.

Arlene shook her head, went to the refrigerator, and began pulling out covered dishes. "I'm not saying as it was or it wasn't. I'm only saying there's no way to know."

That made Miranda feel a little better. To her, it made perfect sense that David would come here if he needed a safe haven. Except why wouldn't he trust Arlene, ask her for help?

"You're sure there's nobody in the house now?" Eddie asked.

"I am." Arlene gave a pointed glance at the broom in the corner—apparently her weapon of choice as she'd searched. "I told Agnes in no uncertain terms that there was no reason for you all to come traipsing up here."

Again, Miranda thought, with the Wise Ones trying to orchestrate her love life. She slid a sideways glance at Eddie, but he was scanning the grounds past the wall of paned windows and sliders that separated the kitchen and the rear patios.

"Now that you're here, though, I'm glad for the company." A smile broke free on Arlene's face. "Let's eat."

"I'll feel better if I double-check the house before we sit down," Eddie said. Arlene narrowed her eyes, but Eddie said, "I'm not taking any chances when it comes to keeping Miranda safe."

"Fine. It'll keep," Arlene said, and Miranda could tell he'd won points despite the brusque tone.

"Great," he said, patting his abdomen, "because I plan to do my part when I'm done." He winked—actually winked!—at Arlene, who fought a smile. He definitely had a way with the ladies, and Miranda was hardly immune. She found the dual play of overlying charm and underlying intensity fascinating.

Miranda watched Eddie go, boots silent as a cat's paws on the hard floors, the power in his frame just asking to be unleashed. She didn't miss the bulge of his gun under his worn denim shirt, and shivered. She didn't feel danger here—not with happy memories of vacations and holidays with her multigenerational posse. No—it was excitement for this dangerous man.

Which *should* worry her. But she couldn't face that right now. If David had been here, somewhere, she wanted to know. Any proof that he was alive would go a long, long way to settling her worry. If he was actually still here—God, what she wouldn't give.

And if it wasn't David, just some random coincidence—well, that would blow. She'd be crushed. But it wouldn't stop her. David was her baby bro. She'd been watching out for him forever, and she wouldn't stop now.

Turning to Arlene, Miranda set about extracting every tiny detail she could about the break-in.

———

Having already checked the detached garages and rarely used cars, along with the closed-for-the-season pool house—a sweet hideout if Eddie had ever seen one—Eddie and Miranda headed for the stables. Apparently Aggie hadn't boarded horses since her granddaughter Max had graduated from college, so Eddie figured it was possible the barn could have been overlooked by most of the staff.

"Max used to sneak boys out here in the summer," Miranda said.

"Somehow that doesn't surprise me."

"Yeah, somehow with her, men just sense…" She waved her hand and turned away, reaching for the big sliding door of the barn.

"Uh-uh, stitch girl," he said, as he nudged her away. She ducked her head, avoiding his eye.

He tipped up her chin and forced her to meet his eyes. "You're every bit as sexy as Max. More so, if you ask me, because you don't advertise." He let every bit of attraction show in his eyes, and was rewarded when she drew a soft breath.

He gave her a slow smile, one that he hoped she understood meant *later*. Later, as soon as he broke and ravished her. Or later as in maybe never, if he managed to keep thinking with the head on his shoulders instead of the one in his pants.

He put his weight behind a shove of the oversized door. It needed maintenance, but he cleared room enough to let the some of the midafternoon light in.

He heard the scurrying of small animals—mice, probably—and the flutter of wings in the upper rafters. But the second Eddie stepped inside, he knew that no one had been here. The air was too stale, the dust too undisturbed, the wildlife too startled.

He shook his head at Miranda, who got a hard set to her mouth and stormed into the place.

"David?" she called, peeking in the tack room and heading for the center aisle. "David?"

She looked in every single stall on the right, while Eddie took the left to humor her. Okay, and to be thorough.

She stomped back the way they'd come, and Eddie trailed. He was glad she was getting ticked. But it wouldn't last. She'd take it hard if they found no sign of her brother.

Instead of heading out, Miranda turned and grasped a rung of the loft ladder.

"No you don't," he said.

She stepped back and swiped an angry flourish through the air with her hand. "By all means."

Hardly trusting the aged wood to hold him, Eddie tested each new rung as he went, before committing his full weight.

At the top, he hopped up. Piles of hay, some old farm tools, a few wooden crates—nothing out of the ordinary. No sign whatsoever of recent activity, unless you counted all the bird shit.

He leaned over, and sure enough, Miranda was looking up expectantly. He shook his head, and her face fell. She was marching out the door before he was halfway down the ladder, so he dropped to the ground, boots thudding on the dirt flooring.

Miranda was skirting a fenced-in area, heading for an open field of short grass and, he assumed, the tree line. Eddie trailed her, thinking she must be healing well, if she could walk that fast, rear end swinging. Or maybe she was just so determined that she was heedless of her injury.

"David!" she called, cupping her hands at her mouth. "David," she yelled again, facing another direction. "Come out!"

She walked farther east. "It's safe... Daaavid!"

Eddie continued to scan the fields, the buildings, the woods beyond, keeping an eye out for any movement. He didn't expect David to show, found it hard to believe that her brother had even been here.

That didn't mean, however, that someone who wanted David and Miranda both out of commission hadn't followed them from the city. He'd been careful, constantly checking his mirrors, but he'd been trained in combat, not espionage.

He gained on Miranda, feeling the need to be close enough to shield her if necessary, still looking for that telltale flash of reflected sunlight.

She kept calling as they circled the outer rim of the property—or at least the portion of land that was tamed. Who knew how much acreage Aggie actually owned?

Miranda's pace had slowed and her shoulders slumped. Finally, as they came around the opposite side of the house from where they'd started, she turned to him and shook her head. Eyes as big and sad as a puppy's.

"I had my hopes up," she said, squeezing her eyes shut when her voice broke.

"Hey now," Eddie said, unable to resist putting his arms around her.

After all, he was only comforting her, right? He wasn't going to notice how good she felt, how sexy she smelled, how perfectly she fit. He would definitely ignore the signs of life in his dick—a hazard every single time he got too close to her.

"It's good to have hope, think positive thoughts."

And what the fuck was he saying, anyway? He should be telling her the hard truth. *Your little bro isn't going to show because he's dead as a doornail, his body dumped in some god-*

forsaken hit-man graveyard, like that undeveloped swamp on the Jersey side of the tunnels from Penn Station.

Tucked into his neck with her voice muffled, she asked, "You really think so?"

He opened his mouth, but couldn't make himself say the words, torn between the truth, easing her mind, and the inadvertent hip thrust she'd launched against his all-too-happy-for-this-conversation groin.

She looked up, again with the eyes, big and green and pleading for a treat—in her case, something she could latch on to.

"Never give up." *Semper Fi*, he thought.

A shadow passed over her eyes—she knew he was holding back. Her nose quivered, turning pink, and then her eyes welled. But there was fire born of anger in her expression, too.

"Shit," she said, and pushed away, turning her back on him. He heard her sob, despite the fact that she was trying to hold back. She took off running, and it was his turn to swear, because he felt like an ass, but also, she was going to make that damn wound bleed.

"Miranda—"

"Stop following me!"

"Goddammit," he growled, yanking her to a stop as gently as possible. "I can't."

"I need to be alone," she demanded in a choked voice.

"I swore to protect you. If you need a good cry, let's go in—"

The first blow to his chest surprised him—Miranda was stronger than she looked, and fueled by frustration and extreme worry. Eddie stood there and let her whale on him, fist after fist, until she broke and sobbed. Her knees gave way, and he picked her up, retreating to the side porch.

Eddie kicked a wicker chair into a corner—back to the wall, protected on two sides, and a halfway-decent visual.

He sat, tucking her in on his lap, against his chest, like a child. Her sobs were ugly and loud and nearly broke his heart.

Whoever had done this—to Kathleen, to David, to Miranda—would pay.

CHAPTER 19

EDDIE AND MIRANDA declined Arlene's offer to stay at the country house, but he hadn't driven back to the city, either.

"I need to check in at home," he'd said, then called his friend Aiden. They discussed their martial arts school, and Aiden agreed to bring Stripes, Eddie's dog, over later that evening.

Miranda suspected it'd feel awfully strange—rather intimate—being in Eddie's home, but hey, turnabout was probably due. He'd invaded her space, had his fingers in her hair—fed her, even. He'd seen her cry, twice now, and he'd seen her in her absolute worst moment of weakness as she'd succumbed to her phobia.

And—if she were really going up close and personal with this line of thinking—he'd had his mouth on her breasts, and he'd made her come like nobody's business.

She squirmed in the passenger seat and shot him a sidelong glance, wondering if they'd end up repeating that little encounter in the privacy of his home.

She should keep her distance. Despite his sweet compliment, she knew she couldn't compare to Max. She wasn't comfortable with a purely physical give-and-take. No-strings arrangements weren't her thing. She was the kind of girl who wanted the future. But she didn't have that to give right now either.

Not until she overcame her fear of the underground. Because she wasn't whole.

She couldn't expect a man like Eddie to be saddled with half a woman. A woman who'd always be working around something, spending too much time and money to avoid this or that, declining invitations because it meant she'd be faced with public freak-outs, and—she glared at the overstuffed backpack at her feet—prepping daily like she was evacuating a war zone.

Really, if the truck went over a ravine this instant, she could probably keep them both alive for weeks. A good trait in a psycho girlfriend.

No, as much as she liked him—and her body really, really did like him—the timing sucked.

She had to get her life in order before she could even think about a real relationship.

She bit her lip. Would a hottie like him still be available when she was ready? Doubtful.

He was such a perfect combination, all the things a man should be. A protective alpha, charming and scorching hot on the outside, yet sensitive, caring, and thoughtful on the inside. The likes of which she'd never encountered before. Or probably would again.

God, but she was an ass. She had a damn long way to go, and her progress over the last seven hundred and thirty-eight days hardly boded well.

"We're here," Eddie said, and Miranda's head snapped up.

His house was one of those funky contemporary ranches with flat roofs, but somehow its earth tones and modern lines nestled into the greenery like it belonged. Very private, sitting amongst lots of trees and bushes, with the neighbors on either side a good distance away.

She smiled at him. "It fits you."

He didn't smile back, however. Instead, he looked horrified. "Jesus, Miranda, you're bleeding."

Crap, she was—her T-shirt was red right over the wound. Not a ton, but it looked fresh. Before she'd even processed that, Eddie had her door opened and was lifting her down. "It's okay," she said. "It doesn't hurt."

But he carried her inside, disabling an alarm and depositing her in a kitchen chair.

"Let me get the first-aid kit," he said.

She eyed the kitchen. Contemporary and simple, but done in warm tones, with shiny new appliances and an uncluttered countertop that looked like something more casual than granite or marble.

Eddie was back before she could investigate, flipping the kit open on the counter. "Stand up," he ordered, and peeled up her sticky shirt as he pulled a chair under him.

She gathered the material and held it up and out of the way, trying to keep the bloody bit from ruining her bra. "Ouch!"

He snorted as he peeled the rest of the tape off. "You overdid it at Aggie's."

She shrugged. She'd apologized for pounding on him, and he'd sworn it was okay. He looked up, seemingly working to drag his gaze past her chest, and she realized he was likely getting an eyeful from that angle.

He cleared his throat. "The stitches are largely intact. One end bled a little. But mostly it looks like you just scraped off a chunk of scab."

His breath fanned over her bare midriff, so she only managed a nod. His hands were efficient, the antiseptic cool. It ran in a rivulet toward her jeans, and he swiped it, tracing from the dip above her hips and upward. Goosebumps erupted.

"I have the bandages in my bag," she said.

"Pretty sure you have your whole apartment in that bag." He ripped open a large rectangle of gauze and pressed it to her side. "Hold this," he said. Their eyes met at the same time as their hands, and heat erased those goosebumps like magic.

Miranda held her breath as he smoothed out the first length of tape, just under her ribs, his knuckles brushing the underside of her bra. The next piece, and another caress.

Miranda watched his blond head bent close to her stomach, and her muscles clenched tight with anticipation. The final piece of tape, and then his large hands spanned her sides, both thumbs smoothing from the center outward, once, twice, three times.

"I just can't figure out what changed," he murmured. He sat up straight, hands dropping to her hips.

My God, but having Eddie's hands on her was so perfect. Both the most natural thing in the world, and the most exciting, even if he didn't intend—

"I mean," he said, "what happened? To put you in the line of fire like this?" A crease appeared between his eyes. "I hadn't asked any more questions, was just keeping to myself, figuring out my next move. Maybe just my presence—but then why *you*?" He gave her hipbones a squeeze. "Why not me?"

With effort, Miranda dragged her brain from the feel of his hands and thought back to that day. She'd gone to work, filming the soft piece at Gracie Mansion…

"Oh my God," she said, dropping her shirt and grabbing Eddie's arms. "It was me—and maybe David."

Eddie's gaze sharpened, and she shook her head, searching her memory for the details.

"Earlier that day—the day of my attack—we did a soft piece at Gracie Mansion. You know, filming the mayor and his wife at home. David was up to something. He asked me to cover for him and snuck off."

"For what?"

"I don't know. He only asked me to cover for him if he was missed. The mayor did ask where he was, but Annette made some flip comment, which deflected him."

Miranda felt the tension in Eddie's forearms, all hard muscle under her fingers, as he waited.

"The thing is," she said, "while it was just me and Annette, *I* was asking questions. Pushing her."

"About?"

"Jeremy Rashorn. You had just told me about him." She felt herself pale, even as Eddie's face hardened like mountain stone. "Also, the likelihood that Kathleen *didn't* commit suicide. She got angry and was adamant that I stop asking questions."

"Holy..." But he didn't finish, only jumped up, both hands going to the top of his head.

"Do you really think... Could she really have..." Miranda stumbled around the words, resisting. "My God, maybe it *is* Annette. Maybe she's..."

Eddie, his tone deadly serious, finished that awful thought: "A killer."

CHAPTER 20

EDDIE WAS STILL chewing over the possibilities when he went to get their overnight bags from the truck. His first instinct had been to pin Annette a murderer. But they'd discussed her strange behavior at Miranda's home. If his theory that she'd thought the flowers were bugged was correct, then it followed that Gracie Mansion could be bugged as well—or possibly Annette herself.

He slammed the car door, blew out a frustrated breath, and detoured to the mailbox, much as he didn't want to. Digging out an armful of junk, he shook his head.

He reminded himself that despite the tension he felt, he was home. Breathing crisp, clean autumn air, the woods alive with the noise of living things. Here, there were no blaring horns or sirens, no crowded city streets, no memories.

He looked up at the lit windows of his little house. He could see Miranda tucked up at his kitchen table, those soft curls backlit a little, making her glow. He felt a sense of rightness settle around him.

Immediately, he talked himself down. *Uh-uh, man. Keep your head. Women are dangerous territory. Just keep her whole until this is all over, so you can go back to your peaceful, solitary life.*

Because if there was one thing Kathleen had taught him, it was that even the supposed good ones couldn't be trusted.

Eddie gritted his teeth and forced his boots to move. The picture of what could be was so tempting, but surely deceiving.

"Can I borrow your phone?" she asked, as soon as he stepped inside. "I forgot about an appointment I'd scheduled for early tomorrow morning, and I need to look up the number." She wrapped her arms around herself.

"Sure." He dumped the mail on the table, instead of chucking it in the back room like he usually did, and set down the bags.

When he handed over the phone, she met his eyes, and then her gaze skittered away. "It's, um, a new therapist, to help with the, you know." She waved her arm.

"The PTSD."

Her eyebrows rose. "You know…everything?"

He nodded. "Came across the ETD footage when I looked you up. Sorry."

She shut her eyes, and her hand fluttered again. "It's fine, at this point…" She attempted a smile. "You've seen me at my worst more than once, and you're still standing here, so…"

"I know guys who've dealt with it. I'll ask, see who they talked to."

"No need. I think this time I've found someone that will be a good fit." She shrugged.

"If it doesn't work out, I'll get you some names. In the meanwhile, if you want to talk…"

"Thanks." She glanced away, looking beat, every bit of this long day showing in the slump of her shoulders.

"When you're done with your call, I'll show you around and then we'll get you comfortable." He grabbed the bags and headed for the bedroom. She'd have to take his. And yeah, he'd love to join her there, but he'd be a smart boy and take the couch.

When he returned to the kitchen, Miranda was standing—eyes wide and face way too pale.

"What?" he said. The room was clear, his phone on the table. Some of the mail had slid to the floor.

Miranda grasped a plastic bag—one of those clear ones from the grocery's produce section—wrapped around something thin and square.

"I recognized this—my slip case—in your mail. It's the DVD of Kathleen. The missing confession video." She held it out to him, hand and voice both unsteady. "There's blood on it."

The smear did look like blood. Like some had dripped on the coated cardstock of Miranda's preprinted case and then been manhandled before it had dried. Eddie's mind raced. Who did he know that could run fingerprints and DNA? How much time would that take?

"This is your handwriting?" he asked, because there was a white rectangle with "Kathleen Mackey" written in permanent marker.

"Yes. That"—she pointed to the early May date—"was the second visit."

He slid the disk out carefully. Same handwriting, same date inside. Miranda squeezed his arm, offering comfort.

Because she'd heard Kathleen's affair confession once already.

A fireball of emotion surged—humiliation, anger, dread. He spun, stalking toward the living room.

All along he'd been asking why. Why would Kathleen have committed suicide? Then, if she hadn't, what the hell *had* gone down?

He had to watch this for information. Where had Kathleen been coming from? What had possessed her? Maybe there was a clue—something perhaps that Miranda hadn't remembered, or hadn't thought important at the time.

He also had to come to terms with this other Kathleen— the one he didn't know at all, his beliefs about their marriage, and the harsh reality that it had been over well before she'd died.

Later he'd return to the other questions, like who'd put the disk in his mailbox? And why?

Eddie stabbed buttons on the remote and waited impatiently for the disk to load. He felt Miranda hovering, and shot her a look.

Arms crossed, she asked, "Do you want me to go, or stay?"

That goddamn pitying look ticked him off. He sneered, then shook his head and looked away. It wasn't her fault his wife cheated on him. It wasn't her fault he was looking for a murderer.

"Stay," he said, his voice tight. "It might jog your memory."

A black screen with the date came on, then Kathleen flickered onto the screen. She'd gained a bit of weight and her color looked better. A marked difference, really, considering the first video had been filmed only six weeks earlier.

Kathleen took a deep breath. "I've thought long and hard about whether to do this. I think I've been given a second chance here. It's too early to be sure, but then again, things are…never quite what you expect. If I get to see you in person, you'll never see this. But if I don't…I need to come clean, because it's been torturing me." She drew a deep breath. "Either way, I need to do this, for me, and for you."

Then, in a rush: "Eddie, I've been having an affair." Kathleen shut her eyes. "I'm sorry," she whispered, "so sorry, because I didn't set out to hurt you. But I was so sad and so lonely. I'd been planning on talking to you about divorcing, but you were home so infrequently, and then…" She opened her eyes and looked directly at the camera. "I didn't mean for it to happen. I found something I needed. I found what made me whole. You and I tried, but we were young… God, we were still maturing, still getting to know ourselves. Well, hell, maybe you weren't, but I was. And so much happened in those years, too. But asking for a divorce… It had nothing to do with you, really, so I don't want you beating yourself up."

Eddie felt Miranda tug on his arm. "Sit."

Woodenly, he folded himself in half in order to sink to the couch.

She sat too, right up against him, body to body from knee to shoulder, and splayed her hand on his thigh. He was grateful for the contact—a tiny tear in the cloak of disgust and fury he felt.

"It's not how you think," Kathleen said. "Not sexual, really, not really. I've never felt so loved and cared for. And that's not your fault. It just is."

Eddie's throat felt choked, like her words were lungfuls of sand—a challenge to breathe through, yet impossible to keep out, no matter how tightly you protected yourself.

"And our marriage sure was put to the test." She sighed, then seemed to gather her thoughts. "Nine-eleven affected us differently. You determined to fight back, to go on the offensive, to avenge the dead, and right wrongs. I did what I had to down there because I considered it part of my job. And then I…tried to squeeze the life out of what I had. I was scared for you, but I was also scared for us. There was already distance growing between us. And I knew much of it was me pushing you away, but I couldn't seem to help it." She shook her head, obviously remembering.

"I should have let you go way back then. This new relationship—it's helped me see all that. I need to apologize for my weakness—in not being truthful earlier, and for what I've put you through. I know you'll hold your own feet to the coals, Eddie, but I don't want you holding on to regrets, wasting time. We did enough of that." Kathleen's gaze became unfocused, then she rubbed her hands over her upper arms and looked straight at the camera. "I have a bad feeling that I'm out of time, despite the second chance. But you're not. You're a good man. A loyal one. But you deserve so much more than I was able to give you. So I'm releasing you, one way or another." Her eyes darted away for a second. "No matter what happens."

Kathleen smiled. "Find a stronger woman than me next time. Okay?"

Eddie jumped up the second the video went black, but sensed Miranda right on his heels. When he spun, she wrapped her arms around him and squeezed hard, her cheek pressed into his chest.

A hug?

Jesus. A hug was so *not* what he needed.

What he needed was—

Fuck it all, was Eddie's only conscious thought as he tilted Miranda's head up and took her mouth in a searing kiss. Like a man possessed. Mouth seeking, hands roaming, body straining hard against all her softness.

She rose on her toes, gave it right back, and kaboom, they were on fire.

Without breaking the full-body contact, Eddie picked her up, crossed the room, and kicked open the door to his bedroom.

She pushed up his shirt, and he ripped it off. Her hands slid over him, leaving a trail of need. He didn't bother with the buttons on her shirt, but tore it over her head, had her pretty little bra on the floor in no time. He bent to press a quick kiss to her fresh bandage, and then forgot all about it.

Her fingers had traveled south. She unfastened his fly and pushed at the material over his hips, only to abandon that effort upon a moan as he sucked a tight nipple into his mouth. Her hands slid into his hair and he nearly tossed her onto the bed—but remembered just in time about her wound. Lowering her gently, Eddie took her mouth again, then stripped off her jeans.

God almighty, but she was beautiful. Flat tummy, long legs, perfect breasts, and skimpy purple panties he put his mouth right over.

"Eddie," she said, pressing her mound upward, as her hands locked on to his head. He slipped under the edge of those panties to taste her.

"This round *won't* be one-sided," she said, voice husky.

He slid back up over her to see her eyes. "Definitely not," he said, and was rewarded with a brilliant smile.

She wrapped her legs around his hips and thrust upward, and he felt his body strain toward her core, even as he tried to keep the bulk of his weight from crushing her.

He put his palm on her side, thumb touching her fresh bandage. "You gotta tell me if you hurt."

She kissed him hard and slid her hand into his pants to squeeze his ass. "Don't you dare go easy."

He groaned. "Promise me."

"I'll promise, if you'll stop talking."

Amazing, this woman, he thought as he took her face in his hands and kissed her for all he was worth.

He wanted to be inside her now, thrusting like mad, feeling her warm, wet walls clenching him—but Jesus, he'd fucking explode in seconds if he didn't slow them down.

He'd been wanting her so intensely—every waking second for days now—and he meant to get his fill.

Eddie sat back on his knees and took in the glorious sight. Miranda's reddish curls fanned on his pillow, her green eyes sparkling with challenge and warm with desire, a sexy curve to her already swollen lips, and his scarred hands caressing those soft, sweet breasts.

"Gorgeous," he said, pulling a finger straight down her middle. Her stomach muscles clenched.

He pushed up and off, intending to lose the pants.

Miranda smiled, making him doubly hard—how that was possible, he didn't know. He couldn't remember ever wanting a woman more.

"*Woof.*"

Eddie spun and Miranda gasped, as Stripes bound into the room, tags clinking.

"Wait!" Eddie commanded, and the dog—*good girl*—halted on a dime.

Aiden was slower to react, however, coming two steps into the room before he clued in. "Ho—"

Eddie had already shifted, arms spread, shoulders back, making himself as big as possible to block Miranda, heedless of the boner tenting his briefs behind the unbuttoned fly.

Aiden spun and whistled. "Come, girl."

Stripes whined, head swinging back and forth between the men.

"She's fine," Eddie managed.

Aiden yanked the door shut behind him.

Miranda scrambled for her clothes.

"Shit, I'm so sorry." Eddie squatted, wincing because his sausage felt like it was in a press. As hard as he'd been for her, it was gonna take some time to calm that beast. He pulled Miranda's shirt out from under the dog's paws and handed it over. Despite the fact that he was still supercharged for her, he was already supplying all the reasons a rain check was a good idea.

Eddie turned to greet the wriggling mass of fur at his feet. "Hello, trouble. Couldn't wait to see your daddy, huh, girl?"

Man, he'd missed this pup. He doled out rubs and endearments and got some face licks in return. Miranda looked at him, eyebrow raised, as she righted herself. Yeah, yeah, he knew he was talking baby talk—or puppy speak, at least.

Stripes, who practically vibrated with excitement, pranced around him and sniffed at Miranda. She tossed Eddie his shirt, and then bent to rub his pooch hard behind the ears.

"Hello, beautiful," she said. "It's nice to meet you, too. Yes, it is."

Eddie had to laugh—she was the goddamn perfect woman.

Then the temporary good humor and sexual high was shot to smithereens in an instant. Because he'd thought the same of Kathleen.

He'd been so wrong. Copping to an affair in that video was only the icing on the cake. He'd figured that out already, of course, but hearing it from her somehow made it worse. She'd lied to him—or withheld, same difference—about the cancer. Jesus, that was fucked. And of course she'd lied about her reasons for wanting a divorce, too. It wasn't about him leaving, or them growing apart, or her giving up. She just wanted to be with someone else. She wanted an easy exit.

Once, he'd have trusted Kathleen with his life. Hell, he had—he'd given her his heart, his love, his future.

No—there was no such thing as a perfect woman. He wouldn't make the mistake of thinking there was again.

CHAPTER 21

MIRANDA DETERMINED NOT to act self-conscious or embarrassed. She was a single adult, after all, right? So after a visit to the bathroom to put herself to rights, she entered the living room head held high.

Except there was no Aiden to meet.

And Eddie, eyebrows lowered and jaw hard, was pointing the remote at the TV.

"Where's Aiden?"

"Heard him pull out."

"Oh." Awkward moment avoided, she relaxed. Yet she was a bit disappointed. She'd been curious to meet this person—Eddie's best friend.

Stripes trotted over for some attention, and Miranda reached down to pet her, even as she eyed Eddie. "How'd this cutie get her name? She's not exactly striped."

"It was better than Stars."

Stars and Stripes. She smiled. "Ah, I see." She rubbed Stripes a bit, then asked, "What are you doing?" Besides glaring at the video of Kathleen, in reverse, she meant.

He didn't answer until he hit pause.

"There," he said, taking a step forward to peer more closely at the tube.

She frowned. "There what?"

"Kathleen's necklace."

"What about it?"

He cocked his head at her. "You don't recognize it?"

She shook her head. "Should I?"

His jaw clenched. "I saw Annette Thompson wearing it."

Miranda frowned and took a closer look at the screen.

"That day I saw you in the office, I'd just come from talking with Annette. She had a habit of sliding it back and forth." He mimicked the motion and angled his head toward the screen. "Kathleen had it on in both videos. Just like you'd place your hand over your heart, she pressed on the necklace." He laid his big hand over his chest, and Miranda could just see it.

Eddie was right: Annette did make that motion, and Kathleen did do that in the video. Clients' physical tics were often obvious when she edited. But the necklace itself wasn't something that had stuck in Miranda's brain. Classic and understated. A thin chain with a gold slider that looked like a sideways figure eight.

She'd never noticed it on Annette, but the woman's style was very much buttoned up. High necklines and scarves, very politician's-wife appropriate.

"That's an infinity symbol, not uncommon," she said. "I suppose they could both have one. Although this one is rather unusual the way it's mounted." The chain didn't slide through the loops of the figure eight; instead, the tube did, and the infinity symbol was mounted on that tube.

"It's Kathleen's." The absolute surety in Eddie's voice made a terrible sense of foreboding crawl down Miranda's back.

"She had it on in both the videos—what? About six weeks apart?" Eddie said. "But she *wasn't* wearing it when she died."

"I take my jewelry off when I bathe," Miranda said, feeling the need to play devil's advocate, instinctually fighting wherever Eddie was going with this.

Eddie's expression was hard. "It wasn't in her things from the morgue, wasn't in her jewelry box or on the vanity or dresser or anywhere in the apartment. Trust me. I had to go through the place. I had to make the decisions about her things." He drew a breath. "She was buried only in her wedding rings and a pair of pearl earrings her parents had given her on her sixteenth birthday. I know because my mother-in-law tortured me about the jewelry, whether this or that was special." He looked pained, every line of his body rigid. "In most cases, I had no idea."

Eddie turned to face Miranda full on, like he was gearing up for a major confrontation. "But I can tell you with one hundred percent certainty that *that* necklace"—he jabbed the remote at the TV—"*never* came up."

Miranda shook her head, struggling with the implications of this. Kathleen had gifted it to Annette? That'd be weird, to give your boss a gift you'd been wearing. Or vice versa? Also strange. "Then you think...what?"

"I think Annette took it. As a prize. I've seen it before. Seen men rip off their enemy's dog tags, cut off a bit of a uniform, steal a personal item, pocket whatever—some keepsake."

Miranda felt almost as sick as when she stood at the top of the subway steps. She said quietly, "Like the movies or books. A serial killer would take something to remember a victim."

"Yes." His eyes were hard. "A memento. A killer's trophy."

———

Given that he had no fresh food in the house yet, Eddie and Miranda ordered Chinese takeout and sat down to discuss things. Hard conversations had never stopped his appetite.

The whopper of a discovery about Kathleen's necklace had, however, screwed his head back on straight. Not to mention finally and thoroughly destroyed his boner.

Not that he didn't still want Miranda—hell, the vision of her nearly naked and very demanding was practically seared on the inside of his eyelids—but this situation was seriously fucked up.

Miranda seemed to be having second thoughts anyway. He was sure she'd purposely avoided touching him when they'd maneuvered around the small kitchen. He couldn't blame her. Like a missile locked on target, reason had come crashing into his brain as well. First and foremost was the fact that already he'd fucked up. He didn't think he had long-term in him again. And she wasn't the kind of woman you just took out for a test drive—yet he'd almost done exactly that, dammit.

Not that he'd have come out unscathed. Hell, if he couldn't trust Kathleen—and she'd damn sure proven he couldn't—he couldn't trust anybody. Certainly not some woman who'd started out lying to him. A woman he'd known for such a short time, and only under high-octane circumstances.

"So Kathleen's affair must have been with the mayor," Miranda said. "It's the only reason I can think of for Annette to kill her."

"Yeah," Eddie said. "It was personal."

"But why me? And David, too, for that matter?"

"The confession video meant you knew about it. David must have known as well. The cleanup of loose ends. Just business."

"I just can't see her..." Miranda had a bad habit of gnawing on the cuticle of her thumb when she was upset. On her, it was somehow cute.

"She hired someone," Eddie said.

Miranda saw him watching, and stuck her hands under her thighs. "How can you be sure?"

"For one thing, she's weak and small. A friggin' gnat. For another, I saw your attacker. Definitely a male, over six feet and broad, *and* he knew what he was doing. Even disguised, Annette couldn't achieve that."

"How do the others come into this, though? Jeremy Rashorn? The campaign finance people and the corruption commissioner guy?"

"I don't know. If the mayor's got a bad habit of sleeping around, then I suppose he could've been doing wives, girlfriends, somebody's daughter…" Eddie rubbed his hands over his short hair and sat back in the chair, legs wide, hands resting on his head. "Jeremy? Maybe the mayor swings both ways. Or maybe the kid knew too much, or threatened to expose the affair, and Annette couldn't bear that. Like David, he would have been privy to insider knowledge. Hell, he might have been in the rotten position of scheduling rendezvous."

"Wouldn't the mayor start to notice? People dropping dead all around him?"

"You would think." Eddie grimaced. He dropped his hands to his thighs and shook his head. "Who knows? Maybe I was stretching with some of those."

Miranda pushed the food around on her plate. Eddie wondered if she always ate so little, or if it was the extreme stress she'd been under.

Finally, she dropped her fork. "If there's any hope for David at all, we have to go to the police."

Once again, he wasn't going to comment on what he thought David's chances were, but he agreed overall. "Yeah, we go to the police."

A giant whoosh of air left her, and she slumped in the chair. "Thank God," she said.

Maybe, Eddie thought, he hadn't realized just how hard this was on her—investigating on their own and not telling the police everything from the get-go.

He was sorely tempted to keep matters in his own hands. Go guerrilla and take down Annette Thompson in the dark of night. He'd killed more times than he was willing to count, so what was one more? One who most definitely deserved the fiery pits of hell.

But he was in America. The United States of. Where there were laws, courts, procedures, proof, and—yeah, when it came to all that, he was way out of his element.

In order to put Annette Thompson behind bars, paying for her crimes in a way that society approved of? They *had* to involve the police.

———

Throughout the rest of the evening, despite the fact that Eddie had tried his best to look anywhere but at her, Miranda felt the sexual tension between them as if it were a tangible thing. Never had she wanted like this.

There was no spray can or positive prayer to the universe in her arsenal for something like this.

Not that she would have used it. If Eddie had shown any indication that he intended to pick back up right where they'd left off—hot and desperate—she'd have launched herself at him.

But he didn't. So she'd been careful. Because he had to be in a helluva spot emotionally right now. When he'd kissed her and stripped off her clothes—God, she got squirmy just thinking about it—he'd acted on impulse, from a deep-rooted need and reaction to hurt, and partly, she suspected, from anger. She hadn't cared. She'd wanted to ease his pain. But then Aiden and Stripes had inadvertently provided a clarity break. And it was obvious Eddie was struggling. She had to refrain from touching him—Lord, they'd combust—and give him the space he needed.

He'd helped her get settled in his room, claiming he could sleep anywhere and that the couch was comfortable. He vacated with a quiet "Good night." But in the wee hours, she'd heard him watching Kathleen's video again.

She'd tossed and turned, restless and needy and alone in his bed and wishing she could give him comfort. She figured at least he had Stripes for company out there.

She sighed. If Max had taught her anything, it was that casual sex did exist. You could even remain friends, or repeat hookup partners indefinitely. Sex didn't have to mean a loaded long-term commitment.

For once, she'd been willing to test that—no matter what it cost her...

But she suspected she'd missed her chance.

———

In the morning, Miranda stole glances at Eddie, who stared straight ahead through the windshield. They were on the way to Aiden's through a gorgeous riot of fall colors. It would have been the most natural thing in the world to lay her hand on Eddie's thigh, or smooth it down his neck and rest it on his shoulder. But she worked to keep from touching him at all, which was harder than it might have been because Stripes claimed the window seat of the truck. Happy as could be, this sweet dog—hanging her head out the window, tongue lolling, fur blowing.

Even happier when they arrived at the stunning lake house. Stripes leapt out of the truck and raced for the lake. A kid burst out the front door and around the house after the dog.

"That's Aiden's stepson, Luke," Eddie said.

Aiden and his wife Tori stood up from a porch swing, coffee cups in hand. Obviously, they'd been expecting them.

Introductions were made. Tori was warm and welcoming, but Miranda knew she was there to size her up. Okay, well, maybe not. Maybe just for curiosity's sake. Either way, Miranda felt her cheeks heat, because surely Aiden had told her about last night's awkward oops.

Eddie asked, "How's my pal Luke? Keeping up with his training?"

"Says it's a cake walk without you," Aiden ribbed.

"What, you're going easy on him?" Eddie asked.

Tori explained to Miranda, "Luke has taken up martial arts at Sunrise, their school. He idolizes Eddie."

Miranda could relate.

"That's only because of that kung fu marathon they had," Aiden complained.

Eddie hadn't told her much, only that Aiden had fallen hard for this woman and her son. Miranda watched their joyful smiles, the looks they shared, the ease with which they touched each other, and felt a small pang. Someday, she wanted that. All of it. From hot sex to tender moments to children and a home. She sighed. Casual sex would only accomplish one of those things. And she had a ton of personal work to do before the others could fall in line.

"Let me introduce you," Tori said. "You should see the lake while you're here anyway."

Miranda suspected it was a ploy to give Aiden and Eddie a few minutes alone, but went along. Luke and Stripes looked like they were having a grand old time. Miranda wanted to say goodbye anyway. She might never see the adorable pup again.

———

Eddie could see Aiden had something on his mind. "About last night—it wasn't what it looks like."

Aiden said, "Pretty sure it was exactly what it looked like."

He looked at Eddie like he was a bona fide asshole—no, wait, that was how Eddie *felt*.

Then his friend's expression turned sympathetic. "Why not? You're allowed."

"Dude," Eddie said, "I can't. Kathleen—"

"Screw that. You can and you should."

Eddie's blood pressure rocketed, and he clenched his fists. Aiden made a settle-down motion with his hand, and Eddie took a step forward, spoiling for a fight.

"Just hear me out, Mackey," Aiden said. "Think of what Kathleen *did* and *hid*. And even what she *didn't* do."

That little speech should have sounded like a riddle, but Eddie knew exactly what Aiden meant: Kathleen's affair and her lying to him about her illness, not to mention the simple fact that she hadn't honored her vows or their relationship.

"You don't owe her jack shit," Aiden said.

"I—"

"I get it, I do. You'll do right by her, no matter what. Find out what really happened, take the fucker down. I'm even happy to help—but after that?" Aiden inclined his head. "Seems you've got a good woman in the here and now. Plain as day that you already care for her. I mean, hell, you even chose her over poor Stripes."

Eddie rolled his eyes.

"Couldn't resist." Aiden laughed. "Seriously, though, when this is done, cut the past loose, man."

Eddie scowled, but that didn't stop Aiden Miller's official life lecture. "You got a lot of years to live. And you *do* have a choice in how you live them, if you'd only get that through your thick skull." Aiden nodded toward the lake again, where Miranda played with Stripes. "There is a damn fine future ahead, my friend."

Easy for Aiden to say, being that he was all gaga over his own new love, like the honeymoon that never ended. But Eddie sat squarely in a place of serious mistrust of the feminine race. Okay, maybe that was unfair, surely there were honest women, good women out there—but he wasn't sure *he'd* ever be willing to take the risk of trusting a woman again.

Eddie tried to explain. "Listen—"

"Maybe Miranda's a part of it, maybe not. I'm just saying, numbnuts, that if you keep your head up your ass, you'll never know."

CHAPTER 22

MIRANDA COULDN'T HAVE been more surprised upon meeting the detective who'd been working David's case. So far, she'd spoken to Danny Iocavelli only on the phone. His accent was full-on New York Italian. Except he was sandy-haired and fair-skinned, with freckles and softly rounded features. Like Little Italy had taken up residence inside St. Patrick's Cathedral.

More disconcerting was the fact that, young as he looked, he seemed jaded—like the Big Apple had cranked him into applesauce at a tender age.

Miranda had been hoping for eager and driven, though she should have clued in. It'd been Eddie's bulldozing, not Iocavelli's willingness, that had gotten them as far as the detective's desk in the twenty-second precinct on the Upper West Side. Utilitarian and crowded, with numerous officers set up in one room. Another room—just the same—was visible, the two workspaces separated by a half-wall-half-glass divider that probably did little for the noise level or the general sense of chaos.

"Miss Hill," Detective Iocavelli said, "I hate to keep telling you the same thing, but there has been no movement whatsoever on your brother's case." He leaned forward, shoulders hunched, forearms resting on a cluttered spray of folders and papers. His hands flipped open to illustrate the *nothing* he had, or maybe in apology.

She was close enough to see the grooves in his palms, her knees and Eddie's wedged against the desk because they'd pulled up chairs and squeezed in.

"Have you put out missing persons reports? Flyers? Notices?" Her voice sounded thin even to her own ears.

"Flyers? No." His tone spoke volumes: tacking up flyers was not in his job description. "A report goes out to all the other precincts, the hospitals, and the morgue."

Miranda wrapped her arms around her heavy backpack, which sat on her lap. Eddie reached over and squeezed her knee, leaving his warm palm there.

Iocavelli went on, "He turns up, I promise you, you'll be the first to know."

She and Eddie had discussed their next move—they'd share any and all information and suspicions with the police. If Annette was caught, the police would get her to admit what she'd done to David. Then Miranda would know whether he could be out there somewhere or…

She took a deep breath, gathering courage. "We have some—"

Eddie squeezed again, harder this time and asked, "You've shared David's case information with your superior?"

"Deputy Inspector Getts receives regular updates on all our actives."

God, Miranda thought, if they didn't do something, some-day David's case would be *cold*. How long before that happened and no one was even looking for him?

"That him?" Eddie angled his head toward the biggest of the offices that actually had doors. "We need a minute with him. Unrelated—no need to add to your workload. Rather have you focus on finding David." He took Miranda's hand and pulled her to his feet, then turned to the detective. "She's really torn up. Anything you can do."

Iocavelli stood, nodded, and shook Eddie's hand.

"Thanks," Eddie said. "Introduce us?"

Iocavelli made it plain when he knocked on his superior's door that this was not his idea. But they'd known this would be an uphill battle.

Deputy Inspector Robert Getts had a broad build, a squared-off gray buzzcut, and a direct gaze that was both sharp and assessing. The bags under his eyes, however, were as dark and soft as specialty tea bags. But his smile was nice, Miranda decided, as hope gathered steam inside her.

Iocavelli clicked the door shut behind them, and the metal slats of louvered blinds banged against the glass window. Eddie wasted no time.

He laid out their suspicions and their evidence, start to finish, in an organized, non-emotional manner. Getts had leaned back in his chair, jaw working back and forth like he was sawing wood. His eyes narrowed fraction by fraction, as Eddie ticked off bullet points.

"So you mean to tell me," Getts said, "that you think our fine mayor has a habit of bedding staffers and his lovely little wife has a habit of offing them?"

"Yes, sir." Eddie displayed none of the turmoil that roiled inside Miranda's tension-filled muscles.

Getts just wagged his head. "That's rich. That is really..." A smiled erupted. "The most entertaining thing I've heard all month."

"Sir, I assure you, I would not be here if I—"

Getts halted him with an outstretched palm, all trace of humor gone, and in a louder voice than Eddie's, he said, "And I assure *you*, I've heard crazier that has proven to be true." He laid that hand on the desk, pressing it down. He looked hard at Miranda, then at Eddie. "But the fact is, you've got jack shit. The mayor's the mayor. And an investigation that pokes at the king of the hill sounds like a surefire way to get me and my hardworking, dedicated, underpaid detectives canned without our pensions."

Miranda fought to keep from screaming and tried to think of something that would sway this rock of a man.

"Now," Getts said, "if you had some kind of absolute, undeniable, no-two-ways-about-it proof we couldn't ignore? That'd be another story."

He nailed Eddie with a hard look. "Uh-uh, son. I saw that flash in your eye. Don't even think about it. Assuming you aren't batshit, then this is not a matter for civilian interference. You understand me?"

"Loud and clear, sir." And Miranda thought by the narrowing of his eyes that the deputy inspector heard the underlying note of sarcasm in Eddie's comment as well.

Getts leaned back in his chair and kept Eddie in the direct line of that sharp gaze. Miranda waited, sensing he was making up his mind about something. She wasn't sure if Getts saw something in Eddie's face that swayed him, or if something they'd told him had gotten under his skin. But finally, he said, "Here's what we're gonna do. I'm gonna get Iocavelli back in here—"

"With all due respect, sir—"

"Mackey," Getts said, and Miranda found it interesting that he'd lost the Mr. and was treating Eddie like one of his own. "There is not one officer in the NYPD who isn't over-worked, underpaid, and at risk every single day. And yet they show up every day and do their damnedest."

The men had a short staring match, until Eddie said, "Roger that."

Getts nodded and leaned back in his chair. Miranda remembered that she'd been surprised when Eddie had introduced himself with his rank. Now she understood. No matter that they were different branches on the serve-and-protect tree, they drank from common ground.

"You are going to tell this all over again to Iocavelli," Getts said. "He will continue to work your missing persons case." He shot Miranda a sympathetic look. "But he needs the heads-up on the rest of this, if something creeps up that connects."

Getts looked up at the ceiling before readdressing them. "Problem is, everybody you've mentioned is in different precincts, different divisions. We start pulling files and asking questions, we're back to that unemployment line. But I've got a friend I can trust in the police commissioner's office. I'll fill him in, just so there's an ear to the ground somewhere higher than me."

He picked up the phone, punched in a button, and said, "Get Iocavelli in here with his notebook."

Then he looked at Eddie and Miranda. "I am very sorry about your brother, Miss Hill. And I'm sorry I can't do more to put your minds at ease, but you two gotta know, I think you are barking up the wrong tree. On the off chance I'm wrong, I'll do what I can to help you."

———

No longer preoccupied as they exited the station onto West Ninety-fourth Street, Eddie wanted to smack himself upside the head. They were being watched. He felt the eyes on his back. And they sure as hell weren't friendlies. His own damn fault. They should have gone directly to the precinct when they arrived in the city. Instead, they'd stopped at Miranda's place. And Eddie had chalked the bad feeling he'd had ever since up to unease about the impending meeting with the authorities.

Eddie snaked an arm around Miranda's waist and pulled her close, careful to avoid her healing wound. On full alert, he scanned: stoops, doorways, trees, parked cars, people.

"What's wrong?" Miranda asked.

"We've got company."

Annette, or her hired thug, must have been watching Miranda's apartment. Damn his big, shiny truck, which he'd now have to leave on the street. Eddie knew all too well how fast and easy it was to plant a bomb. Which meant he couldn't drive his vehicle until he could sweep it, and no way could he do that with eyes tracking them and Miranda exposed.

Eddie hustled them across the street. There weren't a whole lot of pedestrians, but he joined a small cluster, aiming for safety in numbers. There was a subway station at Ninety-sixth and Central Park West, but Miranda's phobia was going to be a serious liability. Could he just scoop her up and carry her down there, even if she was as stiff as an I-beam?

"Where?"

"Don't know yet."

The prickly sensation was getting worse.

"Be ready for anything. Follow my orders."

She jerked her head in a tight nod.

Hitting Central Park West, he turned north but kept to the

east side of the street. The traffic lights had been with them so far, and they moved quickly—Miranda keeping up without trouble. Eddie still hadn't spotted anyone. Unless Annette had all kinds of unexpected skills, this had to be her lackey.

Most of the buildings in this neighborhood were security access or doorman. Only two decent options, then—the subway station or the park.

Central Park didn't lack for crowds or places to hide—but it had wide-open space, too.

Goddammit, he wished he knew exactly what kind of threat they faced. Close and tight like Miranda's attack? Man, how Eddie would love to get his hands around this fucker's jugular. A hit-and-run by one of these vehicles? More than one had tinted windows that concerned him. Or maybe gunfire from a distance? That idea he didn't like at all—no body armor, and too many innocent pedestrians.

This time they got caught at the light. Eddie was just about to stop traffic and take off running when an unexpected bonus appeared from the side street. Young kid, about Miranda's height, knit cap, earphones on, chowing a sad-looking sandwich from a piece of tin foil. Best of all—beat-up rollerblades slung over his shoulder.

Under his arm, Eddie could feel Miranda rigid with worry. He slid his wallet out as the light changed, and tugged the cord for the kid's right earphone.

"Dude—"

"Two hundred for your blades," Eddie said just loud enough.

The kid's eyes bugged and he almost stopped in the crosswalk. Eddie wrapped his hand around the scrawny arm and moved him along.

"I've got a situation. Two bills."

The boy reached for the laces of the blades at his shoulder.

"Wait," Eddie ordered, nodding at the entrance to the park. They kept with the crowd. The second they passed the stone wall, he yanked both the kid and Miranda down behind it.

"Put these on," he barked at Miranda even as he relieved the boy of his blades. He thrust money into the kid's hands, and Miranda scrambled out of her shoes, wide-eyed.

Hand on the kid's shoulder, Eddie said, "Stay low and behind the wall. Go north. Do *not* exit here no matter what."

He tried to slip Miranda's backpack off her arms to take the weight himself, but she said, "No! I need it." She looked panicked, so he let it be and simply tied Miranda's shoes to her pack.

She buckled the last cinch on the blades, and he pulled her to her feet. Taking quick stock—the path was clear—he nodded. The second her wheels hit pavement, she pushed off and he ran.

Crack, crack. Peeng, peeng.

Fuck!

Bullets. Ricocheting off the pavement ahead. Only a few, but enough to create panic.

People screamed and ran. One or two spun erratically, looking for the threat. No one hurt, thankfully. Not yet, anyway.

Miranda gasped and braked, but he shoved her forward.

"Weave," he ordered Miranda, and did the same. The shots had come from behind, aimed at chest level. They'd hit well ahead of them, only because they'd missed.

The path split ahead, and then would join with the park's main circle. There, the shooter would lose his angle and they could really make tracks. But dead ahead, a clump of tourists blocked their way. And as badly as they needed some coverage, Eddie sure as hell didn't want civilians in the line of fire.

Another *crack* and *whiz*, this time damn close to Eddie's ear.

Miranda swerved and ran—on wheels—through the patchy ground to cut right. The move both avoided the pedestrians and cut off distance. Eddie cracked a smile, even as he followed.

They both leapt onto the paved circle and picked up speed.

Eddie craned his head, watching to see if the shooter burst through the entrance to the park...

No—no one.

And blessedly, no more shots fired, either.

CHAPTER 23

ONCE EDDIE WAS sure they were out of danger, they'd argued about where to go. Eddie voted for a randomly chosen hotel. Miranda, shaken up as she was, held her ground. She insisted that she'd need her recorder, her equipment, and her security pass if they were to pin down Annette, get proof the police could use, and finish this thing.

That he understood. He wanted it done, too.

So they exited the park on the east side and hauled ass to her place.

Hopefully they could hole up before the shooter could take position nearby and try again. And once inside, they'd make it look as if they weren't even there—at least until they had the items she needed and a solid plan in place.

So far, so good.

"I just can't believe all this. I just can't." Miranda shook her head.

For whatever reason, being shot at seemed to have more impact on her than being injured. He suspected that she'd been still holding on to hope that the first incident had been coincidental, a poorly timed mugging. That she hadn't been targeted, even if the rest of it was true.

Eddie pressed a glass of wine into her hand, hoping that just a little would help calm her. He'd make sure neither of them drank enough to let their guard down.

With the lights and television off, the only light was the life of the city that edged in around the blinds. They made do with canned soup and crackers. Eddie had subsisted on far less. No big deal.

Despite Getts' warning, Eddie *would* take matters into his own hands. He'd started this to make things right for Kathleen.

But there was so much more at stake now.

Miranda.

Aiden and his big mouth.

Thanks to him, Eddie couldn't shake the idea that maybe Miranda could actually be his—for good, for keeps. That maybe it was unfair to judge her because of all the shit Kathleen had pulled. That he maybe didn't need to stay wedded to the past forever.

Not to mention the fact that *he'd* put her in danger by awakening the enemy. Future or no future, Miranda was his to protect now.

The only way to do that was to take the enemy down—because no way was Annette Thompson just going to roll over. No. Someone who'd killed before, who probably didn't even get her hands dirty most of the time, if ever? She'd keep on eliminating threats—probably as simple for her as checking off boxes on a to-do list.

And the casualties were piling up. Kathleen, David, and whoever came before...and who might come after.

Eddie shook his head. Once, those not yet in the line of fire might have mattered to him. But he no longer wanted to save the world. Only one sexy, redheaded woman, who made him want to haul her into his arms, even during the direst of discussions—even when she was opposing him.

Gradually, Eddie saw Miranda shift from disbelief and horror to anger and determination. Probably a good time to discuss what tactic to take with Annette tomorrow.

"We'll have the element of surprise if you come with me, as if I'm just heading to work," she said.

"If security is doing their jobs, they won't let me in, and you'll end up in there alone, unprotected." That thought made him crazy, and his muscles strained like they wanted to pull a Hulk and bust out. "I should go alone. Pretend I have an appointment."

"No." She leaned forward, breasts straining against the thin T-shirt she worse, and another part of his anatomy—already bulging—strained a little more. "They'll let you through because they trust me, and you're with me. Inside, Tara won't bat an eye, because she's already met you. If you do the mixed-up appointment thing, Annette will have way too much time to prepare, or it's possible she won't agree to see you."

Eddie took a sip of wine, discarding possibilities as quickly as dealing cards.

"Besides, the screener will flag you if you carry in a recorder," Miranda said. She cocked her head, eyeing him. "I'm not sure you can sell the Big Apple tourist thing, and they've seen you before. But they check my equipment all the time."

He'd like to check her equipment, and yeah, he knew the immature thought was his subconscious's way of trying to avoid thinking of her in danger. His body didn't care, though.

Now that he was considering the fact that he might actually be willing to put his bruised heart at risk to have her in his life, his libido saw no reason not to get started on the perks.

It didn't care that he intended to wait until all this was over to decide.

"I'll bring the small camera bag," Miranda said, "and just flip it on inside its case after they check. We won't get video, but we will get muffled audio. Best we can manage, short of whipping it out."

Goddamn, did every word out of her mouth seem to have a sexual connotation? Sweetheart that she was, she seemed to have no idea what she was doing to his body.

Eddie scraped a hand back and forth over his hair and forced himself to focus. Unfortunately, she had a point. A recorder might not hold up in court, but if they could get enough to convince the police to investigate...

Eddie could see the determination, and even eagerness, in Miranda's green eyes.

"If there are two of us there, Annette won't be able to try anything."

Eddie took in the hard set of her plump lips, the smooth, pale skin glowing over her cheekbones. This was how she must have looked back when she was covering breaking news: passionate.

This was how she'd look underneath him. Every night of his life, if he was willing to take the chance...if he could get it right this time.

No way would Annette try anything. Eddie wouldn't let it get to that. If she came anywhere near Miranda again, he'd strike—consequences be damned.

———

Eddie insisted that Miranda stay on the sofa and relax with her wine while he cleaned up. He felt her gaze warming his back the whole time. Although they'd sat in the dark, the normalcy of having a meal and a drink, and the muffled sounds of city life outside, all worked to make them feel safe, like evil wasn't out there. Or so he thought.

Instead, when he returned to Miranda, pulling her feet onto his lap so he had somewhere to sit, he saw that a heaviness had returned to her eyes. Eddie knew what that was like. It could be hard to maintain the adrenaline when you had to kill time, lying in wait for the skirmish. Confidence flagged. Doubt crept in.

He rubbed the soles of her feet through her fuzzy socks. Lids half closed, she rested her glass on her thigh. Still on antibiotics for the wound, she hadn't drunk much.

"Mmmn," she murmured. Her head fell back against the sofa and he thought she might fall asleep. But her gaze lingered on the movements of his hands, traveling up his arms, across his chest. Long moments on his lips.

Eddie felt the heat of that gaze, noticed the strum of his blood as if she'd awakened every cell in his body.

When her eyes met his she smiled, slowly, the sexy minx, like she knew secrets he didn't.

He saw her breathe deeply, lips parting, chest filling, then she set her wine glass on the floor and tucked her legs under her. Green fire lit her eyes now, and those lips curved up ever so slightly. The tip of her tongue touched her teeth, and he swallowed hard.

She caught his eyes then came up on her knees, breasts at his eye level, and—God help him—straddled his lap.

"I don't have a dog. And I don't expect my best friend," she whispered.

Eddie raised his hips, shifting where he'd needed only a bit of encouragement—except it only served to nestle him against her. Her stretchy workout pants—God help him some more—left little to the imagination.

She rocked against him and fit her lips over his in a warm, wet kiss.

He groaned and slid his hands up her thighs and around to that sweet ass. He pulled her in, tighter. The kiss went from zero to sixty just like that.

"Miranda." He took her face in his hands and nibbled at her lips, kissed her jaw line, her ear. She kept pushing for more. He tried to think.

"This isn't what you want." He did. He wanted inside her fast and hard, more than he wanted to breathe. But his protective instincts had reared up, too.

"You don't know what I want," she said, nibbling his neck.

"You're at a low point, sweetheart." He stroked her back, keeping his hands in a safe zone. "Scared. Off balance. This isn't going to solve any of that. I *do* want you…"

Did he ever. He closed his eyes. But he needed to square things before he'd be able to give her the future. "I'm working on putting the past behind me, but—"

"I know." She took his hand and touched a finger to the wedding band he still wore. "I have some work to do, too. Maybe even more than you," she said. "Let's put it all aside. Just for tonight." Those moss-green eyes brimmed with understanding, yet glinted with determination.

"Give me this," she said, and leaned in to kiss him, sucking slightly on his lower lip.

"And this." She stroked her hands down his arms, then smoothed them over his chest and down to his abdomen.

When she neared the waistband of his pants, a grunt escaped him.

He'd tried to take the high road, be considerate, but damn, she was making it—and him—so hard. The look in her eye, her soft, sure touch, the press of the heat between her legs—all of it creating a maelstrom of need, building like—

"I also need..."

Miranda arched, thrusting out her breasts. Momentarily distracted by that gorgeous sight, he didn't realize that she'd snaked an arm behind her back. Until she pressed hard with the heel of her hand—directly on the base of his cock, while her fingers squeezed his balls through his pants.

"This."

———

"Fuck sainthood," Eddie growled, and stood, his hands supporting her under her rear. Miranda grabbed a hold of his neck and wrapped her legs around him. *Yes*, she thought.

He carried her like she weighed nothing, claimed her mouth hungrily, and still navigated the dark hallway to her bedroom in the back.

He set her down, and they each whipped off their shirts. Eddie didn't wait, leaning in to kiss her as she shimmied out of her jeans. He shucked his cargo pants—not government issue, but still so damn sexy. Someday she wanted him inside her while he still wore them. Those and bare feet, like the first night he cooked for her, but bare-chested, too. Eddie shirtless was a sight she'd never get enough of.

But this was now, and she already had the soft skin and

hard muscle of his tight ass in the palms of her hands, his erection pressed flush against her belly.

They kissed like they were possessed. Hands roving, pressing, pulling. Couldn't get everywhere fast enough.

He walked her backward to the bed. She waited on her knees while he dug in his pants, like a large shadow. She heard a crinkle as he stood. Condom.

They were really doing this.

Thank God—because she'd wanted him since day one. A feeling that had only swelled and deepened since. Circumstance certainly had something to do with it. She'd been fighting to stay hopeful about her brother, on tenterhooks about the unknown threats, struggling to reconcile Annette as the evil force she was. All the while, Eddie had protected her, cared for her, held her.

He was the real deal. The whole package.

She didn't know what would happen tomorrow. Tonight might be it. "I want to see you," she said.

He flipped on her bedside lamp—there were no windows in this room—and his body glowed in the soft light. Ridges, valleys, bone and muscle. So virile, incredibly formed, and honed to absolute perfection. Dragging her gaze from his body, she saw a burning need in those blue eyes warring with tight restraint on his face.

Miranda had chucked all her reservations. She wanted him, even if it all went horribly wrong tomorrow. Wanted him, if it all went perfectly right.

Which was almost scarier, she realized, sucking in a breath as she held his eyes. Daring to hope. Daring to believe they could have a future together. It'd be brutal, making herself well enough, whole enough, to be worthy of this man.

"Miranda?" he asked, his voice raspy with need, his body nearly vibrating with the urge to move.

For Eddie, she'd do it—she'd go to war against her demons with everything she had.

A smile erupted on her face. Pure joy in her heart.

"Come here, soldier," she said, and reached for him.

CHAPTER 24

TARA WAVED THEM toward Annette's office Monday morning and said, "I let her know you were coming."

Eddie ushered Miranda forward. Her lips were pressed into a tight line, her eyes looked jumpy over pale cheeks, and her gait was choppy. She also white-knuckled the handles of her equipment backpack—recorder already turned on and the bag unzipped—which she'd chosen to hand-carry. The ever-present—and very heavy—everyday backpack, she wore.

Eddie knew how she felt—all senses on high alert, every muscle poised for action. He suspected Miranda struggled with a great deal of fear as well. In his case, any unease was channeled into planning for every possible scenario.

He was feeling even more protective after bedding Miranda last night. She was all Eddie had imagined and more. So sexy, both fiery and sweet. Soft and curvy and so incredibly responsive. And when he had looked into her eyes, their connection was so deep, so intense—just like their lovemaking. And that's what it was. Not sex, not banging, not screwing, not getting lucky or laid. This was mind-bending, soul-touching lovemaking.

Had it ever been like that with Kathleen? Eddie didn't think so, but it was possible that there'd just been too much time and crap between them dirtying the memories.

He wasn't going to let that happen with Miranda. He wanted her, every night, forever. He didn't need time to decide. She wasn't Kathleen. And she wouldn't be perfect—hell, he wasn't either.

Miranda could hurt him. But maybe she wouldn't. And he knew already—relationships took work. He was essentially retired other than running his school. He could put her first, do whatever he needed to keep things solid.

Like Aiden had so wisely pointed out, he had a choice. Eddie intended to make the most of it—which meant he had to keep her safe now and put an end to this whole mess.

The door was wide open. Eddie chucked manners and stepped in ahead of Miranda.

Annette stood behind her desk, watching the doorway. She forced a smile, her hands clasped tightly together in front of her.

No gun aimed at their heads, no weapon on the desk that he could see, but he'd feel a whole lot better if she'd step out from behind all those drawers and hidden spaces.

"Mr.—" She shook her head. "Eddie, Miranda. How nice to see you both." She spoke a little too fast, and her gaze landed on Miranda. "I trust you are feeling much recovered."

After the bogus mugging you orchestrated, or the spray of lead?

Eddie's every cell strained to leap across the room and wipe that placid expression off her makeup-caked face. Instead, he reached behind him to shut the door.

Miranda hadn't said a word, just stood there, like she was still trying to reconcile this tiny, coiffed, suited woman with a cold-blooded murderer.

The silence went on too long. A flicker of—what? Unease, dismay, realization?—crossed Annette's face at the silence.

"I don't believe we're scheduled for any tapings today, are we? What can I help you with?"

"You can start by telling us the truth," Eddie said.

Annette's eyebrow twitched.

"We've been busy, Annette," Eddie said. "We know your husband had an affair with my wife."

Annette looked stunned, mouth dropping open and eyes bugging. He had to give her credit.

"Bernard most certainly did not have an affair with Kathleen. Or anyone. He wouldn't stoop to something so pedestrian." The words dripped with disdain.

Eddie looked at Miranda, who looked grim. They hadn't expected a full confession without some serious prodding. In fact, he expected they'd have to threaten her before it was all said and done. They just needed *something* to use, something damning. And he wouldn't mind some closure while they were at it. He could guess what had had happened to Kathleen, but Miranda had no answers whatsoever about David.

"We know what you did, and we're not leaving here until you tell us how," Eddie said.

Annette's eyes jumped from one to the other of them. Her hands shifted to fists at her sides. "I have no idea what you're talking about."

"You murdered Kathleen."

Annette looked even more shocked than when he'd suggested the mayor had had an affair, going so far as to stagger backward. Eddie sneered. She should've tried Broadway.

Annette recovered quickly and rushed around the desk. Eddie primed himself but let her come—better that she was close to the recorder.

She stopped just short of them, her eyes welling with tears. "Never! I'd never hurt her. Not Kathleen."

"She was the other woman, and you took her out."

Annette shook her head furiously.

"How many others have there been, Annette? I'm thinking your husband must have a real hard time keeping his hands and secrets to himself, given the number of dead bodies littered around the mayor's office."

"No!" she cried. "He doesn't have affairs. He considers himself above something like that. He never forgets for an instant that he's in public office."

Miranda finally found her voice. "We have proof."

"You don't. You can't. Because you're wrong. Wrong about everything." Tears spilled down Annette's cheeks, as she reached up and wrapped her fingers around her necklace.

That damn necklace. Fury rose inside Eddie. He wanted to reach out and tighten it on her scrawny neck, twist and pull until every sickening detail popped out.

"I loved Kathleen—truly I did. I would never ever hurt her." Her eyes pleaded with them, and she dipped as if her knees had nearly given way. "You'll see," she whispered, then seemed to stand taller as she reached some decision in her mind.

She scampered around the desk and yanked open a drawer. Eddie was nearly on top of her, but she came up with only a small notepad and pen, which she quickly tucked under her arm.

Oddly, she didn't put the items on the desk, or even approach Miranda again. She skittered over to the corner of the room, pad tight to her chest, back to the corner, as she scribbled away.

Eddie's mind raced. He looked up—careful to only move his eyes, not his head—and sure enough, above her was a tiny camera. He and Miranda weren't the only ones recording.

So she'd spill, but she wouldn't do it aloud, not here.

Quickly, Annette peeled off the paper. She dropped the pad and pen to the floor. She folded the sheet she'd written on twice, and tucked it into her palm.

Composed once more, she walked toward them. Eddie felt Miranda looking at him for direction.

"It's okay," he murmured.

"This conversation is over. It's time for you to go," Annette said, very precisely. "Take care, please." Both phrases spoken with force, as if she were warning them.

She reached for Eddie's hands, and he let her, wanting that note. Sure enough, the paper was pressed into his palm. She held his eyes. "I would never have hurt Kathleen."

Miranda burst out, "What about my—"

"Shhh!" Annette hissed. Her back was to the camera. She dropped Eddie's hands to grasp one of Miranda's.

Miranda flinched and made to step back, but Eddie knew now that Annette wouldn't hurt her—not here, at least.

"David is safe," Annette whispered, and Eddie could see that she squeezed Miranda's hand hard.

Annette's gaze darted back to Eddie's. "You must go. Now. Before you make it any worse."

————

Noon. Columbus Circle Station. 1 train. Uptown platform.

That was what the note said, and that was where Eddie was.

He'd arrived early and already checked both ends of the

platform. No Annette. She'd chosen well. Numerous trains converged at this station, meaning there were multiple exits and transfer options. Consequently, there was a constant flux of people and noise.

He'd already considered all the various ways Annette could approach the station. Directly from city hall or via a roundabout route? It would depend on her motivation. Was she ready to talk, or was she setting them up? Was she concerned about being seen, or was she the only one pulling all the strings?

From a spot where he could see most, if not all, of the action, he put his back against the wall and waited, every nerve ending on high alert. Body primed to move, eyes peeled, ears attuned, mind focused—and yeah, he was packing, ready for anything.

But Eddie had serious reservations about leaving Miranda unprotected at street level. However, she wouldn't, or couldn't, come down. And they had to have answers. She had her mace, but that was very little consolation to him.

Local trains came screeching to a stop, a new outpouring of people for him to scour. Express trains barreled through on the same track due to construction.

Annette would find him. Or—

There. She was early, as well. Eleven fifty-two, by his watch. Annette approached as if she'd come from another train. But unlike everyone else hustling to make the Uptown 1 that'd be pulling away any second, she paused and reached up behind her neck to unfasten her necklace.

Hiding proof? Wasn't it a little late for that?

Bong. The doors shut, and a roar filled the tunnel as the train accelerated.

Annette walked slowly in too-high heels, with her hands

fisted at her sides and the tails of her dress coat flapping. Her head swiveled, searching the platform, but he'd chosen his spot well.

Reaching the yellow safety strip at the edge of the platform, she crossed her arms. One fisted hand at her sternum, the other hand holding that wrist tight. Okay by him. If her hands were hidden in her pockets, that'd be bad.

Every so often she'd lean out over the track, as if she were looking for a train.

Eddie scanned again, concerned she had a hit man ready and waiting to take him out. Spotting nothing, he gritted his teeth. He didn't like it, but he didn't have much choice. He waited until he heard the distant sound of a train, prayed it was a local and would stop, then approached at a fast clip, aiming to arrive at the same time as the train.

If someone started shooting, he'd yank her onto the train. That would leave Miranda alone longer, but getting himself killed wouldn't help either of them.

Annette shut her eyes for a long moment. When she opened them again, she spotted Eddie and offered a sad smile.

The train was still approaching, but it wasn't decelerating. Express, then, dammit. Eddie scanned again for a shooter, keeping Annette in his sights.

People poured in, city dwellers attuned to the sound of an approaching train and determined not to miss it.

Eddie's attention was caught by a man, moving just against the pack—angled, possibly, to cut Eddie off. Dark clothing. Hood up. No briefcase or backpack.

Eddie picked up speed even as he assessed the threat.

Then he took off, and the assailant launched into a full-out run, too. He saw Annette's confusion, and pushed hard. He had to get to Annette before this fucker got to him. Get her in a stranglehold—her body in front of his. He'd have to count on this guy not putting a bullet or knife through his bread and butter. And just maybe, if she felt physically threatened, she'd give up and spill.

His mind raced as he ran. Why didn't Hoodie just take out his piece and pop Eddie? Why come in close for the kill?

Annette spotted the other man. Eddie couldn't hear for the screaming of the full-throttle train bearing down on them—but he saw her gasp, rearing back. An ankle seemed to give way—her skinny heels surely off balance from the raised dots of the warning strip. Her hand opened as she scrambled for balance, and the gold chain fell.

Eddie won the race, but he needed extra inches to get behind Annette. Instead of launching himself at Eddie, Hoodie shot out an arm—at Annette. He caught her square in the chest and shoved hard.

"No!" Eddie lunged, but only grazed her shoe as she sailed over the edge, legs and arms flailing.

The train hit her before she'd even hit the tracks.

The sound was as awful any he'd heard in battle—maybe more so, because it had been so unexpected. Eddie clamped down on the urge to hurl, even as he gained his balance.

A blur of metal whizzed past his nose, and he heard the screech of brakes applied hard. But Annette was...already gone.

Expecting Hoodie to strike again, but unsure of his position—focused as he'd been the last few seconds on Annette—Eddie dipped fast into a squat. The necklace glinted near his boot. He grabbed it even as he spun and rose, ready to attack.

But the man had run, and—*fuck!*—he had a solid head start.

———

From just inside the Shops at Columbus Circle, Miranda saw a man shoot from the subway steps and leap into the street like he was running for his life. Eddie!

She burst out of the glass doors, then stopped short.

He'd crossed the pedestrian divider at a full run. Then weaved and dodged traffic as angry horns blared and brakes squealed.

Not Eddie. A man in black, hood flapping behind him.

A hood.

No!

She followed his path in reverse, rushing toward the subway entrance, but stopped short as if there was a force field at that first step. As always, her legs began to quake and a sickness erupted in her gut.

Was Eddie down there? Was he hurt?

My God, what had Annette done?

She gripped the railing hard, determined to find Eddie. Just as she'd mustered all her will and dipped a shaky foot over the ledge, Eddie burst out of the gloom below.

She gasped and jumped back, heart leaping.

One long-legged stride and someone vaulted from behind him, tackling him at the legs. He twisted with a kick and came to his feet. Arm already swinging, he seemed to falter.

Uniform. A cop—he couldn't strike a cop.

Another officer jumped onto the steps, gun drawn.

"Don't shoot, don't shoot!" Miranda screamed, but her

throat was so tight, she didn't know if they even heard her.

Half crouched, Eddie stood in increments, hands held high and visible.

"Hands in the air. Turn around," both officers shouted. "Turn around! On the ground, on the ground!"

Eddie moved very slowly, completely controlled.

He spotted her when he turned. His face was tight and hard, like set concrete, but his eyes—all twisted pain.

"Hands behind your head. Now!"

She opened her mouth—he shook his head ever so slightly. His eyes shifted to his left hand, back to her, and back to his hand, which was, oddly, partially fisted. The thumb and first two fingers were splayed, but the pinky and ring finger were tucked into his palm.

"Hands behind your head!"

Eddie opened his fingers. A string—no, a gold chain—slipped out of his palm and to the ground, landing one step above his feet.

He dropped to one knee—directly over the jewelry—and then the other. She looked up and saw that his hands were now clasped behind his head.

The police pushed him down. Eddie held her eyes as long as he could, then turned his face just in time to avoid smashing his chin into the step.

An officer put a knee in his back to cuff him. Eddie did not resist.

"We got him," one said into the radio, even as more police rushed past her from up top.

Miranda heard somebody read Eddie his rights, but she could no longer see past all the uniforms.

Oh, Eddie, she thought, biting back a sob. What the hell had *happened* down there?

She shuffled to the outside edge of the railing and gripped it hard, hands and feet anchoring her solidly in place to wait.

He meant for her to take that necklace, if the officers didn't find it first.

She'd have to go down there.

And for Eddie…she would.

CHAPTER 25

MAX'S APARTMENT WAS nearer than her own, and thankfully, she was home—because Miranda really, really needed her.

After Miranda's disjointed and shaky retelling—peppered by shocked expletives—Max insisted they both do a shot of whiskey to calm down. Somehow, it actually helped. Miranda gathered herself together enough to realize that they had to have more information. The women held hands as they flipped through channels. Over and over the news stations repeated the breaking news.

Annette Thompson, the mayor's wife, had been killed. Pushed to her death in front of an express train. Not an accident, but murder. The networks aired the footage, which was horrible in itself, but also horrifying to watch.

In fact, they showed the grainy clip so often it may as well have been looped. And God help Eddie, because it actually looked like he'd rushed Annette and sent her flying. His back was so broad, you couldn't see his hands or her body until she shot out. Miranda gulped, swallowing tears, and sank to the couch.

She knew the man in the hooded sweatshirt had done it. He was on the surveillance video too, coming into the footage at the last second, also partially blocked by Eddie as they converged. From this angle, a viewer really couldn't be sure who'd pushed Annette.

However, Miranda had seen that man with her own eyes, running like the devil was on his heels, up and out of the subway station. He had to be the same man that attacked her.

Had Hoodie decided to take out his boss? Silence the only person that could tie him to Kathleen's—*please not David's, too*—murder?

"This is not good," Max murmured for the umpteenth time.

And Miranda, yet again, insisted, "He didn't do it. He didn't."

Max turned the TV off. "You're sure? One million percent sure?"

Miranda wiped her eyes and said, "A billion. Squared. Yes."

As badly as he wanted justice for Kathleen, Eddie was simply not capable of an act like this. It didn't matter that he was trained to kill, or that he had killed in the line of duty. He'd done all that to protect people. Miranda had seen his soft side. He was tender and protective and caring. Smart and stable, too. Not rash, not rage-filled, not insane or insanely desperate.

"Max, he didn't do it. There's not a single doubt in my mind."

"Okay, then. What are we going to do about it?"

"I don't know." She got up and moved, trying to gather her wits. But her mind was on a nonsensical loop.

"Goddammit! Think, think," she told herself, slamming a fist on her thigh.

"Calm down. Getting worked up is not going to help," Max said. "You got down those steps to get that damn necklace—an act of supreme power, by the way. You can handle this, too."

Miranda nodded, drawing air. Max was right—she never

imagined she could do that, but she had. She could do this for Eddie, too.

"How did you make yourself do it, anyway?"

"A homeless woman spotted it while I was trying to talk myself past the second step."

The corner of Max's smile kicked up. "Your competitive nature kicked in?"

"More like desperation. I knew if she got to it first, I'd never talk her out of it. And I had very little cash on me." She shrugged, even as she marveled. Seven hundred and forty days, and she wasn't even sure how she'd done it. "I just kept thinking I had to get it for Eddie, that it could be *very* important, and when she bent over and reached for it, I just sort of lurched forward and practically fell down the steps, my heart pounding like it would explode." Miranda shook her head. "If she hadn't had three pairs of gloves on, it'd be hers."

Max put her hand to her mouth, stifling a giggle. She had a habit of laughing whenever it was most inappropriate.

Miranda knew the last tidbit would tip her friend over the edge. "She chased me."

Yep, that did it. Max howled.

Miranda joined her, and in seconds, they had tears streaming down their faces again.

"Oh. My. God," Max said, winding down to minor snorts. "You are so meshugana."

She was. A totally crazy woman. "Oh, man." Miranda got up and grabbed tissues.

Inappropriate and ridiculous. But she did feel a little better—she'd needed a release.

Tissues bunched in her hand, she crossed her arms and stared at nothing.

"All right," she said after a moment. "First I'm going to call the deputy inspector we talked to yesterday. Then, well, I don't know—let's see what he says."

She reached him on the first try—probably glued to the news like everybody else—and assured him Eddie didn't do it.

Getts sounded pissed off. "I told you two to stay out of it."

"Sir, is there *anything* you can—"

"No way. He's not in my jail, and the mayor is already pushing hard. Wants your man to fry."

Miranda explained that the man in the hoodie had to be Annette's hit man, who must have turned on her.

"I hope for Mackey's sake you're right." Getts sighed. "But you'd better hope some undeniable proof turns up. *Fast.* There're plenty of good men in the NYPD, but there's always somebody who'd like to dole out their own brand of justice, too. Mackey's a sitting duck. No way he'll get bail with the fucking mayor's wife dead."

Miranda's heart sank. She hadn't even thought of the danger Eddie faced.

———

Proof. Undeniable proof. She needed something every bit as convincing as the footage the news stations were rolling.

Miranda gaped at Max as it hit her. "That's it," she said. Excitement surged, displacing the overwhelming sense of panic she'd been swamped with.

"What's it?"

"Footage. The opposing view." Miranda spoke as fast as the ideas were forming. "Subway platforms have multiple cameras, from multiple angles. There has to be one that shows what we can't see."

"That will surface eventually, right?"

"Eventually. We can't wait for eventually."

"How do you get it? Maybe call one of your old reporter friends?"

"The MTA." Miranda's head snapped up. "I know someone at the MTA."

"From your reporting days?"

She grimaced. "From the ETD."

In fact, it was the son of Chuck, the man she'd performed CPR on. Everyone had seen that footage. Chuck Jr., who went by Charles, had gotten in touch well after the fact. Grateful for his dad's life, he'd promised that if she ever needed anything...

Well, she did.

Charles had worked for the MTA. While she and Chuck Sr. had been stuck in that subway car, Charles watched the disaster unfold and spent painstaking hours working the other side of things.

Miranda went for her bag, then realized she still didn't have her cell phone. "Shit." She turned, heading for Max's laptop.

Luckily Charles was on shift, and surprised, but pleased, to hear from her.

"I need a favor," Miranda said, and explained.

"That already exists. It's all we've been talking about here."

"You've seen it? It shows clearly that my friend didn't do it?"

"Sure does. The guy in the hood is the bastard who pushed her. Looks like your guy tried to grab her back."

"Oh, thank God," Miranda said, crumpling onto the couch.

"Not so fast," Charles said. "That clip went to the police not a half-hour after they snagged the first one. We've been watching the news and nobody's said squat about it."

Miranda sat up, gripping Max's phone with all the anger she felt. "Goddamn—"

"Uh-huh. I figure they want people thinking they got their man. At least until things calm down."

No way in hell was Miranda waiting for that. "Can you get it to me? Email or disk or anything?"

He hesitated. "I sure can."

"Charles? You aren't going to lose your job over this, are you?"

"Don't worry, girl. The police already have it, so I don't see any harm. I was thinking about the how." He laughed. "Besides, I hate this damn job."

Not ten minutes later, she was able to watch the alternate footage on Max's laptop and thought, *God bless, Charles.*

Max whistled behind her. "I'd say that's pretty undeniable."

Miranda nodded.

"So what now?" her friend asked. "Take it to the cops?"

"They already have it, remember?" Miranda smiled. "*Now,* I get to call my old reporter friends. We generate a new story and put the pressure on."

"Just your old station? Or you want me to look up numbers for the others?"

"No need. Channel 8 will run it, and the others will scramble to piggyback. It'll be all over in no time. The cops will be forced to release Eddie, and I'll be there to bring him home."

Miranda squeezed her eyes shut. Daring to hope. They were almost out of this whole nightmare. If only David—

Max's phone rang. Picking it up from the desk, she checked the screen, and her eyes shot to Miranda's face.

"What?" Miranda said, wary.

"It's from—you. Your home phone. The ID says Goodbye Angel."

Miranda's stomach dropped out and her mind raced.

"Answer it," she demanded, even as Max was putting the thing to her ear.

"Hello?" Max said, and a second later her eyes went wide, and she gasped. "It's David!"

CHAPTER 26

MIRANDA STRODE INTO the Upper West Side South precinct feeling like she'd conquered the world and tucked it tidily into her pocket. With Annette dead and her killer surely disappearing to parts unknown—probably congratulating himself for offing the one person that could nail him for all her dirty work—the danger she and Eddie had faced had vanished as quickly as the pop of light from a flash. Miranda had proof in hand—not to mention already airing on multiple news networks—that Eddie was innocent. She'd managed some subway stairs. No doubt she had a long road ahead of her there, but now she knew she could do it. Maybe she'd be doing it with Eddie. And, last but not least, David was alive—*alive*!

She didn't have the whole story yet, but he'd been on the run, hiding mostly. He was now safe in her apartment and had agreed to wait there. Relief made her nearly giddy. Although after she interrogated David, she might consider wringing his neck for not revealing he was okay sooner.

First things first, though. If the police weren't already in the process of releasing Eddie, she would be forcing the issue.

Captain Carl Klein—tall and skinny, with a protruding face and belly, large Adam's apple, and saggy skin—looked like a turkey with teeth. He had recognized her name from her harrowing five minutes of fame, and greeted her warmly just outside of his office. All what-can-we-do-for-you-Miss Hill.

When she told him, that tune changed and he ushered her into his office and shut the door.

"Hometown hero or no, you can't go messing with an investigation."

"What investigation?" She threw out her arm at the TVs in the bull pen. The very same footage she had on disk in her bag was airing on at least two televisions that she could see. Men, some in uniform, had been clustered around watching when she arrived. She'd seen one or two shaking their heads. Her arrival had stirred a ripple effect: low murmurs and uneasy glances her way until, one by one, they returned to work.

"It's clear you've got the wrong man." She tried not to think too hard about Annette's hit man. Miranda *believed* he'd just disappear now that Annette wasn't around to pay him for risking his neck, but... She squashed that thought. "Eddie Mackey should have his walking papers by now."

"It's more complicated than that." He shook his head. "We've got protocol. The paperwork takes time."

"Paperwork, protocol, procedure. Quite frankly, Captain Klein, I don't give a shit." Miranda stood, heat blazing in her cheeks. "Either you start that paperwork right now, or I go directly to Channel 8 and put my hometown hero face on screen and my hometown hero mouth to a microphone."

"Hold on now—" He stood too, stretching his chin upward as if to release the skin of his neck from his collar. He put his hands out like he was going to try to placate her.

Miranda didn't give him the chance. "All of a sudden I have a helluva lot to say about the Upper West Side South Precinct.

None of it good." She remembered what Deputy Inspector Getts had said, and cared about, when she and Eddie had met with him. "You want to do that to your men? They deserve better than that, don't they? You think your position is secure enough to withstand the pressure of the media? Maybe this story goes national, huh?"

Captain Klein glared, eyes round and buggy over lips pressed flat.

A staring match ensued.

"You've made your bed," Miranda said, and reached for her bag. Hefting the backpack onto her shoulders, she stomped toward the door.

From behind her she heard a grudging, "I'll see what I can do."

She turned to face him. "Right now."

He curled his lips in, biting back a curse, she thought, and gave a tight nod.

"Then I'll wait."

He pointed to some chairs outside his office, and as she passed through the doorway, she heard him mutter, "Royally fucked either way."

Miranda sat in a crappy plastic chair, bag gripped tight on her lap. Klein sat at his desk, already on the phone, shoulders slumped and head in one hand. He straightened up at one point, expression looking angry. A second later, he slammed the phone down, walked over to the window, and snapped the slats of the blinds closed.

Miranda stared and stared at those vertical lines and willed him to hurry up. Eventually, an older cop came over and handed her a coffee. He seemed familiar somehow, but she was too distracted to place anybody.

"It's crap, but it'll keep you upright." He smiled.

"Thank you," she said, shifting her shoulders back and straightening her spine.

"I let Mackey know you're here. Told him he's clear. Shouldn't be long now."

Relief flowed through her, far warmer than the paper cup between her hands.

"Thank you"—her eyes went to his chest, then snapped up to his face—"Officer Getts. Any relation to—"

"My brother. Just spoke with him." He winked. "You take care now, Miss Hill."

Miranda smiled and sipped her coffee. She doubted Deputy Inspector Getts had told his brother all the scary details, but he'd at least declared her a good egg. She'd gotten coffee out of it.

By the time Klein came out of his office, she was starving. She hadn't wanted to use her water bottles or granola bars, however. Instead, she'd taken advantage of a little paper cup from the station's water cooler.

She stood and saw Officer Getts *and Eddie* at a desk.

He faced away from her, but what a sight for sore eyes, gorgeous man that he was, whole and unharmed.

An envelope slid over the counter, and Eddie shook out his wallet, cell phone, and wedding ring. It bounced across the Formica, and he slammed his hand down on it. Picking it up, he started to slide it onto his finger, then hesitated. He stuck it in the front pocket of his cargos.

Miranda's heart thumped.

An officer retrieved a hard plastic case from a separate room, and took out Eddie's handgun. Eddie checked it, ripped the tag off, and slid it in the back of his pants, then flipped the tail of his faded jean shirt over it.

When he turned around, she realized she'd been holding her breath. Their eyes caught and held.

He didn't smile, but she felt the need and want in him, reaching out for her.

A smile burst onto her face—one she felt all the way down to her toes—and he strode forward.

Eddie wrapped his arms around her. She gulped—suddenly fighting a sob of relief—and buried her face in his chest. His big hand cupped the back of her head, and she felt his lips on the crown of her head.

For Miranda, the bumpy film of a terrifying ride had finally settled and steadied.

———

Eddie hadn't had his fill of Miranda when the door burst open behind her, and the mayor strode in, two suits right on his heels. His face looked like an approaching sandstorm in the Middle East. Menacing.

Eddie yanked Miranda to his side, blocking her slightly, and he felt the energy change in the larger room behind them. Men coming to alert, standing, shifting, entering ready mode.

Captain Klein—Eddie assumed—shot out of his office to intercept, but the mayor kept coming, dress shoes slapping the hard flooring, his upper torso leading the charge.

"Why the hell isn't this murderer behind bars?" He lunged, dress coat flapping wide.

Eddie *would* protect Miranda, and he was prepared to stop the mayor without inflicting any damage. But two officers caught the mayor by the arms just in the nick of time.

Miranda gasped. Likely Thompson never lost his cool.

Today, however, his tie and shirt were undone, his normally slick hair stuck up everywhere, and his eyes were wild.

"You *will* pay for this." Thompson strained toward Eddie, the officers holding tight.

"Mayor Thompson!" Miranda put her hand on his arm, and Eddie wondered how the hell she'd managed to get in the middle of this scrum. "He didn't kill your wife. Haven't you seen the new video?"

He sneered. "Looks like he did quite a snow job on you. Where's your loyalty?"

"Mayor." The captain settled a hand on his shoulder and tried to turn him. "New evidence has come to light."

Miranda yanked the flash drive from her bag and slapped it flat on his chest. "Proof."

The mayor's eyes flashed and his jaw ticked. "Can't keep your nose out of trouble no matter what, can you?"

Eddie could see Miranda warring with herself, trying hard to remember that Thompson had just lost his wife in an incredibly brutal way. Eddie, however, fought the urge to knock sense into the asshole. One more shitty word to Miranda and he would.

The captain snagged the flash drive and gave them a warning look.

Thompson held Eddie's eyes, fury running hot, as he was all but dragged into the captain's office.

CHAPTER 27

AS SOON AS they hit the street, Eddie took her hand and pulled until she rounded to face him. "Getts tells me you were the one to get me out of there." He stroked a thumb over her cheek.

"They would have had to release you eventually no matter what." Miranda said, stepping closer. "They had the evidence already and the captain was feeling the pressure. I only sped things up."

"Tenacious and ballsy." He tipped her chin up. "You're incredible."

Her eyes looked like they were about to spill over, glinting in the waning evening light.

"I was so worried about you," she whispered.

He took her mouth, his hands anchoring her tightly to him. He managed a grateful "thank you" when he came up for air. Otherwise, he kissed the hell out of her, right here for all the NYPD, the mayor, and God to see.

Amazing, strong, sexy woman.

Unlikely and surprising as it was, sneaking up when he wasn't looking, he realized it was love.

Holy shit.

He'd never thought that'd happen again—or that he'd want it too—but it had. And he couldn't get enough. He didn't want to get enough. Tonight, tomorrow, and all the days to come, he wanted to have Miranda's back, just like she had his.

"I need you," he said, his voice completely raw. "Let's go to your place."

"How fast can you get me there?"

He smiled into the next kiss, gratified to hear her own voice was raspy and heavy with need.

Then she shook her head and pulled back. "Wait. You don't know yet." She grinned and gripped his shirt. "David's alive."

"No shit?" Eddie was genuinely shocked. He'd thought the kid was a goner. "That's fantastic."

"Isn't it? He's at my apartment."

"What did he say?"

"He hasn't yet. I was at Max's when he called. I had to deal with your situation first. I told him to just stay there and go to sleep. He sounded exhausted."

"Think he'll sleep through me ravishing his sister, or should we get a hotel room?"

"Let's take our chances." She went up on tiptoes and pressed her lips to his. "I'm dying for answers, so I'll know if I should smother him with sisterly love or kick his butt."

She would, too. He laughed and slung his arm around her shoulders, above the ever-present backpack, as they began to walk.

"Either way, Miranda, I'm glad he's all right."

"Thanks to you, everything is all right," she said, eyes shining.

"We're getting there."

"What are you talking about? It's all over. I've got my brother back. You're free. You found Kathleen's killer—and though it would have been better to send Annette to jail, at least she's no longer a threat." She looked up at him, her brows knitting at his frown. "No more hiding in my apartment or looking over our shoulders. I can even go back to work."

What the hell? Was she serious?

"Once the mayor has seen the footage, he'll never give up. He'll find that hit man. You can be done."

"That guy is going to disappear like smoke," he said. "The mayor doesn't have a shot in hell of finding him."

"The police, then," Miranda said. "They have the resources."

He grasped her shoulders. "Miranda. It's up to me."

"Why does it have to be you? And how? How are *you* going to find him if you don't think that even the police can?"

He shrugged. "I won't have to. He'll be coming for us."

She shook her head hard. "No. He'll disappear—you just said so. And he'll stay gone, because the only person who can really identify him is Annette. And she's dead!"

"We're witnesses. A guy like this doesn't take chances."

She kept shaking her head.

"Miranda." He reached out to hold her arm. "He is just as responsible as Annette."

"Why can't you just let it lie?" Miranda asked. "Walk away. Let your wife rest. Let yourself off the hook. What could it hurt?"

Eddie went hard all over, tensing at her words. "Kathleen deserves justice. There's only me to give it to her. Don't you see that?"

She looked up at him with big eyes and drew a shaky breath.

"I can't do this anymore," Miranda said.

"What are you talking about?"

"Please listen, Eddie." She looked pained, gripping his

arm tightly in her hand. "If we stop pushing, go back to work, things will just die down. It's not worth all this."

Eddie twisted his arm out of her grip.

She latched on to her backpack like a lifeline, white knuckles grabbing the straps near her shoulders. "I need my life to be calm and"—she faltered—"and safe. I *need* a normal life."

The realization hit him with the force of an explosion. He'd been wrong, so totally wrong. He'd worried about trusting her—and he was apparently right to. She wasn't lying like Kathleen had, but she was bailing like Kathleen. Hell— she was jumping ship far faster than Kathleen had, the very minute she felt like she didn't need him anymore. Miranda wanted her life to be easy. She wanted smooth sailing. If she wasn't willing to see *this* through with him—Christ, it was so clear cut in his mind that Annette's hit man had to be dealt with—she surely couldn't be trusted to stick through the ups and downs of a marriage...

Jesus, he'd thought being incarcerated was the lowest point, but man.

"What's normal, Miranda, huh? Mistresses murdered? Heads of departments just keeling over dead? Staff silenced— slashed on the street like you, or beaten like Jeremy Rashorn? You don't think those families deserve justice? That they don't deserve to know who robbed them of their loved ones?"

She shook her head, tears welling.

I can't *love a woman who can't—or won't—stand by my side, somebody who's not all in*, Eddie thought, horrified. *I already did that once, and look what a shit show that landed us all in.*

He said, "It's too late for *normal*. Be done if that's what you *need*. If this is too *hard* for you. Or you're too *scared*." He knew every bit of disgust showed on his face, but he was way past giving a damn. "But I won't stop. I can't rest. I owe it to Kathleen. I have to make it right, or I can never move forward."

Ha—what there was to move forward for now, he had no idea.

"Until Kathleen's death certificate says homicide instead of suicide? I'm in this." Eddie took one last shot. "And if you think you are *safe*, Miranda? Think again."

CHAPTER 28

THE CAB RIDE to her apartment so that Eddie could retrieve his duffel and get the hell out of her life—as he put it—ranked as one of the worst ten-minute chunks of her life. The tension between them weighed so heavily that she wouldn't have been surprised if the vehicle had been unable to roll. Worse was the anger rolling off Eddie.

He'd taken a call from his friend Wik, but didn't share the info with her. In fact, he didn't speak to her at all. Kept his eyes trained out the window.

When she'd locked the door behind them, she peeled out of her backpack and set it near her bigger backpack that always waited there. Eddie squatted down and unzipped his duffel bag. He'd kept it in near the door in what he called "ready mode."

What a pair they made. Convenient now. He'd be out of here in two seconds flat.

"I want to see your brother before I leave," he said without looking at her, and headed down the hallway.

Miranda squeezed her hands together. She also desperately wanted to lay eyes on David. She didn't want to see Eddie leave.

She followed and heard snoring before Eddie pushed her bedroom door open.

Sprawled across her bed, David looked haggard and pale.

He had the beginnings of a real beard. Unlike the patchy one in his younger partying days, this one was full. He'd borrowed one of her T-shirts and a pair of yoga pants, both ridiculous-looking because they were way too tight.

His own clothes sat in a disgusting—she could smell them from here—pile in the middle of her floor, along with one of her towels.

Just what had *he* been through?

Miranda bit her lip, as tears threatened. She worked not to fall apart.

Eddie stalked to the bed, grabbed a fistful of David's shirt, and lifted him up enough to wake him.

David startled, looking nearly panicked, then relaxed when he realized who it was. Eddie bent down and said something Miranda couldn't hear. David nodded.

Eddie crossed the room. She backed out into the hallway.

Eddie looked over his shoulder at David. "You're awake enough to remember this?"

Miranda spun and fled down the hallway before David could answer. In seconds, Eddie had joined her at the door, tension visible on his face, his eyes stone cold. She came close so close to blurting out *forgive me* and *I take it back* and *I was wrong, please, please don't leave*…but she couldn't.

She was buckling—finally—under the pressure of all they'd been contending with. She simply couldn't do it anymore.

Eddie hefted his bag, stepped around her packs, and opened the door. One stride and he was in the foyer. He looked back and opened his mouth, before clamping it shut. His eyes were hard, his jaw as tight as she'd seen it.

"Lock up," he said, and shoved outside.

She shut her door quickly, unwilling to watch him walk out of her life.

Tears welled fast.

Lock up.

He was still protecting her. He still cared.

He shouldn't.

She flipped the locks, heard a faint snore from her bedroom, and went to the phone and turned the ringer off so David could sleep. She wandered around, then found herself staring at the door, seeing only Eddie's back as he left.

She sank to the floor where she stood and buried her face in her knees.

She'd thought that if she could just fix herself, have life calm enough to start working through her fears, making progress on her fucked-up psyche, that she'd be whole for him. For later. She'd lost sight of *now*.

She should have realized that there was no pause button on a relationship. Once that film started rolling, it existed. They existed.

They'd been through so much in the short time they'd known one another—what was one more life-threatening event, like facing down a hit man?

She half laughed, half sobbed. She'd blown it so thoroughly—so focused she'd been on righting her safe little cocoon.

And what had it gotten her?

She turned her head, eyes cutting to her ever-ready bag.

Like a hoarder, she was forever stocking up against the future and all its what-ifs, desperately afraid of actually using what she had now. Her safety nets had become a prison.

The bulging pockets and straining seams of that damn backpack mocked her. Coming up on her knees, Miranda ripped open zippers one after another.

With two hands, she flipped the thing upside down, shaking madly. Packs of batteries, a flashlight, chargers, and a first-aid kit all hit the floor with heavy thuds. Water bottles bounced and rolled, and plastic-encased edibles poured out like candy from a piñata.

She shook and shook that bag long past empty. Then she doubled over the mess, empty nylon clutched in her fingers, and sobbed.

Managing her fears had gotten her nowhere, nothing.

Holding on to those fears, letting them use her...had allowed her to ruin everything.

Her automatic refusal and complete unwillingness to stand by Eddie, work alongside him, support him in what he needed to see through, what he believed was the right thing? That *sucked*.

Okay, yeah...Eddie had walked, too. He hadn't stayed and tried to convince her, hadn't tried to help her work through her fears. He'd been angry, and probably shell-shocked. She figured half of that was a knee-jerk reaction born of self-preservation. Despite the fact that his wife had been gone for well over a year, Kathleen was *still* putting him through emotional hell...all those confessions and revelations were fresh to Eddie. Almost like the woman was walking out on him—in one way or another—over and over again.

Damn. Here Miranda had to go and do the same. Albeit for totally different reasons. If only she'd had more time to think it all through, to come to terms...

Eddie was such a good man, with a big heart and a moral compass so calibrated that it never wavered. Sexy, smart, and capable, yes, but so much more important, he was steadfast, protective, and caring. He made the hard choices over and over again, always doing what he believed was necessary and right, no matter how inconvenient, how tough, how seemingly impossible...

He was everything she ever wanted in a man, and more. Absolutely one in a million.

But he'd *never* be back, and she wasn't sure she could blame him.

———

Wik, techie genius that he was, had unearthed some very interesting information. So Eddie hightailed it down to Chinatown on the subway, his bag in tow, as soon as he left Miranda's.

Good timing, he supposed. Because not only should Chang be back from that conference and at work, but Eddie was off the hook now. He'd given David strict instructions to protect Miranda until the hit man was no longer a threat. Eddie wasn't entirely comfortable with that, but it would have to do. David was all he had at the moment, and he'd at least proven himself tougher than Eddie had first given him credit for. Hell, he certainly hadn't expected the kid to turn up alive.

Eddie was now free of babysitting somebody who didn't want him around to mess up her tidy life, free from being stuck behind bars, and free to do what he needed to in order to finish this. Hopefully, fast.

Back to stalking unsuspecting targets, then. This time, he staked out the route Winston Chang was most likely to use to reach his apartment, assuming he was coming straight home from work.

The steady stream of people and traffic lulled Eddie, turning his thoughts inward. He struggled to come to terms with Miranda's choice. He was ticked, and yeah, it fucking hurt to be cut off like that. He felt like a damn fool for trusting her, for beginning to think…

Eddie kicked the bag he'd set at his feet and scowled,

before he remembered he shouldn't look so menacing while he was trying to blend in.

Then—there was the coroner, squeezing between a fruit cart and a storefront. Eddie threw his duffel over his shoulder and crossed the street fast, coming up alongside Chang and clamping a hand on the man's shoulder.

"Winston," Eddie said.

Chang startled, then relaxed when he recognized Eddie's familiar face. Just as quickly, his posture tensed and his expression turned wary. He said, "What do you want?"

They both kept walking, keeping pace with the crowd of people on the street. Eddie smiled. "I want to know what you know."

"I don't know anything." Chang didn't look at Eddie, but the corners of his mouth pulled down.

"I think you do."

Chang stopped and turned to Eddie. "I *can't* help you."

"Could you have helped Jeremy?"

Chang's eyes widened, then narrowed. He looked over his left shoulder and then his right as people swerved to go around them. "Not here," he said, and continued walking. Eddie followed Chang into a fish market. Chang nodded to a woman and then a man, as he passed bin upon plastic bin of raw fish of all kinds. Whole fish, heads, tails, squid, pink grays, white. The smell was overwhelming. Fresh fish—thankfully—overlaying years of old scents that had surely permeated the walls.

Chang stopped in the back corner where they could be somewhat alone. The fishmongers hovered up front, but there was enough noise and chaos from the street that the rear of the store felt insulated.

"Why didn't you tell me you had a connection to Jeremy Rashorn?"

"Why would I? You weren't asking questions about him. Only about your wife."

Eddie scrubbed a hand over his hair. "You didn't think I'd want to know?"

"Know what, exactly?"

Eddie clenched his jaw. "Stop dicking around. You and I both know there's more to this than just the official stamp on Kathleen's death certificate. Otherwise you wouldn't have sent me to your family's restaurant."

Chang put his hands on his hips. As before, he worked a piece of gum nervously.

Eddie asked, "Was Jeremy murdered?"

Chang stopped chewing and inhaled enough that his scrawny chest puffed out. Gathering his resolve?

He held Eddie's eyes. Finally, he said, "I think so, but I can't prove it."

Eddie's breath stopped for a moment. Holy shit. "You can't or you won't?"

"Both," Chang said, sounding resigned. "Listen, Jeremy answered my ad for a roommate. I didn't know him that well, but he was a nice kid. Smart and hardworking. He paid the rent on time, picked up after himself, kept his social life elsewhere. After a while, he landed a new job. He was really excited about it."

"At city hall," Eddie supplied. He shifted his bag further onto his shoulder, antsy for Chang to continue.

Chang glanced around them and then nodded. Eddie could have told him they were still alone—just them and the fish crammed together.

"Over the course of the year," Chang said, "he changed little by little. Always brooding, even more serious. He withdrew from talking to me at all—not that we were buddies, but you know." He waved a hand. "Then he got agitated. Couldn't sit still. I'd hear him up at all hours of the night. He'd check the locks and shut the blinds." Chang rubbed his eyes. "Anytime I asked him, he wouldn't say anything except that his job was very, very stressful. And then he was jumped one night, and although it was random by all appearances..." Chang shrugged.

"Did you do the autopsy?"

"No, but the ME that did is good. And I did get a look at her report. It is what it is. There's no solving it. Not yet."

"What the hell does that mean?" Eddie asked.

"It's like your wife's case. It means there's no red flags, no reason—other than my suspicion—"

"Isn't that enough?" Eddie asked.

"You must understand." Chang held Eddie's eyes, "I *need* to keep my job—and my *life*. I can't go chasing wild theories. And I certainly can't go poking at the *mayor's office*." Chang blew out a frustrated breath.

Eddie opened his mouth, but Chang cut him off. "You do what you want," he said. "What I can do is go to work. Every day. I will take the cases that come to me and get closure for other people. I will catalogue all the data, thoroughly, so that someday, when DNA evidence surfaces and a match is made or a pattern is identified"—he pounded a fist into his other palm—"there *will* be dots to connect. It's the only way I know how to get justice for people like your wife and Jeremy, people like my sister."

"All right." Eddie inhaled, then nodded. "I get it. But what's with the cryptic note, then—that proof might exist?"

"I'm sorry...I didn't want you to give up."

"Great," Eddie muttered.

Chang shook his head. "I couldn't say anything at work. I think there are some people who've been...influenced."

By money? Threats? Political influence? Eddie figured it didn't much matter.

Chang held his left hand aloft. "It's as I was trying to explain. It's challenging to connect dots when only one half exist—those pertaining to the victim. But if there were also dots from the"—he lifted his right hand, palm facing the other—"perpetrator—*then* there might be something worthwhile to compare."

Eddie felt a keen disappointment. Yeah, he'd gotten some questions answered. But damn, he'd been banking on something more concrete from a guy who dealt in science at its purest every day.

Chang tilted his head at the bins of fish in the center. "You should buy something."

"I'm in a hotel," Eddie said. "Not even a hot pot."

Chang flashed the first real smile Eddie had seen from him, and said, "Sashimi?"

CHAPTER 29

EDDIE HEADED BACK uptown and bypassed two diners before he found a true Irish pub—because no, raw fish was not going to do it. He figured he was about two meals behind and needed to remedy that. He probably could have made do on a street vendor's hot dog, but he was hoping a real meal would settle the roiling in his gut.

Eddie sat at the bar toward the back, where he could make use of the rear exit if need be. He could still see the door to the street via the large pub mirror. His duffel sat upright on the stool next to him like an old, silent companion. Not such a comforting one at the moment, though. Eddie felt uneasy. A nasty mix of guilt, worry, disappointment, frustration—

Aw, fuck. He shook his head.

He signaled the bartender and ordered up a large steak and potato dinner, and some hearty soup. He must look like shit, because another beer just appeared.

Aiden's pop, whom Eddie had been closer to than his own dad, had always said, *There's nothing like red meat to make ye feel like a king.* Course, he was also fond of *Tipping into the foam of a Guinness is like losing yourself in a cloud.*

Eddie should be celebrating his freedom. And losing himself sounded mighty fine right this second, though he'd chosen a Harp—no head of foam.

Wait until he told Aiden about jail—oh damn, had they

seen that news in the Poconos? As soon as he'd charged his phone—it'd gone dead in police lockup—he'd call Aiden and let him know he was okay.

Bizarre how jail suddenly seemed like a minor event all of the sudden. Even after the chat with Chang, Eddie's brain space was still consumed with Miranda's little bombshell.

He'd thought she was amazing, just struggling in that one area—which was understandable. PTSD was a wicked illness, and a very real one. But how she was about going underground? He hadn't realized that that's how she was about *life*. Consumed by her fears, well beyond the scope of the actual disorder. She couldn't see beyond herself and her needs. She couldn't put herself out there to help him, to see this crazy mess through.

Or she *wouldn't*. That was more likely, given that she didn't even consider trying. Certainly not for him.

Maybe she'd only been using him—a free bodyguard, with benefits. And the minute she felt she was out of danger... What an idiot he'd been for thinking they had something real, something once-in-a-lifetime. He should have known. A relationship that had kindled out of danger alone was bound to reek like burned plastic when you stuck it into the fire.

How had he not seen it? Because he'd been distracted. By gorgeous green eyes, a sexy bod, full lips saying shit he'd wanted to hear...and his own needs.

Eddie felt nearly ill. The soup arrived, and Eddie forced spoonfuls past his tight throat, determined to fuel himself.

Food did help, a bit. But he couldn't turn off the sickening refrain in his brain.

If he was so done with Miranda Hill, why did he still have severe misgivings?

His subconscious was definitely rearing up. If she'd been

that heartless, she wouldn't have descended on that jail like some avenging angel. And that had taken real guts.

And he'd blown up pretty fast. He could have...hell, stayed long enough to give her time to work it through. Talked more. Reacted less. It probably wouldn't have mattered, but then he'd know for sure.

What else was he grappling with...residual worry over her safety? Loose ends? Something they'd missed? A foreboding? Or instinct?

Whatever it was—*something* didn't feel right. Sitting in that cell, he'd had plenty of time to replay Annette's words, her strange actions. But it was all a mixed-up mess. Things didn't quite fit, and yet the locks wouldn't tumble into place in his mind.

Maybe the iron in the steak would help him think clearly, he decided, and he set to slicing, stabbing, chewing on auto-pilot, more like a machine than a man. Before long, he shoved his plate away. He craved a scalding shower, but the thought of another hotel room in this damn city sucked.

Still, he had to stick around. Make himself available for a hit.

Eddie cracked his first smile. It would feel damn good to tidy up this mess physically.

He refrained from ordering another beer. No losing himself in Patrick's cloud until this was all over. He'd get a coffee to go, retrieve his truck—Christ, where the hell was his truck?

Oh yeah—a couple of blocks from the twenty-second precinct. They'd left it there when they'd been forced by bullets to flee. It only *felt* like he'd parked it there a year ago.

———

Eddie stared at the compact cars jammed nose to tail in the block where his truck should have been and let loose a torrent of choice swear words.

Could this day blow any harder? Christ. It probably could. As sucky as hitting a New York City impound lot would be, if the vehicle was stolen, that'd mean he'd be back at a police station. Eddie nearly shuddered at the thought.

Although he'd expected a hefty fine, since he hadn't paid today's meter, he'd never expected a tow, because it'd been a choice day: suspension of alternate side of the street parking—meaning he hadn't been required to move it.

He headed for the coffee shop he'd passed a few blocks back. The city had a number you could call in these situations, but Eddie had to be able to plug in his phone to find it. There'd been no outlet anywhere near his seat at the bar, but coffee shops, especially the chains, usually had plenty.

Ten minutes later, Eddie realized he'd been wrong. There was a serious level of suck between the two outcomes.

For some ungodly reason, they'd towed his car to fucking Masbeth in Queens instead of Pier 76 in Manhattan.

He'd been to the Queens impound lot years ago. Under the Kosciusko Bridge and in a largely industrial area, there was no fucking way to get all the way to the godforsaken shithole via public transportation—at least not fast. And he had to move fast. They closed at ten p.m. on Mondays, and in his experience, there was *always* a wait.

Eddie hailed a cab, then seethed the whole way. He debated what to do after he retrieved his truck. Head for the hotel he'd stayed at before? Or the first hotel he passed, even if it was a dump? Get some shut eye, and then early morning, when the streets were still largely deserted, go for a run—with his 9mm and a couple of knives? Or stay out all night? Tempting, but only because his man might be more inclined to strike at night.

Jesus, Eddie thought as the cabbie let him out. The place hadn't changed a bit. Fucking no man's land, with lots of chain link fencing coupled with giant corrugated metal and a cutout for an entrance. A depressing, desolated kind of place.

Soon as Eddie walked through the door, he heard a yell from somewhere behind the glass.

"Go lock that damn door, or we'll be here all night."

And sure enough, yep, a line. But only four people in front of him, and there was an energy to the place. An hour to closing and *everybody* wanted out.

When it was his turn, he pasted on a smile, paid—imagine that, they took credit cards these days—and headed for the waiting area, where a cop came to escort you to your car.

Except he didn't, really.

The patrol car pulled up, and Eddie stepped forward. Just as he reached for the door handle, the officer tossed his keys through the passenger-side window.

Eddie caught them on instinct, then watched with disbelief as the cop peeled out.

What the fuck? The jerkoff headed for the exit, red taillights bouncing.

The lights started flicking off one by one inside.

Fuck.

He yelled in to the woman.

"He *what*?" she replied.

And there it was.

They hadn't changed policy. The guy *was* supposed to escort him to his vehicle.

This was it, then. Eddie's senses went on high alert—almost like he put out feelers behind him.

The woman shook her head and sucked her lips. "You got ten minutes only, 'cause I ain't staying here one extra." She was sorry for it, but she wanted out.

"Which quadrant?"

"To the right. In the middle somewhere."

Christ. The lot was fucking huge.

Eddie bent, setting down his bag like he was getting organized for the long walk.

Which he was. Giving his eyes time to adjust to the dark. Slipping a KA-BAR knife out of his bag and into his hand, tucked up straight along the inside of his forearm where it was virtually impossible to see.

Nice and dark, this lot. Lots of pockets of deeper shadows. No witnesses.

Eddie smiled. Bring it on, Hoodie.

He hit the key fob occasionally—when he got close enough, the truck lights would flash and the horn would beep.

Either Hoodie had paid off that cop or it'd been one of his own, but chances were that Hoodie knew exactly where the truck was, too. He might be waiting there—though if it were Eddie, he'd eliminate the possibility of escape and attack well before his prey reached wheels.

Eddie stayed close to the bumpers. Possibly closer to Hoodie, but also nearer to cover.

Eddie felt the warning tingle on his scalp even as he heard the slightest shift of a body.

A shot rang out.

Eddie dove between two vehicles and dropped his bag as he rolled. He scrambled forward and then over the hood of two cars—they were parked bumper to bumper—to loop around. Over another and—

Ping, another shot rang out and bounced off the car he'd just slid off. Eddie knew where the guy was now for sure. Back and left, about ten o'clock, and staying low.

He threw a pebble behind him, to ping off a car further back. It worked.

The dumb shit ran across the aisle at an angle and darted between two cars. He popped up, trying for a visual, looking exactly where Eddie had led him.

No hood today. But there was just enough light here—it was definitely the guy from the subway platform who'd taken out Annette. Caucasian, close-cropped dark hair, hollow cheeks, hawkish nose, day's growth of beard. Late twenties or early thirties, maybe. No earring, no tattoos that Eddie could see.

Hoodie crept forward in a crouch, and Eddie timed his own footfalls to match as he crept back out into the aisle, then rounded the end of the car.

The guy looked hard and intense. Depending on the choice of clothes, he could pass for an uptight Wall Streeter or an attitude-prone thug. In another ten seconds, he'd pass only for mincemeat.

Eddie took a peek. All good. Hoodie still crept forward.

Three, two, one.

Eddie rounded and launched himself forward, aiming both to tackle the dude and wrest control of his firearm.

But Hoodie caught on fast, turning and firing all at once.

Airborne as he was, Eddie couldn't correct course much.

———

Utterly heartsick, Miranda had shut her eyes and wallowed in misery. She woke hours later, shivering on the hard floor, one leg tingling painfully.

She forced herself up and hobbled to the end of the apartment to assure herself that David was still there.

She traipsed back to the living room and peeled out of her coat, tossing it over the arm of the couch.

She heard a clink and a slither, as something hit the hardwood floor. Miranda turned on the side lamp.

The damn necklace.

The very one that Kathleen had worn, Annette had claimed, Eddie had somehow saved and dropped, and she'd—miraculously—retrieved.

She shook her head, sank onto the couch, and reached for it.

Elbows on knees, Miranda ran it through her fingers, the lamplight glinting off the gold. Like pirate treasure, tainted by treachery and death. Cursed, she thought, but then, so was she.

Huh. There was a marking on the back. Tiny, though, so tiny. Probably a jeweler's mark.

"How did you get that?"

Miranda jumped, her hand slamming to her chest.

"Jeez, David, you scared me."

"Sorry." He advanced, frowning. "How did you get Annette's necklace?"

"You mean Kathleen's necklace."

"No, that has to be Annette's," he insisted, the serious tone to his voice in stark contrast to his kooky outfit.

"Just because Annette was wearing it," Miranda said, exasperated, "doesn't make it hers. She took it from Kathleen."

He shook his head. "She couldn't have. Kathleen's was tossed into a trash can on Thirtieth and Park."

"Are you saying... You mean..." Miranda's mouth hung open. "Kathleen and Annette had *matching* necklaces?"

David nodded. Miranda's heart clenched, freezing for a second from shock.

Two necklaces—matching necklaces.

The implications were...staggering.

CHAPTER 30

MIRANDA WAS STILL wrapping her head around the facts. Kathleen and Annette had had matching necklaces commissioned and inscribed, as a symbol of their love and commitment.

Not only lesbians, but both still married. Both in high-profile positions. One working for the mayor of the city of New York. The other his wife.

David couldn't believe that Miranda hadn't known. "But you came to me. You knew about the affair."

"At the time, I thought *you* were the one she was having an affair with, asswipe."

"Gee, thanks for the vote of confidence, sis."

"You came with her to her goodbye video." She gestured emphatically. "You were all caring and comforting and touchy-feely."

"She was dying!" He threw his arms out. "And we were friends. We talked—a lot."

"Okay." She breathed deeply. "That explains that."

David shook his head. "So, I knew Kathleen and Annette were lovers. I knew the mayor wouldn't like it—okay, well, what husband would, but you know what I mean."

"No, David, I don't. I need you to spell out everything. In detail."

"Okay, well, I had already seen how...particular he was.

Careful and controlling. You know, about how he and his wife were presented, how anything—from a risky political stance all the way down to a choice of restaurant—could matter."

Miranda thought back to what Annette had said about Bernard Thompson. *He never forgets for an instant that he's in public office.*

David grimaced. "I imagine Kathleen knew that, too. Probably why she didn't tell me that she'd gone to see you again. Mayor Thompson had begun having me accompany his wife places. Like somehow it'd become this big part of my job description, even though I was hired as *his* assistant. I think he was hoping for information, but I wasn't about to tell their secrets. And Annette didn't confide in me anyway."

He blew out a long breath. "Kathleen though was starting to talk about divorce. She and Annette were seriously happy, you know? Like, it wasn't some teenage boy's girl-on-girl fantasy thing."

Miranda screwed up her face. She did not want to know her brother's inner fantasies at any age.

"They were, you know, best friends, like you and Max, just…more. I think with such asshole husbands—"

"Eddie is not an asshole."

He held up a hand. "I know that now, but back then I only knew that he was MIA when she was in treatment. I didn't know until later that she'd kept him in the dark. Anyway, they both needed the comfort and companionship." He shrugged. "Just so happened they found it in another female. And it was solid. They were really good for each other."

"So Kathleen was pushing Annette to get divorced too?"

"I don't know who was pushing who or if it was just this big, idealistic wish. I couldn't see how they'd manage it without a shitload of fallout. I told her to forget it. By then I had this feeling that something wasn't right." David shook his head. "That maybe the mayor was controlling more than he had any right to."

Miranda had been grappling with this ever since David had started talking. She *really* did not want this to be true. She wanted it to fit in the outline she and Eddie had made. The one where Annette had killed Kathleen.

"But with all of us grieving Kathleen, and the intensity of the job, it was easy not to look too close. Like with the necklace."

David explained that he didn't know the details, but the mayor had visited the morgue after Kathleen's death. He'd seen the mayor tuck a small manila envelope into his chest pocket—only to toss it in a garbage can a few blocks later. David knew it was the necklace, because he'd overheard the mayor make the call about it in the first place.

"It was shitty, yeah, but I almost couldn't blame him. With Kathleen dead, it did seem best if her affair with Annette didn't come out. I never thought…" David swore under his breath. "It wasn't until you came to me with Eddie Mackey's suspicions that I really got it. Like, you know, a sudden test of the emergency system—this unreal blaring in my head. Suddenly way too loud and disturbing to ignore."

He ran a shaky hand over his face. "That's when I started digging, going back to things I hadn't thought much of before. Like that disk that disappeared from your apartment."

"The confession video."

"Yeah. Months ago, I'd seen the mayor squatting down in the corner of his office—not his real office downtown, but the one in Gracie Mansion. There's nothing in that corner, you know? He claimed he'd killed a spider, but it was just odd. He didn't have a tissue or paper towel or anything. I'd forgotten about it, until you told me about Kathleen coming to see you again. That's what I was doing, when I asked you to cover for me that day we filmed there."

"The day it all went south."

"Uh-huh. He's got a hidey-hole. The carpet pulls up, and there's a hatch underneath. There are all kinds of disks and flash drives in there, neat as a fucking library. I found the confession video fast because I knew what your Goodbye Angel covers looked like."

Dread was creeping in past her resistance. "So it was the mayor—or he hired someone—to break into my apartment and take it. But why wouldn't he destroy it? If he's so concerned about his appearance and his career, why would he keep it?"

"Blackmail. In case he decided it was better to threaten his wife." David shook his head, looking much older than only a week ago. "Or maybe in case he needed a scapegoat."

"For what?"

David shrugged. "Anything, really. To him, it's probably just business. Like insurance." He added, "And it's a big policy he's got. That hole is filled. I don't know with what or who, but he's definitely covered his ass."

He stopped pacing and plunked down beside her.

"When I was young," he said, "I'd always imagined being a hero. You know, saving the day. Righting wrongs. Rescuing curvy women and cute dogs."

He laughed, a bitter, brittle sound. "But the mayor was way ahead of me. And you. I figure he knew right away that I'd taken that DVD. Maybe the room has cameras or he just got suspicious, but he wasn't about to let us save the day. Once he knew Mackey was digging, and we'd been clued in?"

David made a chopping motion with his hand.

Holy shit, shit, shit. She and Eddie had been wrong. One hundred and fifty percent wrong.

Miranda jumped up from the couch as the ramifications of that error hit her.

The threat to all of them was still very much alive.

———

Eddie slammed his elbow hard into Hoodie's solar plexus, even as he pushed his gun arm up and over his head.

Dude punched him in the side, but he'd asked for that, leaving his middle exposed. Eddie crammed his forearm into the guy's throat, pushing, crushing.

"Drop it and we can talk, shitbag," Eddie said even as he twisted the guy's arm down and snapped his wrist. The hand went limp, and Eddie shook the firearm free.

Hoodie's legs scrambled ineffectively, but he did manage to get the free arm up, aiming a fist at Eddie's Adam's apple. Eddie shifted, making it a glancing blow, and doubled down on Hoodie's windpipe.

His eyes bulged and his mouth worked, but he didn't last long.

When he started to black out, Eddie pulled back just enough to allow the guy to suck air and keep a functioning brain. "Why take me out after you killed Annette? I couldn't have ID'd you."

Hoodie's eyes shot hatred. "No win for you here, asshole," he rasped. "Won't talk and won't go in."

Eddie leaned in, fucking ticked. He wanted something other than the upper hand from this.

"You will."

A plop of red—blood—fell on Hoodie's face. Eddie knew

he'd been hit, but had been ignoring it. His head hurt like he'd been blowtorched, but his limbs worked fine. The only life threatened at the moment was Hoodie's.

Despite struggling to breathe, dude actually grinned. "You are one stupid fuck," he managed to say, the look in his eye practically gleeful. "Won't end till you're dead."

Hoodie reached for Eddie's neck and squeezed one-handed, but his strength was waning—too low on oxygen.

Adrenaline and black anger brought Eddie so fucking close to permanently removing this blot from humanity. This shit had nearly killed Miranda. Likely had a hand in Kathleen's death, and who knew how many others.

It'd be so goddamn easy—oops, self-defense—to press just that much harder. But Hoodie's death didn't mean justice for Kathleen, nor would it provide answers.

Breathing heavily with blood thumping in his temples like a drum and every muscle still poised for the kill, Eddie waited.

Finally, Hoodie lost consciousness and Eddie yanked his arm up, disgusted.

He pulled some ripcord from his pocket, flipped him over, and trussed up the asshole like the pig he was.

Eddie squatted down, back against the cold metal of a car, and blew out a hard breath.

Hoodie might not talk to *him*, but, as Eddie had learned, bars really made a man think.

He pulled out his phone. Damn. No charge. He'd only been able to plug in long enough to call for impound information. Eddie tied Hoodie to the nearest vehicle, and set out for the building.

No surprise: it'd gone dark. Luckily, the security was for shit. Eddie kicked the door in.

He called 911 to relay the necessary details. Then he told

the dispatcher, "Alert Deputy Inspector Bob Getts at the twenty-second precinct and Captain Carl Klein at Upper West Side South. This fucker is the one they are looking for. He attacked Miranda Hill and killed Annette Thompson."

He heard the intake of breath on the other end from the operator. But she only said, "Understood. Are you injured?"

Eddie took stock. He had that warm, sticky feeling from his ear all the way inside the neck of his jacket. Pain radiated from his head. He raised a hand and felt around. Raw flesh, but not too much. Head wounds always bled heavily. He'd been grazed, but he'd do.

Much more pressing was Hoodie's comment. He'd called him stupid and claimed it *won't end till you're dead.*

But Hoodie had known he was losing this battle when he'd said it. Was it one last dig? Or…the truth? If it wouldn't end with Hoodie dead or in custody, then—

Holy mother of—

Not Annette in charge, but someone else.

The someone he and Miranda had considered all along, but discarded when they'd discovered that Annette had Kathleen's necklace.

No. Oh fuck no.

Eddie nearly exploded—fury, frustration, and fear blasting up from his gut like screaming rockets.

It wasn't Annette Thompson who'd been giving orders. It was *Bernard* Thompson.

CHAPTER 31

AFTER SHE STOPPED swearing a blue streak, Miranda planted her hands on her hips and faced David.

"All right. There's still a ton of blanks. Fill me in."

"On what?"

God, sometimes she still wanted to knock him upside the head.

"Like, duh, what happened to make you disappear? Why the hell didn't you tell me you were safe?" Tears sprang to her eyes—jeez, she'd been more emotional the last two weeks than she'd been in the last two decades. "Christ, David, I was afraid you were dead."

He got up and hugged her. "Sorry. Really. I tried. But your stoop was mobbed. Those reporters are piranhas, and I was afraid that if Thompson discovered I was alive…just, you know, thought it safest to stay under the radar."

He looked ashamed, but Miranda was glad he hadn't risked his life, and was supremely thankful he was standing here next to her in once piece.

"Anyway, I saw Mackey at the front door in guard dog mode." He grinned. "I've seen him in action, so I knew you'd be all right. I figured if I could just manage to get him the video, he'd deal with it. Do whatever he would. Maybe *he* could save the day, and I could keep my skin." David's eyes slid away and his expression turned grim. "Until Annette was killed. Even if... Well, there's no standing by any longer."

"No, there isn't." She took a deep breath, wishing like hell that realization had come before she'd pushed Eddie away.

"Okay," she said, "I need all the info so I know what I'm dealing with here." God, what to ask first. "Why? Why is the mayor doing this?"

"Been asking myself the same question. I think he wants to stay on top. So he won't let anything or anyone get in his way."

"He considers himself above..."

"What?"

She waved her hand. "Something Annette had said." She frowned, thinking. "Helluva way to stay on top. Awful risky, killing people left and right." She shuddered. "I guessing this isn't a new hobby."

"No. Probably not," David said.

"Do you know anything about Jeremy Rashorn? Eddie suspects the mayor may have..."

Now David looked as disturbed as she felt. "I'd say it's possible, even probable. It's awfully hard to work as someone's right-hand man and not eventually start putting two and two together. I should know. I'd only just figured it out and I was..."

Miranda reached out and squeezed his hand. "There could be even more."

"God, I don't know. But yeah, maybe. He's twisted. Seriously, I'm not sure he even has a conscience."

Miranda shuddered. "Great."

She crossed her arms. "Okay, so the same night I was attacked, you disappeared. What happened?"

"Annette called me. She said something like, 'I don't know

what you did, nor do I care to know. It doesn't matter now, because he's coming for you.' She also said that 'everything she feared was true.' She warned me to get out—immediately—and then she hung up."

Dear God, Miranda thought. The note that had come to Eddie's hotel room—that had to be Annette, too, trying to warn them. Poor Annette.

"I'd been sitting there, trying to figure out what to do with the damn disk now that I had it, so I was distracted when the phone rang. Really thought it was a prank call," David explained. "It wasn't Annette's number, and her voice was all shrill. But I went to look anyway. A few flights down"—he gulped—"there was a man creeping up the stairwell—I could just see the nose of a gun. Adrenaline kicked in, and next thing I knew I was out onto the fire escape. Dropped the disk in my panic—landed right in the dumpster. The man was already climbing out the window above, so I jumped in after it, then scrambled out and took off running." David looked at her with big eyes, and she could see his little kid self as clear as day. "He shot at me. I couldn't believe it. If it wasn't for Annette, I'd have hitched a ride to some landfill where scavengers would be jabbing their beaks into my bullet holes."

"God, David. I really didn't need that visual."

"I *really* didn't want to be dead that way." He squeezed her hand. "Tell me what happened to you."

She did, and though she'd kept it brief and to the facts, he must have heard something in her voice.

"You really like him, huh? Mackey?"

"I do, but—"

"Miranda and Eddie sittin' in a tree. K-I—"

"Shut up, you idiot." She slapped his arm. "And we're not sitting in a tree any longer."

"Why not, you just said—"

"Because I totally blew it, okay?"

She rubbed her forehead. Shit. She really had. If she hadn't been so quick to bail on him, they could have been sitting here together, in the proverbial kissing tree. Figuring out what to do—together.

She might have had all that good, lovey-dovey stuff. Like regular sex. Foot rubs. Flowers. Someone to bake for, eat with, share good news and bad with. Hug and hold. Eventually, maybe even a ring and wedding cake.

"Sorry," David said. "Maybe it'll work out when all this is over."

"No. I killed it but good." As it was, she might as well have stuck the flowers in acid, thrown the ring into the sewer, and tromped all over the cake.

Not that she really gave a crap about any of that material stuff. She just wanted Eddie.

David reached over and took her hand. "What are we gonna do?"

She fought tears. "I have no idea."

"Me either." He rubbed a hand over his face and scratched at the beard. "Is there more on your end that I should know?"

Miranda gave him the rundown of what she and Eddie had been up to, and why they'd suspected Annette. From her attack, to Annette smashing the flowers on the floor (David agreed that the flowers and her office were both likely bugged), to thinking he'd been at Aggie's place (he had—he'd needed both distance and shelter), to finding the video at Eddie's (with no phone, no identification, and no wallet, David had had a helluva time finding Eddie's address and getting there).

"That's why your clothes smell so awful. You've been living on the streets."

"Nearly. I was afraid to go to the apartment or access my money or involve anybody else."

"Oh, David."

"I won't deny it was a nightmare, but we've got more important things to think about now."

She took a deep breath. "You're right. I'll put those in the laundry for you."

"I'd rather burn them."

But she was distracted, going back over the last of her thoughts…a pattern.

The flowers, she thought…something about the flowers.

"What?" David peered at her.

Miranda held up a hand and squeezed her eyes shut. Annette had smashed the flowers Mayor Thompson had sent—bugged flowers. And Miranda had been thinking about flowers and weddings…

Flowers for get well, flowers for celebration, flowers for everything—even death. Grief and funerals. And Annette was gone.

Her eyes popped open. "We can bug the flowers."

David looked at her like she'd said something completely nonsensical.

"The only way out of this is to get proof, real proof, like Eddie and I tried to do with Annette, except we had the wrong person. We need the mayor to admit he killed Annette, killed Kathleen. Tried to kill you and me."

"Have the *police* get the proof," David said.

"They can't. Eddie and I already tried, remember? Even with what you know, I still don't think we have enough solid evidence." Miranda thought of Deputy Inspector Getts. He wasn't exactly unwilling; he just needed a damn good reason before he stuck his neck out against their mayor. Could she force his help—one way or another?

"It's done, then." David threw up his hands. "The mayor wins."

"No, I can't allow that." Thompson had killed. Eddie's wife, David's friend, her coworker…and others, probably. It would go on and on. They *had* to stop it.

"And why are you giving up so easy?" Miranda asked. "You said Annette's death made you realize you couldn't stand by any longer."

"Because I see that look on your face," David burst out. "I don't want it to be *you*, Miranda." He took a deep breath, puffing out his chest. "It doesn't *have* to be you."

Miranda squeezed his hand, then stared at the bit of light coming around the blinds from the street lamp outside.

She'd lost so much already, traded it for a false sense of security. Risk was the only way now. And yes, it had to be her. At least if she made it to spinsterhood, she could hold her head high.

Returning her gaze to David, she said, "Besides the fact that Eddie is probably busy lying in wait for the hit man, Thompson wouldn't agree to see him anyway. And he'd be suspicious if you showed up all of the sudden. It has to be me."

"But," David said, frustration evident in his voice, "Thompson will never admit something like that out loud."

He didn't necessarily need to, Miranda thought, but she wasn't going to terrify David further.

"I'm doing this, David. Period. So help me figure out the logistics."

He swore and kicked her couch, then spun, putting his back to her.

"I can bring flowers to the funeral, or no—wear a corsage or boutonnière or maybe a hat with flowers, and get him alone. Use his own trick against him, see? And there's safety in numbers, so—"

"You'll never get him alone at an event like that. And I'm telling you, he'd never talk." David shook his head more emphatically. "He's too careful. He'd never risk it."

Miranda bit her lip, then grabbed David's arm. "Now. I'll bring him flowers now. He's grieving, right? And I'm close enough staff, it'd make sense for me to offer comfort. And if we're alone, he *might* talk."

"You're not even full-time staff. I'm not sure they'd let you in at a time like this."

"Security knows me. They trust me."

"Wait." David shook his head. "City hall is closed tomorrow for observance. The news said he's grieving in private at home."

"Even better. And it's not tomorrow anymore. It's today." Miranda pointed at the clock in the kitchen. Well after midnight.

"They did say skeleton staff, but somebody will still be on security detail. His gate is gonna look like your stoop last week. Why would they let you in?"

She took a deep breath and let fear speak. "Because Thompson will tell them to. He'll want to get me alone."

She looked at David, her resolve already hardening.

"He's been trying to kill me, remember?"

CHAPTER 32

ONCE HOODIE HAD regained consciousness, he hadn't stopped with the shit-eating grin. He couldn't wait for Eddie to get his—and was sure it was coming.

Which only cemented Eddie's previous realization—because the only person in this maelstrom with enough power and resources to keep up this insanity, this bizarre string of picking people off one by one whenever it suited his purposes, was Bernard Thompson.

Harder for the asshole, now that the hand actually carrying out the dirty work was in custody, but still.

Although they'd taken a statement at the scene, the police had insisted Eddie come to the station in Queens. Eddie was not happy to be spending time in his third police station in as many days, but he had little choice. Finally, when his stomach was screaming for breakfast and his brain was beginning to feel the effects of being up all night, he'd thought *fuck it*, and simply got up to leave.

Getts, who was still there arguing to have the dude—name still unknown—moved to his own precinct, grabbed Eddie's arm just as he hit the doors.

"You can't just go, Mackey."

"Have to." In fact, it'd taken all the reserve he'd had to sit there for hours, wondering if Miranda was in danger. He had his dead phone in his pocket, but the charger was in his bag, which was in his truck. He tried her home at one point in the wee hours from the station's landline, but didn't leave a message. He assumed it'd take Thompson time to regroup, to come up with a plan or to hire a new man. However, it was also feasible that the mayor could have more than one paid killer on his roster. Then again—he wouldn't know Hoodie been arrested. Would he?

Eddie just needed to check on Miranda—assure himself of her safety—and then, if the police still couldn't get dick from Hoodie, he'd figure out how to prove Thompson was behind everything.

"What the fuck now?" Getts barked.

"You don't want to know."

Getts' eyes had narrowed. "This is over. Do not—"

"We were wrong. This is nowhere near fucking over."

Eddie stormed out, leaving one furious deputy inspector glaring after him. He didn't give a shit. He didn't know what or how to handle this fucking mess next; he only knew he had to get to Miranda.

Because she'd buried her head so deep in wishes, she wouldn't even know she was in danger.

The police had his truck in their garage, and Eddie retrieved it quickly. Unfortunately, traffic crawled despite the early hour. Everybody trying to beat rush hour into the city.

Eddie gritted his teeth. This was going to take forever. Eddie plugged into his car charger. As soon as it charged enough for a call, he called Miranda, not caring if he woke her. He just needed to know she was there, and in one piece.

———

Finally, Eddie bounded up the stoop steps and hit Miranda's door buzzer hard. There'd been no answer when he'd called. Not home? Sleeping? Too angry to answer?

He waited, then pressed it again, harder and longer.

"Who is it?"

Eddie reared back at the unexpected voice—a man's— then immediately realized it must be Miranda's brother, David. He'd practically forgotten about him with all the crap that'd been going down. Eddie gave his name and ordered, "Let me in."

A buzz followed, and Eddie pushed through the vestibule. He heard locks flipping on the other side of her door and waited, breath held in anticipation.

His anger at Miranda had waned over the long night. He was still disappointed in her reaction, but he realized that not everybody had the reserves of strength they needed to handle intensely stressful situations. Eddie had been trained for long periods of wicked stress. Miranda hadn't. He'd been shot at so often, he barely blinked. For all he knew, Miranda had never even been in a fistfight.

He definitely shouldn't have judged her so swiftly. She'd come to his rescue, after all. He should have at least given her some time to come to terms with things. She may have made the same choice. But by walking away so damn fast, he might never know. He hoped he could at least apologize for that.

And he recognized the strange duality he felt now—that she'd let him down, and yet he pulsed with the need to see her. That pretty face, eyes wide with surprise. Healthy and whole, maybe with mussed morning hair.

But it was David who opened the door, looking...

"What are you wearing, man?" Eddie asked. He'd seen him earlier, of course, but hadn't been focused on his clothing.

"Miranda's." David waved a hand.

Eddie strode in, scanning for Miranda. She must be in the back.

David said, "Man, am I glad you're here."

Eddie moved down the hall, in search of the face he needed to see, and felt David practically on his heels. "You too." He shot a grin at David over his shoulder. "Congrats on being alive. Where is she?"

David's footsteps stopped. Eddie spun and took one look at David's serious expression, and his gut clenched with dread.

"Tell me."

David tensed up like he was getting ready to take a punch. "She went to Gracie Mansion."

"What?" That was the last thing Eddie had expected.

"She's trying to get information. The mayor is the one behind it all."

"I know that."

"You do?"

Eddie rubbed his face. "The guy Thompson hired to try to kill us is in custody."

Relief showed clearly on David's face. "She's got a chance, then."

"What the fuck is she thinking?"

"I think"—David's expression turned belligerent and his hands clenched—"that she feels she has something to prove. To you."

"Fuck."

"My sentiments exactly. But she wouldn't be swayed. Listen, I tried to reach you earlier, but now I gotta—"

"Why the hell aren't you with her?" Eddie crowded David, bearing down on him with all the frustration he felt. "Why would you let her go in there alone?"

"We—"

"You goddamn chickenshit. When I'm done rescuing your sister's ass"—*God, don't let him be too late*—"I'm going to beat the ever-living crap out of you."

David held his ground and shot back, "What about you, Mackey? Why the hell didn't you stick around and help her?"

Eddie stopped in his tracks, his arms and fist pulsing with anger—because he'd been asking himself that very question. Kicking himself.

He turned and yanked open the front door. "What time did she leave?"

"Not even a half-hour ago. She should be just getting there. I'll try to—"

But Eddie was already in the vestibule. He calculated quickly as he bounded down Miranda's front steps. Gracie Mansion was mere blocks from here, but he had to hit the truck's lockbox for more weaponry.

Or would taking extra time to prepare cost Miranda her life?

That wasn't an outcome he'd consider.

Assuming he made it in time, it was entirely possible that Eddie would be forced to end the mayor's life.

He might well lose any chance at justice for Kathleen. And he'd likely lose the chance to provide answers to those families that had come before, or protect those to come.

But it wasn't always a numbers game.

Sometimes you could only save one—the most important one…

Miranda.

CHAPTER 33

MIRANDA HADN'T BEEN to Gracie Mansion nearly as often as she'd been to city hall, or even as frequently as she'd accompanied the mayor and Mrs. Thompson about town. Still, the guard in the security tent recognized her.

"You're on the short list," he said, and gestured her through the metal detector.

Miranda gulped.

The young man radioed to the house to let them know she was coming. Just like the weather, dreary and cold, both she and he were somber—the guard surely grieving Annette, Miranda secretly quaking with fear.

Because now that she was here, past the gate and its growing shrine—so many bouquets of flowers, photographs, signs, and letters that it put her own to shame—she realized her plan was the ultimate in stupidity.

She was waltzing into the lion's den, offering herself up like a piece of raw meat. She was relying on her wits, her instincts, three cell phones purchased first thing this morning, a can of mace if things got violent, and the flowers.

Risky.

Dangerous.

Incredibly stupid.

She forced her unsteady legs up the walk and clutched the vase of flowers to her chest like a cold security blanket.

The cell phones were perhaps the only saving grace. She'd worn a small purse—with almost nothing in it. Scary to have only one water bottle, some nuts, and a thin wallet with only a little cash. But the point was that one of the cell phones was clearly visible in the front purse pocket. She'd also donned a light windbreaker with deep pockets. Another phone was within easy reach of her right hand, set not to go to sleep and primed to dial 911—she had only to hit a single button to call for help. The other hung in a chest pocket, well below her breast, and held an open line to David.

They'd tested it en route, but she heard David's voice again now. "Miranda?" he whispered.

His phone was supposed to be on mute, so he could hear her, but couldn't be heard on this end.

"This is a bad idea. Turn ar—"

Miranda agreed wholeheartedly, but said, "Shhhh!"

David pleaded, "Listen for one minute."

"I can't! I'm here! Put your phone on mute again *now*. Do *not* give me away."

She heard him swear, and the sound cut off midstream.

She took a fortifying, if shaky, breath and placed a booted foot on the first wooden step up to the veranda. Then another. Scary as it was, her heart pounding like a jackhammer, it was up instead of down, so her legs actually complied with orders—unlike trying to go underground.

She had to attempt this. For Kathleen, and for Annette, and for who knew who else that came before, like Jeremy Rashorn.

She tried hard not to think about Eddie. He would have been a real asset at a time like this, as would his gun.

Would he have been furious at the risk she was taking? Or would he have been pleased that she had yanked her head from the sand and was actually taking action?

As she reached the top step, Miranda clenched her teeth to keep them from chattering.

There was no point in wondering. Eddie couldn't protect her now. She didn't even know where he was. Shame surged, seeping in around the fear. The blow she'd dealt him had been as devastating as if she'd pushed him off the Verrazano Bridge. She'd seen his face. Shock, disbelief, anger, hurt…

Even if this stupid attempt went horribly, inexorably wrong—*don't think about that*—she just hoped she'd get David enough. A parting gift she could give Eddie. Something the police could use. Some kind of confession, or at least enough doubt to start a real investigation. Remove the bastard from office. Ideally, lock him up. Strip him of power, keep him from hurting anyone else.

She thought of how she'd felt when David was missing, imagined how much worse it would have been if she'd had no hope of seeing him again. If he'd been killed by this monster. Eddie had had to face that, and more, when he'd discovered that Kathleen had been murdered. And he'd have another reconciling to contend with when he was told it was the mayor to blame, and not Annette.

Eddie deserved the truth, however. So did the others. And there was only her—her and David now—to do it.

Miranda pried one of her hands from the vase and reached out to knock. The door swung open before she managed it, making her jump.

Another guard. This one older, with a hard-lined face and lips pressed flat.

"This way," he said, staring right through her with dead eyes.

Oh, God. Was he in on it? Did he know what the mayor

had done, kept doing? Was he paid or threatened to keep quiet, to *not* see?

Miranda's heart beat so loud she couldn't hear her own footsteps on the inlaid sundial on the marble floor of the foyer.

The guard led her to a room they hadn't covered in the feel-good piece. A room that had never, to her knowledge, been shown to the public.

The large wooden door was closed, and the guard rapped, then waited.

The mayor himself opened it. He wore a dress shirt with the sleeves rolled up. His power tie had been loosened and the skin around his eyes was red.

Miranda had never seen Bernard Thompson not *looking good*, as he so often put it. He slumped inward, it seemed, with grief and exhaustion, and he sounded genuine when he said, "Miranda, I appreciate you coming."

She blinked, thrown off. Then reminded herself that a man who could kill and pretend nothing had happened was a consummate actor.

To the guard, the mayor said, "Take the flowers."

Uneasiness came roaring back to her. "But sir, wouldn't you prefer—"

"The fewer reminders the better."

"But—" she said, sure the desperation she felt was clear as day on her face, as the guard lifted the vase right out of her hands.

Then he caught the guard's eye and nodded at Miranda's purse. "You know what to do," Thompson said, and the man reached out with his other hand and lifted the purse right over her head.

Despite the fact that she'd planned for that, she was still

shocked. Her mouth opened and closed in protest without words as she watched the guard slip past her.

"Come in," said Thompson.

Arms empty now, she did as he bade. There remained a teensy sliver of hope inside her that she'd been wrong—again. That the man for whom she'd worked for the last year, that had offered her safe haven when she needed it, that had done so much for this city, wasn't—

The door clicked shut. Miranda flinched and pivoted to face him in time to see him flip the bolt closed. Her heart pounded in heavy, double beats of dread.

CHAPTER 34

"HOW CONVENIENT of you to stop by, Miranda." Now the mayor's voice was mocking and cold. "I was debating what to do about you—the last loose end."

Miranda's heart plummeted, as the last shred of doubt was erased.

He checked his watch and nodded once. "I took care of your brother, my wife, that bitch Kathleen..." Thompson smiled, the fake grief gone, as simple for him, apparently, as peeling off a suit jacket. "You're the last one who knows." He spoke as calmly as if he were discussing a new city ordinance.

She made herself suck air. She had no chance at all if she passed out. "You forgot Kathleen's husband. He won't stop until you're behind bars." Miranda raised her chin, feigning a confidence she didn't feel, because Eddie believed he had only to find the hit man. He had no way of knowing that the man took orders from Bernard instead of Annette.

"How could I forget? Your new beau." He smirked. "Some protector. He's already dead and gone—or he will be shortly."

Her struggle to read between the lines must have shown on her face.

He explained. "I sent my man."

"No you didn't."

"Indeed I did. The minute I realized that my dear friend Captain Klein would have to release Mackey eventually."

Was Klein in the mayor's pocket? Or just unduly influenced by his position? Or was Thompson being sarcastic? She couldn't even remotely tell.

"How did you like my acting skills at the station, by the way? Impressive, no?" Another smile. Gloating, as if he were winning a game.

Miranda needed him to back up. "What do you mean, you sent your man?"

"I pulled some strings. Had Mackey's vehicle impounded. He'll have gone to get it and…" He shrugged. "Have you been to the Masbeth impound lot, out in Queens?"

She was dumbstruck at his cunning, at his reach, at the lengths to which he'd go…

The mayor searched her face. "It's an interesting part of our great city. Quite out of the way. Nearly deserted, in fact. A perfect place to be caught unawares."

Oh Eddie, Miranda thought as her heart went from nearly stalled to working overtime. Towings were so common in the city, he'd never expect it to have been orchestrated—a setup with murder in mind. He'd be caught completely unaware and…

Crossing her arms, she clenched her upper arms so hard it hurt, and started praying. *Please, please, please…*

The mayor's expression shifted. Fury and scorn. "A place where goddamn surveillance cameras aren't an issue."

She knew he was referring to the subway platforms. "How could you do that to your wife? And in such a horrible way?"

"I didn't." He crossed to the desk, half sitting, hands loosely clasped. One leg propped him up, the other swung idly, as if he had all the time in the world. Good, Miranda thought. Much, much better for her.

"I merely suggested," Thompson said, "that she was becoming too much of a liability. My associate enjoys the more creative aspects of his work. Too much, sometimes. Annette's dramatic end will do wonders for me in the long run, but really, it was a poor choice overall. Too risky. Under the radar is always preferable, as I'd hate to lose my most valued employee."

"My God, you don't even care, do you?"

"Oh, I care," Thompson said. "I care quite deeply. Just not about the things *you* want me to care about."

"Like your wife."

"A woman bound and determined to ruin me? My cheating wife who couldn't even just have an affair, who had to have a lesbian one? With an employee, no less? Conducted virtually right under my nose in the offices of the city of New York? Practically advertising it to the public?"

His nostrils flared. He was angrier than he let on.

She'd learned so much already, but, furious herself, she wanted more. "What is that you care about, then? If not your wife, your staff, the same people who got you here?" She flung a hand out at the walls of Gracie Mansion. "What is it? Power? Money? Control?"

"So close." He smiled, a smug twist of the mouth. "It's the pinnacle of all those."

He waited.

"Enlighten me," she said.

"The White House."

"The presidency?" She laughed, feeling reckless now. "You'll *never* become president."

"Oh, I will. Annette will help me from the grave, you see."

"You're insane."

"No. I'm a realist."

Thompson checked his watch again, and Miranda wondered just what they hell kind of schedule they were on here. Then he plucked a cigar from the box on his desk and slid it lengthwise under his nose as he inhaled.

"I don't know why I didn't see it before," he said. "I'd worked so hard to rein that woman in, to keep her secrets under wraps, because I'd assumed I needed a first lady at my side in order to be elected." His words picked up pace as his excitement grew. "But just think. It's perfect. The whole nation will grieve with me. Their sympathy will carry me right to Washington." He spread his hands as if he showed a marquee. "The widower president."

Miranda stared, incredulous. "Sympathy doesn't elect presidents."

"Why not? Public sentiment elected me mayor, and re-elected me mayor."

"The hero campaigns," she said.

"Don't look so shocked, Miranda," he said. "You knew there was a political agenda attached. And it's not like you didn't benefit from my hometown hero plans too."

Admittedly, she'd jumped at the chance to make a decent salary while she licked her wounds from the ETD. And yes, she'd realized that hiring people like her was orchestrated. But she'd justified the mayor's tactics, thinking that a greater good was being met. Like the policies he'd passed to better care for first responders.

"I thought you cared." Her voice wavered. "About New York, about its people. About making a difference. About me, and Kathleen Mackey, too." She felt positively sick now, to have fallen so easily into his larger scheme, a gruesome game of power in which people were eliminated at the snap of his fingers.

"Oh, I *cared* about Kathleen. After all I did for her? She betrayed my goodwill, slept with my wife, discredited my office with her sordid actions." Thompson shook his head. "But with the timely cancer diagnosis, I thought I could sit back. Until it became clear that she was getting well. I monitor"—he paused, smiling as he remembered—"*monitored* Annette's conversations, you know. When Kathleen hinted at good news after a doctor's appointment and a possible celebration, I knew I'd made a mistake counting on nature."

So cruel, so without conscience, and so matter of fact. It was as if people were nothing more than papers to shift from his desk to the trash. Miranda couldn't imagine how none of them had glimpsed his evil nature before.

"And the others? Did they know too much about something else?"

He raised an eyebrow.

"Jeremy Rashorn, for instance?"

"I realize it's human nature to seek answers, to need them, but these questions already have you in a tight spot. You know too much."

"You must have already believed that back when you had me attacked."

"Of course. You knew about Annette's nasty affair."

"I only knew Kathleen was having an affair, not with *who*. You stole the video. You must have known she didn't name Annette."

"She didn't tell you off camera?" He made a tsking noise. "Then Kathleen was more discreet than I gave her credit for. A shame. Still, I would have expected your brother to confide in you. So cozy, the two of you were."

"He told me nothing."

"Another surprise. Perhaps he was more loyal than I thought. You have my sincerest apologies."

So, Thompson believed David had been successfully killed by his hit man. Apparently, the mayor's *most valuable employee* didn't share the details of his botched missions.

"Did you really come here to talk about the past, Miranda?" He stood, his eyes glinting. "Aren't you more interested in trying to make a deal? Seeing if you can somehow wriggle out of my plans for you?"

CHAPTER 35

THE MAYOR COCKED his head, obviously listening. Miranda wasn't sure for what, but he appeared satisfied. He circled his desk and opened a drawer, as if it were any other day at the office, and yet Miranda could feel the air in the room change, an undercurrent of charged warning making her tense even further.

There was no way to deal her way out of Thompson's game. She had nothing he wanted or needed. And they both knew it.

Thompson pulled out a gun, and Miranda froze.

Advancing on her, he raised it—a tiny thing, compact. Different than Eddie's. Almost cute, yet surely as deadly as any other.

And then he just stood there pointing it at her like that, making her quake.

"Wh-what are you waiting for?"

"The ferry."

Miranda struggled to follow, until he said, "Coast guard rules. They have to blast their horns every time they pull away from the landings."

Noise cover-up. The East Ninetieth Street ferry was just past the FDR highway. Her mind raced. She'd heard both car horns and ferry horns that day they'd filmed. Loud enough to cover the noise of a gunshot? She had no idea.

"Maddening, really," the mayor said. "But it'll come in

handy now. Extra insurance. Prepare to say goodbye, angel," he murmured with a smirk.

She stepped back hastily, self-preservation taking control of her limbs.

Surely by now, David had done what needed to be done. *She* might have blown it, however, waited too long in her quest for more and more damning information. Allowed herself to freeze with fear when he'd pulled the gun. Miranda slipped a hand into her pocket and slid her thumb over the old-fashioned raised keys, feeling for the right one.

"What about your staff?" she asked, words too fast, full of panic as her back hit the wall behind her, her head bumping a picture frame. "The cook or the cleaners? The guards outside? I'm on the log sheet. Someone will know if I've been hurt if I don't come out."

"So naive you are, Miranda, even now." His smile was condescending, but he liked to brag. "My chef will already be passed out cold—he drinks too much. The guard outside has a habit of falling asleep because he moonlights. And the one just outside this door?" He smiled. "He's in my pocket."

"He does your dirty work for money?" *Where does it end?*

"He keeps his mouth shut because he can't afford for his own secrets to get out. Not to mention that yes, the... bonuses...are allowing him to manage some extenuating family circumstances. So, you see, you are quite alone."

Miranda reminded herself that Thompson didn't know about David. And he didn't know how tough and smart Eddie was—it might well be the assassin who didn't walk away. Even if *she* didn't make it out of here, one of them would see this through.

"In fact," the mayor said, "I'm sure I can enlist my guard

for help getting your body out of here and thrown in the East River. It'll look like you met an unsavory character while out running alone, or some such." He gestured just out the window.

Miranda refused to give up again because of fear. That was a mistake she'd never repeat, whether it was too late for her or not. She pressed down with her thumb, the mayor only two feet from her.

Seconds only and a female voice sounded from her pocket. "Nine-one-one. What's your emergency?"

"I'm at—"

The mayor's expression clouded—he didn't wait for any ferry horn—and he fired.

Click.

Miranda's heart stalled and then jump-started again.

Click, click.

She cringed, her heart stopping each time.

The mayor roared in frustration and hurled the weapon to the floor.

Miranda's mind flew from thought to thought. Had David removed the bullets? The guard—no, the guard was all in, according to Thompson. Annette—bless her—must have done all she could once she realized the full scope of—

That thought was lost as Thompson lunged and latched his hands around Miranda's neck. Her head slammed the wall behind her. The ferry sounded its horn, and the mayor smiled at the timing.

Help, she tried to say, but no words came through the vise of pain at her throat. She pulled and clawed at his hands, but couldn't budge his grip. She reached for his face, aiming for the eyes, managing only to scratch as he angled out of her reach.

Frantically, she tried to get a hand in her pocket for the mace, but couldn't find the opening.

Her eyes watered as she flailed. The picture banged against her again. She grabbed the heavy frame and yanked, slamming it over his head. But it bounced—a canvas, not glass. *No, no.*

His brows lowered, jaw clenched, and he squeezed harder, intent on killing her.

She dropped the canvas and pulled again at his fingers—desperate to breathe.

She kicked, at him and at the wall. Making as much noise as she could, for 911, for David, for *any*body listening. *Please, hear me. Please, help.*

But black swayed into her vision, her thought processes frantic, disjointed.

A sudden, ear-splitting crash came from the window on her left. She could just barely see a figure hurtling through the shattering glass.

The mayor spun and lunged for the gun he'd dropped. Miranda crumpled to the ground, legs giving way, as she desperately gulped for air.

It was Eddie! Miranda came up on her knees as he charged the mayor. *Gun!* she tried to warn him, but her voice wasn't working right.

The mayor aimed, and this time the weapon fired. Eddie was pushed back, hit.

No!

Somehow he kept coming, barreling down on Thompson.

Eddie moved like lightning—with swift, powerful cracks of power. In mere seconds, the mayor had been disarmed, then doubled over. Eddie swung again, and Thompson's head snapped up as his body flew back and then tumbled off the desk.

Another crack of noise and the door burst open. Miranda tried to scream, but it was a SWAT team—finally. Still her heart pounded, as she feared they'd shoot Eddie in error.

But Eddie had already halted his pursuit of Thompson. His arms were raised, palms open, showing complete cooperation. "Pocket pistol in the corner," he told them, his voice shockingly calm.

The mayor had grabbed the desk and attempted to stand.

"Stay down!" one of the officers shouted.

"This is my home," Thompson said in an imperious tone. "These intruders—"

"Shut up, *mayor*." The last word sounded filthy. They *knew*. Miranda sagged with relief.

Three SWAT officers circled him, with their big, scary weapons all pointing at his chest, and more focused on Eddie.

"Who are you?" they demanded.

Eddie told them who he was, why he was there, and where his own weapons were on his body.

One officer relayed information through a radio, but Miranda watched Eddie. He'd been shot. No matter that he stood tall and still, blood poured over his right ear, shards of glass stuck out of his head and face, and he was white, sweating, strained.

She worried he'd topple over. He needed medical care. She pushed up with her arms, making to stand, even though she was still unsteady.

Eddie's voice, so calm. "Fellas, I'm going to move now. Check on the lady."

"Don't move," an officer ordered.

He barked, "Then one of you fucking hurry up and make sure she's all right!"

―――

The second they'd secured a still-protesting Thompson face-down, hands zip-tied behind his back, weapons still trained on him, an officer knelt down to Miranda. Eddie finally relaxed a fraction.

"No, not me. Him." Her voice was a rough rasp, and she pointed to Eddie, still looking panicked. "He's been shot."

Eddie shook his head. *She* was worrying about him? My God, she'd come this close to being strangled to *death*.

Miranda brushed the officer off. He said, "Ma'am, please," but he helped her up, supporting her arm.

She stumbled to Eddie, reaching up to his head wound. "He needs medical attention!" she said.

At the same time, SWAT confirmed by radio that Eddie was kosher and gave him the okay. He lowered his hands and put them under Miranda's chin.

"Your throat," he said. Red finger marks stood out as bright as burns, and her eyes were bloodshot.

"Sir?" the officer said, pulling some gauze and antiseptic from a small pack at his waist.

"It's from earlier. It probably split open."

"Stop it," she said, then looked to the SWAT member. "The mayor shot right at him! I saw it!"

Eddie shook his head and placed Miranda's hand against his chest. "Chest shot. Kevlar. Piss-ant weapon. Barely hurts." Okay, so it hurt plenty, but he wasn't telling her that.

"Paramedics will be here any minute," the officer said. "They'll check out the both of you."

The team hauled Thompson up and out. Eddie noticed one of them remained behind, guarding the door.

Miranda lowered her forehead to his chest, then looked up, tears filling her eyes. "I thought you were going to fall over and die on me." She shook her head. "Even though I don't get to have you, I couldn't bear that. I need to know you are here in the world. Just out there somewhere…doing good…being the person the rest of us are too scared to be."

"What the hell are you talking about?" Eddie shook his head. "Jesus, Miranda, you scared the shit out of me. You shouldn't have risked your life. You didn't need to be such a martyr."

She laughed—or croaked, really. "A martyr or a chicken? Those are my choices? I can't win."

"You are no chicken. You are so strong. And as far as winning? You can, sweetheart." He stroked his thumbs over her cheeks. "You just did."

"Because of you. If you hadn't come when you did…"

"You would have made it. SWAT arrived right after me." He searched her face. "And I didn't call them."

"I did."

Eddie's head snapped up as Deputy Inspector Getts strode into the room, his sharp gaze assessing every inch of the place. "Miss Hill's brother conferenced me in. Heard every word." He looked at Miranda. "Real sorry it had to come to this."

"David?" Eddie asked, still holding on to her. "How?"

"Most stressful phone call ever," came a faint voice.

Miranda laughed weakly and unzipped a pocket on the front of her jacket. She held up a simple black phone. "Say hello to David."

CHAPTER 36

EDDIE AND MIRANDA spent the rest of the day at the twenty-second precinct, and while they were both exhausted, it'd been worth it.

Mayor Thompson's hit man, or as Eddie still referred to him, "Hoodie," had been ID'd. Some guys in this line of work, they were told, lived like ghosts. This one apparently wasn't smart enough to vanish. Ronald Silver, twenty-nine years old, owned property in both New York and Miami. One offshore account linked to him had quickly been identified; likely there were more. The officer that had delivered that news commented that Silver had either been planning to retire early, or he was a workaholic. Silver still wasn't talking, but Deputy Inspector Getts and Detective Iocavelli believed their tech people would be able to make connections between deposits made and cash outlay—no matter how buried—from Thompson's side. Probably the timing of those would coincide with the disappearance of at least some of the mayor's victims, like Jeremy Rashorn.

Eddie had whispered to Miranda that he wasn't worried. If Getts' team failed, there was always his pal Wik to give them a little direction.

Miranda had told them about the hidey-hole David had mentioned. Surely, anything the mayor had felt was important enough to keep would yield clues.

Eddie shared his suspicions about the other deaths—the campaign finance board guys and the one serving on the Commission to Combat Police Corruption—that might also point to the mayor. Getts narrowed his eyes, but didn't ask how Eddie had come across that kind of information. He did promise that he'd personally see to the reopening of any case that warranted a closer look during the course of their investigation.

And Eddie had also explained that he believed there could eventually be forensic evidence supplied by the coroner, Winston Chang. Chang had himself suggested that with comparable DNA from the probable perpetrators, they might have better luck. Maybe too, Chang and his counterparts would be more willing to dig deep now that the mayor couldn't touch them. Regardless, detectives would interview Chang for sure. And if he back-pedaled, they could subpoena.

If all else failed, there was the plain fact that—thanks to Miranda—Mayor Thompson's confession had been recorded.

Getts had initially reamed both Eddie and Miranda out for taking matters into their own hands. But in the end, he'd promised that although he was sure that Kathleen was now resting in peace, he'd have her case reassessed. He also vowed that both the mayor and Silver would rot behind bars for a lifetime. And finally, he ordered one of his officers to give them a lift home.

Miranda's adrenaline kicked up again as they entered her apartment. Although they'd talked some earlier, there'd been no chance for a more private conversation.

Eddie flipped the locks behind him and immediately said, "You took too many risks. An open cell phone connection? You could have lost the connection at any time. What if Getts and Klein hadn't been available? What if they'd refused to cooperate with David and link in?"

He sounded no less upset the second time around these questions, but Miranda couldn't change the situation now. "I had David recording as well. In case I didn't make it."

"Stop saying that like it's no big deal." Eddie's voice was gruff, his expression intense.

Much of the terror Miranda had felt had dissipated. At this point, she was *almost* able to pretend she'd been more confident than she'd felt. "I had the other phone for 911."

Eddie ran a thumb gently over her sore neck. "You waited too long to use it."

"True."

"And you should have called me from the start."

Miranda said, "I know, but..."

"Why?" A new question—one Eddie must not have felt he could ask in front of Getts. "I admit I was furious when I left you, but you knew that I was committed to seeing this through. And that I wouldn't have let you get hurt?" His hands tightened on her arms. "Why didn't you call me?"

She felt like she'd lost that right. Tossed deserving him, his caring, and his protection right into the trash when she'd let fear rule her. Miranda sighed. So many reasons. "I knew the mayor would let me in, that he'd welcome the chance to get me in his clutches—and I didn't think he'd take that chance if you were with me. Me alone he wouldn't have considered a threat."

"David intimated you were proving yourself to me."

Miranda shook her head. "Side bonus. I had more to prove to myself. And I really thought it was the only way. Plus, I was worried about Hoodie. And about you. I thought you'd need all your focus."

Eddie kissed her—quick and sure. "I might never forgive you for scaring me like that."

She took comfort in the fact that he'd barely left her side since the showdown with Thompson. But things had to be said…before he left for good.

"That's okay," Miranda said. "I already knew you'd probably never be able to forgive me—for bailing on you. I know I let you down horribly."

"Yeah, but…" He shook his head. "I put you in a tough position. I held you to a standard I shouldn't have, and I didn't give you time to come to terms with any of it. That wasn't fair. And—I'm sorry—I bailed on you, too."

Miranda gave him a small smile. "I'm just sorry I wasn't holding *myself* to a higher standard earlier. I wish it hadn't come to that. I'm so sorry."

"And what about you?" His expression was grim. "Can you forgive me for walking away?"

"Yes." But she realized the question was born of an older wound, a deeper need. She reached up and put her hand on his face, palm against his two-day scruff, thumb stroking his cheek. "You have to remember, Kathleen forgave you too. She said so in the video, and she meant it."

"Thank you," Eddie whispered.

Miranda's eyes welled up and spilled over, and Eddie reached up to cup her face, big thumbs wiping away the tears.

"Shhh," he murmured, then kissed her so tenderly that she wanted to melt. A puddle of salty tears, right at his feet. The kiss went on and on, breaking her heart, because she still feared it was likely the last.

"I've got an idea," Eddie said, still holding her face, kissing between the words. She couldn't imagine, and focused instead on imprinting him on her memory.

"Let's start over. Clean slate," he said.

Hope flared. Doubt tamped it. Miranda smiled only a little, unsure of his intention. "You mean…what, exactly?"

"Dating." Eddie pressed his lips to hers. "Minus the danger."

She burrowed into his chest and breathed deeply, her heart swelling with love. He was granting her—them—a second chance. No way was she going to blow it. She kept a fistful of his shirt in each hand as she pulled away enough to look into his eyes and asked a very important question.

"Safe dating? Where's the excitement in that?"

He grinned. "In the bedroom."

She laughed. "And the kitchen."

He raised an eyebrow. "The kitchen, huh?"

"I want you to cook for me again. Barefoot like before, but shirtless, too."

"So I should beware of grease splatters? That definitely does raise the stakes."

"Mmmn." She smiled, "I was thinking you might need to beware of me. You cooking is super sexy."

He laughed. "Then I want a replay of washing your hair in the sink. Wet shirt and all."

Miranda felt that telltale blush heat her cheeks. "Deal."

Was it too soon to act on the heat that rose between them so easily? Maybe so. A shadow crossed his scruffy face, and she reached out to soothe it. "What?"

"I realize this is jumping the gun, but you need to know…" He looked serious, and she thought of Kathleen. It was possible she'd always stand between them.

Eddie grimaced and said, "I can't live in New York again. It'd make me miserable. Weekends, or whatever, I can do." He squeezed her hand. "Stripes would love to chase some pigeons now and then."

Miranda's heart swelled again—huge with hope—because

Eddie actually thought they might take this farther than the bedroom. Farther than real dating. Far enough to maybe consider location.

"No worries," she said with a grin. "I'd love to spend some time where subways don't exist." What the hell—she knew what she wanted, and it was him. She was putting it out there. "Maybe permanently."

"You could leave Max and the Wise Ones? Your work?"

"At the moment, I'm rather unemployed."

"I was thinking of the Goodbye Angel work."

"I can do that from anywhere. And I was considering branching out anyway." She thought of her PTSD, and the friends he'd mentioned. "There might be some servicemen and women who'd like to tape thoughts for their families before deployment. Or after. Some things would be easier to explain to a camera."

Eddie squeezed her hand, pressed his lips together, seeming to hold both words and emotions in.

"As for Max and the Wise Ones," she said, "don't for a second think they wouldn't visit regularly. They're part of the package. And it's a short trip, especially when you have access to a driver."

"That part *could* be dangerous."

She laughed. "So we'll just…see where this goes?"

"Yeah," Eddie said, and tugged her toward the bedroom. "Effective immediately."

Thank you for reading,
and I truly hope you enjoyed!

———————

Please consider leaving an honest review of Uncovered
at your retailer and on Goodreads. Besides word of mouth,
reviews are the best way for others to find new reads, and
we authors greatly appreciate every single one!

For more information about JB Schroeder
and her books, visit:
www.jbschroederauthor.com

Newsletter subscribers are the first to receive news and
updates, however, if you'd prefer only new release alerts,
simply follow JB on Amazon or BookBub:
amazon.com/author/jbschroeder
bookbub.com/authors/jb-schroeder

UNHINGED
(Unlikely Series, Book 1)

Tori Radnor is determined to overcome the past with her start-up venture. Mega-successful Aiden Miller agrees to help despite his own obstacles. Inexplicably, as the desire between them increases, so do threats from an elusive villain. When bizarre taunts escalate into terrifying attacks, Tori and Aiden must confront their worst fears—before it all becomes *unhinged*.

UNDONE
(Unlikely Series, Book 3)

Modeling agency owner Maxine Ricci and her body-guard Shane O'Rourke must put the past—and their tangled sheets—aside in order to stop a serial killer who has targeted her models...and ultimately her.

RUNAWAY
(Retrieval, Inc. Series, Book 1)

Detective Mitch Saunders uncovers a disturbing link between his missing sister and one of his cold cases. The runaway—or victim?—now known as Charlie Hart—holds the key to his sister's safety. Except she refuses to help him. Too much is at stake to look back. Nor can she consider a future with Mitch—a man who will expose her to evil, if that's what it takes to bring his sister home. He leaves Charlie no choice but to run—again. Or is it already too late?

ACKNOWLEDGMENTS

Grateful thanks to the following:

AJ Scudiere for going above and beyond with solutions to tricky story problems.

Eli Jackson for keeping my fighting techniques on the up and up.

Charlie Cusumano for a primer on today's videography equipment.

Sue Barry and her husband Sean for helping me authenticate the Chang brothers and Wong Palace.

Jill Rathyen for the info on exploratory laparoscopy, exsanguination, and the liver stab and yank. I was bummed I couldn't use this in the end—but Miranda couldn't be stuck in the hospital for long!

Critique partners and beta readers: Joanna Shupe, Rose-Ann DeFranco, Diana Quincy, Maureen Hansch, D.B. Sieders, Cate Hartzell, Julie Cahillane, and Karen DeJongh. I can't tell you the value you bring to this process.

Bev Katz Rosenbaum for insightful content editing, Arran McNicol for speedy copyediting, and Barbara Greenberg for superb and thoughtful proofreading.

The Violet Femmes for unwavering support.

My dad for the extra help, and my whole family for always believing in me.

And last, but certainly not least, my real-life local Miranda: Kerry Glass of Memories Live (memorieslive.org) for the inspiration!

JB SCHROEDER, a graduate of Penn State University's creative writing program and a book designer by trade, now crafts thrilling romantic suspense novels. Blessed with a loving family and a home in NJ, JB has no idea why her stories lean toward gritty, and her characters keep finding evil—but she wouldn't have it any other way.

JB loves to connect with readers and can be reached through her website:

www.jbschroederauthor.com